DEADLY SWITCH

Also by KAREN DODD

Deadly Switch

Scare Away the Dark

Everybody Knows

DEADLY SWITCH

KAREN DODD

ISBN 9781775122135 (paperback)
ISBN 9781775122142(e-book)

To Glen—for believing in me before I believed in myself.

DEADLY SWITCH

Chapter One

West Vancouver, British Columbia
February 9, 2013

E ven though she was expected, it struck her as peculiar that the wrought-iron gate was wide open. Obsessed with security, Gavin Stone had emphasized she would need to buzz to gain entry.

Jordan Leighton opened the unlocked front door of the mansion at 70 Seaspray Close. She called out as she stepped into the dimly lit foyer. "Hello, is anybody home? Hello?" No reply. She pulled her cell phone from her coat pocket, found his last text message, and hit Voice Call. It rang several times. No answer. She peered into a boldly furnished living area to a wall of glass. Lights glittered from outside, but without venturing farther into the house, there was no way to see where they came from. To her immediate left was a suspended steel and glass staircase.

Annoyed, she started up the steps. *Who has glass stairs*?

1

she mused, as her high heels clattered on each tread. "It's Jordan, are you up there?" *Dammit*. She knew she shouldn't have come and now just wanted to get this over with.

Once past the first landing and at the top, she saw light spilling from an open doorway. Crossing the threshold from the black hardwood floor of the hall, her heels sank into a plush, black and white striped carpet. Judging by the cavernous size of the austere surroundings, it appeared to be the master bedroom.

She gasped, gulping for breath. For a second, she thought she'd caught him in bed at an inopportune moment. But he didn't move.

Her pulse thundered in her ears. Desperately trying to slow down her breathing, she forced herself to move in for a closer look. A naked body sprawled across the king-sized bed. The duvet lay loosely bunched around his feet. Averting her eyes from his exposed genitals, Jordan felt her stomach roil as she saw a syringe sticking partway into the man's inside right forearm.

Her heart pounded as she stifled a scream. She clenched her shaking hands and took another tentative step toward the bed. His neck and head were twisted at a grotesque angle. He stared with bulging, vacant eyes. White frothy spittle had dried in one corner of his partly open mouth. Recoiling, she lurched backward out of the room and fled for the stairs.

In her panic, she stumbled down the glass steps, losing one shoe and then the other on her frantic descent. Her phone flew from her hand and smashed on the floor below as she grabbed for the cold metal banister. Missing the last few stairs, she landed in a heap on the slick marble floor. Willing herself to get up, she bolted through the open front door at lightning speed, stockings ripping on the wet concrete drive-way. Her head reverberated with the sound of her own screams. Dizzy, she felt soggy grass underfoot before she vomited and passed out.

H er mouth tasted vile as she struggled to pull something constricting off her face. Her body throbbed as if someone had used her as a punching bag, and she winced when she tried to lift her head.

"Miss, I need you to lie still. You're in an ambulance, with an oxygen mask on to help you breathe. You seem to be doing all right on your own so we can leave it off for now if you like." He gave her a reassuring smile. "Some neighbors called nine-one-one and we found you wandering around on the grass. Do you remember what happened?"

Jordan looked into the paramedic's eyes and shivered uncontrollably. "I'm so thirsty. Could I have a drink of water?"

"I can't give you anything until we get you to the hospital. We're just waiting for my driver to give a quick report to the police. Good news is your blood pressure has come back up to almost normal."

"Hospital? No, I don't need a hospital. I have to make a call...where am I?" Frantically, she patted her coat pocket under the blanket, feeling for her phone.

"Whoa, slow down. There's plenty of time for that. We're just outside the house where we found you. I'm sure the police have your cell phone."

Someone opened the ambulance door, letting in a blast of cold air. Even as the paramedic tried to keep her horizontal, Jordan was determined to see the goings on outside. Suddenly, she remembered where she was. She squinted to avoid the glare that lit up the front of the house. Her eyes gradually adjusted to the brightness when it registered that the

3

lights were from television cameras. Red and blue flashers from police cars further illuminated the long driveway, the wrought iron gate now closed. For a brief moment, she wondered if she was in the middle of a movie shoot, a sight exceedingly commonplace in what the locals referred to as Hollywood North.

Dizzy, she tried to sit up. Despite the cool air outside, drops of perspiration trickled down her neck. Her stomach heaved. A second paramedic poked his head in. "Hey, Pete, let's close her up and get out of here." He began securing the doors. "Everything good to go in here?"

Before the doors fully closed, Jordan heard a gravelly, masculine voice. "Hey, can I talk to her now? Jesus, I gotta get some information here."

A massive fist pulled the door wide and the disembodied voice came into view. Although dressed in street clothes, she assumed he was a police officer.

Before the paramedic could reply, Jordan interjected. "I can talk to you now, but I need my shoes." She shivered again from cold and shock. "And my phone." Over the protests of the EMT, she struggled to a crouched stand inside the ambulance, shuffled to the door, and dropped to a sitting position on the tailgate. Dangling her legs to the ground, she tested them for sturdiness. Although still wobbly, she pulled herself up and stood before the officer. He towered over her by at least five inches. He smelled faintly of cigarette smoke and looked at her with tired, rheumy eyes. She wondered if they had called him in from off-duty or if, in his line of work, he looked like that all the time.

Ignoring the disapproval of the paramedic, the cop nodded. "Yeah, we can grab your shoes when we go back in the house to talk. Your phone's another story. But we'll discuss that later."

Dodging the hand he put under her elbow to steady her, she resolved to make the trip back into the house under her own steam—something she was not relishing.

"I've got a pair of booties for you to put on. You've probably contaminated the scene, but I'll have one of the techs take impressions of your shoes while we go inside."

Thanks a lot, she thought. *Never mind that I'm an invited, albeit reluctant guest to this place and now I'm getting shit for messing up the scene.* She fought to keep her thoughts to herself as she and the cop made their way back inside. *This can't be real.* The events of the evening closed in on her like a suffocating grey fog.

He led her into an enormous living room, which she remembered seeing when she had entered the house earlier in the evening. Immediately, the grandiose starkness of the room struck her. Her childhood home in the British Properties was equally large. In spite of the fact that she grew up in the "old money" area of West Vancouver, her family home had been warm and inviting. This place spoke of iciness and detachment.

The officer coarsely cleared his throat, and she was jolted back to the present. He motioned to a chic but uncomfortable-looking chair and pulled over another for himself. "So, Ms..." he consulted his notebook, "Leighton. I need to get a few details out of the way."

If he knew her name, he must have run the plates on her car. Indignant, she simply stared at him.

"Leighton. That your married name?" he asked.

"No, I changed it several years ago to my mother's maiden name."

"Oh, yeah? Why'd you do that?"

"Officer is this really necessary?" she bristled. "Shouldn't we be talking about what I just discovered upstairs in my father's bedroom? Aren't you at all concerned about who it is, or that whoever did this might still be in the vicinity?"

"It's 'Inspector,' ma'am—Inspector Dave Hunter. And no offense, but we've done this a few times before. We've secured the scene, and my guys are on it. Whoever that is upstairs either did himself in, or he was murdered. Did something happen recently with Mr. Stone that might have set him off?"

His question hit her like a cold, hard slap across the face. "Set him off? I can assure you Inspector, you could accuse my father of many things, but murder is not one of them. Is that what you're suggesting?"

"Well, I don't mean to be rude, ma'am, but…"

"Well, you *are* rude and please don't call me ma'am."

He coughed again. "I'm sorry, Ms. Leighton, but seeing as how we have a body upstairs and Mr. Stone is nowhere to be seen, that's exactly what I'm suggesting. We won't know for a while if the deceased caused his own demise or was a victim of foul play. Either way, we're obviously interested in Mr. Stone's whereabouts. You wouldn't happen to know where he is, would you?"

A siren howled outside and then stopped suddenly. Jordan shuddered, thinking of the person she had initially feared was her father, lying motionless just two floors away. Vaguely, she remembered going up the stairs, and then slipping on the glass treads as she half-raced, half-fell on the descent. She tried desperately to shake off the horror of what she'd seen.

"No, I have no idea where he is. We haven't been in contact for several years. And then I received a message from him this evening asking me to meet him here."

"How come you haven't seen him for so long? You two

had a fight or something? Why did he want to meet with you?" He rifled through his notebook, not waiting for an answer.

"Inspector Hunter, I don't see how my personal life is any of your business. However, to answer your question, I don't know why he wanted me to meet him. His text just said it was urgent and he would explain when I got here."

"So, if you haven't seen him in a while, I don't suppose you know Mr. Stone was scheduled to meet with the B.C. Securities Commission tomorrow morning." He looked at his watch. "Ah, make that *this* morning."

Jordan also checked the time. Shocked, she wondered where the last hour and a half had gone. "Why would meeting with the BCSC be out of the ordinary? I imagine he and his lawyer had many meetings with the commission." She glanced at her watch as if to emphasize the lateness of the hour and briefly wondered how Hunter had known about the meeting. "Inspector, am I free to leave? I believe I've told you everything I know."

He appeared to be sizing her up and considering his options. Then he flipped his notebook closed. "I'll go see if our techs are done with your shoes. But we're going to have to keep your phone—what's left of it. Then you're free to go. We can continue this in my office, later today."

Without waiting for her reply, he left the room.

Chapter Two

A lerted to the police incident on Seaspray Close by a mutual friend and neighbor, Julius Pinsette left his home in the British Properties and made the ten-minute drive to his client's residence. Parking his car on the road, he headed for the long driveway that wound downhill toward the house on the water. Television camera lights flooded the front of the estate, and despite the press's best attempts to push closer, several members of the West Vancouver Police Department aggressively enforced the area outside the crime tape. A couple of the cops recognized Julius and after he successfully ran the gauntlet of security, they allowed him to duck under the yellow and black tape, which cordoned off the property.

Entering Gavin's house through the kitchen, his heart sank when he bumped into the inspector. Hunter held a pair of women's shoes in one meaty hand. Reluctantly, Julius made the first move to shake the other.

"Nice to see you again, Inspector," Julius said wryly. "As I'm sure you're aware, Gavin Stone is a client of mine. What the hell's going on here? Has something happened to Gavin?"

"Well, if you count a dead guy upstairs and Mr. Stone being MIA as something happening, then yup, I'd say so. You wouldn't know where your client is, would you, counselor?" he asked with one raised eyebrow. "Seems the daughter found the body. Kind of strange wouldn't you say, in that they haven't talked for years?"

"Jordan Stone is here?"

"Yup." He scratched his stubbly chin. "Seems she isn't Stone anymore. Changed her name to Leighton. Maybe she was trying to get away from her old man's stellar reputation, eh?"

Never known for subtleties, Hunter's sneer reminded Julius why he loathed the man. "I want to see her immediately. Where is she?"

"Geez, I only consider her a witness at this point, and she's lawyered up already? No disrespect, Pinsette, but does she know you're not a criminal lawyer?" He eyed Julius up and down. "Looks like white-collar clients pay pretty good these days, though. You been doin' that since you got your license back, haven't you?"

Julius's eyes rested on the shoes in Hunter's hand. He resisted the urge to say what he really wanted to. "Are those Miss Leighton's? If so, are you finished with them?"

As if forgetting he was still holding the shoes, Hunter handed them to Julius. "Yeah, we're done with them. She's in there." He tilted his head in the direction of the living room. "Just so you know, the paramedics offered her a ride to the hospital, but she refused treatment."

Reasonably sure Jordan hadn't yet noticed him, Julius stood in the entrance for a moment before entering the living room. Recessed lighting only marginally warmed the starkly cold area Gavin presumptuously referred to as the "great room." Against her deathly pale face, Jordan's long hair shone a golden auburn brown. A tailored blouse, which at some point must have been white but was now crumpled and grubby, had come partially untucked from the waist of her grey flannel skirt. She sat ramrod straight, embraced by the arms of one of Gavin's Hans Wegner Papa Bear chairs. Her skirt—in fact her entire being—blended seamlessly into the charcoal grey linen of the chair's upholstery. A pile of tissues sat crumpled in her lap, and her long, slender legs crossed at the ankles above torn, stockinged feet. She stared vacantly out the window into darkness punctuated by flashing police lights.

Jordan had grown from an attractive teenager to a striking young woman. Perhaps it was because he never had children of his own that Julius thought of her as a daughter. In fact, after the divorce of her parents, he had in some small way tried to be the father Gavin wasn't.

Awkwardly, he moved toward her. Her eyes were blood-shot when they met his, and her stoic composure crumbled. Appearing on the verge of tears, she looked utterly and completely exhausted.

"Jordan, what happened? What are you doing here?" Julius asked.

Before she could reply, Hunter strode into the room. "More to the point, Pinsette, what brings you here?"

Jordan glared at the inspector as she got up from her chair. "Julius, how could this be real? He sent me a text just this afternoon."

"Jordan, my dear…I am so sorry. I don't know what to say."

"Inspector Hunter said my father may have murdered whoever is upstairs. That's not possible. He would never have done anything like this. Julius, tell him, please."

The lawyer turned his attention to Hunter. "What the hell happened here?"

"Exactly what I'd like to know, Pinsette. I guess that's the million-dollar question now, isn't it?"

Gavin, what have you done? In the back of his mind, Julius had always known this day would come. Not that they would find someone dead in Gavin's home of course, but one day all the things he had been privy to, and probably many more he wasn't, would come out and hurt the one other person Gavin cared about most. Was it possible after everything his friend had been through he had chosen to take care of things like this?

As Julius drove home from the crime scene, it occurred to him if Jordan only knew the truth, she might not be so confident her father wasn't mixed up in this nightmare.

Chapter Three

Earlier that evening

I f she could get the file wrapped up and on her editor's desk in the next twenty-five minutes, Jordan Leighton could call it an early night. In the five weeks following Christmas, she considered "early" as any time before nine.

She felt added motivation to finish up quickly. After six, the building's energy-saving device required anyone working late to manually reset the lights every half hour. Despite the faint illumination at the far end of the twentieth floor, Jordan's cubicle became virtually pitch black each time the lights went off. As the newspaper's newest and youngest reporter, she had forced herself to become efficient in slogging through colossal amounts of writing in half-hour increments.

Tenacious to a fault, Jordan knew her idea of a story being "good enough" was her fellow journalists' idea of perfection. She had no doubt her thoroughness would pass muster at the editorial meeting in the morning. Satisfied, she scrawled a quick note to her boss, Ernie MacDougall, assignment editor for the regional newspaper's city desk, and stuck it to the outside of the four-inch-thick file. Glancing at the clock, she hastily grabbed her purse and briefcase, slipped into her cashmere coat and was about to head down the hall to Ernie's corner office. With any luck, she would make it to the elevator before the next blackout.

A vibrating sound reminded her she'd left her cell phone behind. Returning to her workstation, she grabbed for the phone as it threatened to wriggle off the edge of her desk into the wastebasket. In the seconds it took to enter her password and unlock the cell, her office was plunged into darkness. *Damn!*

A text message lit up her phone's screen. *Jordan, I know I'm asking a lot but pls meet me ASAP at 70 Seaspray Close, West Van. URGENT! Will explain when you get here.* Neither the number nor the address was familiar. She scrolled down. It was signed *Gavin*. Her pulse quickened. After ten years of no contact, how did he even know her number?

She shoved the phone into her coat pocket, carefully traced her way down the hall toward the dim light outside Ernie's office, and deposited the file on his impossibly disorganized desk. Rather than head to the darkened reception area, she let herself out through the private back door of the staff lunchroom and into the well-lit exterior hall. She heard the click of the security-coded door close behind her. Pulling the key card out of her cell phone case, she waited impatiently for the elevator.

Jordan got off on the second floor and threaded her way through the circuitous corridor which led to the parking lot. By sheer luck, she had managed to snag a permanent spot right outside the doors. She wasn't normally nervous when working late, but as a woman recently had been attacked in a nearby underground parking lot, it gave her pause for thought. Once in her car, she hit the button to lock all the doors, pulled her phone from her pocket, and reread the message. Her heart hammered as she considered whether simply to ignore it. She jumped when the cell vibrated in her hand and a second text came through. *Please come, Jordan. Buzz at the gate when you arrive.* Staring at the screen, she realized she needed to make a decision. She pulled her coat closer around her body, started the car, and entered the address in her navigation system.

The rain blew across the road in horizontal sheets as she turned the corner onto Georgia Street. Crossing the Lions Gate Bridge, the GPS indicated she'd be better to take Marine Drive rather than the Upper Levels Highway if she was going to meet him. Otherwise, she could just shoot up Taylor Way and merge onto the highway before taking the turnoff to her condominium on Deer Ridge.

As she drove across the bridge deck into West Vancouver, Jordan considered whether to head directly home. Some warmed-up leftovers were all that awaited her but that, and a glass of wine, was more appealing than the alternative. She jumped when she heard a quick honk behind her, startled to realize she had stopped at a red light that had turned green. She had no option but to carry on straight ahead on Marine Drive. *Decision made.*

The rain continued unabated, but in spite of the poorly lit road, she navigated the twists and turns expertly. It was, after all, where she'd learned to drive as a teenager. Unlike others who found the drive nerve-wracking, especially at night, she anticipated every bump and narrowing of the two-lane road. When the navigation screen told her she would reach her destination in 300 meters, Jordan slowed the car until she saw the house number on a stately concrete pillar.

Surprised the gate was open, she studied the expansive three-level structure sprawled luxuriously across an equally large lot. The interior of the house appeared dimly lit with a few external floodlights providing a bit of warmth to the mansion's perimeter. With clammy hands, she turned down the heat in the car, suddenly aware her face felt flushed. Taking some deep breaths to calm her nerves, Jordan debated whether she should park on the street or pull into the sweeping circular driveway reminiscent of an upscale hotel entrance.

Or should she just drive away and ignore his messages?

Chapter Four

Two days later

Even the caffeine wasn't helping, Jordan thought as she sipped a strong Americano in the Starbucks around the corner from her office. She glanced at the time on her new phone, the police having kept her other one. If they considered two texts from her father to be "valuable evidence," they were welcome to knock themselves out.

She waited a little longer, knowing her boss would be on his way to the airport to catch a flight to Fort St. John. Although she loved her job as a junior reporter, she dreaded the amount of work that awaited her in Ernie's absence. Any excuse to dally was a good one, so she reached for the *Globe and Mail*, which lay discarded on the adjoining table.

Her heart lurched when she flipped to the regional section. The bold headline threatened to jump off the page. A flush crept up her neck, warming her face. Although she was already familiar with the details of the incident, seeing it in print in the national newspaper hit her like a body blow. Two days ago, Manfred "Manny" Smith, a private investigator who was "known to police," had been found dead in a multi-million-dollar mansion on the West Vancouver waterfront. Inspector David Hunter, with whom she had spent too much time in the past forty-eight hours, was quoted in the article as saying the cause of death had not yet been determined, but they had not ruled out foul play. Gavin Stone, a successful real estate developer and owner of the home where the deceased was discovered, was considered a "strong person of interest," and anyone knowing his whereabouts should immediately call the Crime Stoppers anonymous tip line.

She dropped the open paper into her lap and kneaded the tension that crept up the back of her neck. In large part, she had Julius to thank for what *wasn't* said in the article. Given Inspector Hunter's insistence her father had been involved in something unsavory that may have ended in murder, Jordan was sure they were not the inspector's own words in the article. Instead, they had likely been force-fed to him by a police spokesperson, based on legal counsel.

The allegations her father was in any way connected to Smith's death, was abhorrent. In the past two days, her world had been rocked as she learned Gavin Stone had been under investigation for almost a year, suspected of bilking investors in one of his real estate projects out of millions of dollars. Though it was ten years since she had last seen him, after her parents' divorce, she simply could not wrap her head around her father being a suspected criminal. Thankfully, nor could Julius. He'd pushed hard, threatening legal action if some of the allegations against Gavin were made public. However, Inspector Hunter had made it clear they could only count on a temporary reprieve from the prying eyes and ears of the press.

Glancing once more at the article, Jordan considered how

fortunate she was to have Julius's support through what had been a horrible ordeal. Prior to him rescuing her two nights before, she had not seen him since her return to Canada. While at journalism school in Boston, she heard from her mother, Cynthia, that Julius asked about her often. As loyal as she knew he was to her father, he had always been good to her and her mother, even after her parents' divorce.

Julius Pinsette was a tall, gangly man. Even as a child, she thought he never looked comfortable in his own body. What an odd thing for her to think. She could only have been six or seven when she first met him. He often came to the house late at night to meet with her father, closeted behind huge double oak doors of the downstairs study. She used to sneak out of her room when she heard unexpected company arrive after she had gone to bed. Sitting halfway down the front stairs, Jordan had tried hard to hear what they were saying. Her father was often shouting, but she couldn't tell what their conversations were about, and she never heard Mr. Pinsette's voice raised.

Jordan couldn't recall how old she was, but it must have been one of those long mid-summer evenings. She was in her room reading when she heard a car come through the gates of their driveway. Her bedroom was in the new addition, over a generously sized, four-car garage. Hearing tires crunching on gravel, she knelt on the padded window bench just in time to see Mr. Pinsette's shiny black Jaguar pull around the circular driveway in front of their house. Although she hadn't seen her father at dinner or when her mother had left for her ladies' bridge game, she assumed since her father's lawyer was there, her father must be home as well.

She excitedly pulled open her bedroom door, only to freeze when she heard her father shouting. Barefoot, she stepped onto the second-floor landing and closed the door quietly behind her, careful not to make a sound. She knew from experience, if she walked around the squeaky spot in the hardwood floor, she could make it to her perch on the stairs, undetected. Settling into her hideaway, she could see her father through the partially open study doors, his back toward her and facing Mr. Pinsette. She knew she shouldn't be there, but with a peculiar combination of guilt and curiosity, she sat paralyzed.

"Gavin," she heard Mr. Pinsette's terse tone, "I thought it *was* taken care of. I was very thorough. I just don't understand how they could have gotten their hands on this information, but I assure you…"

At that moment, the lawyer caught sight of her through the open crack of the door. "Jordan…" Julius said, as her father spun around to face her.

"Jordan!" Gavin's raged, seeing her on the stairs. "What are you doing eavesdropping outside my study?"

Rooted with fear, she was embarrassed to have been caught. "Daddy, I wasn't eavesdropping, it's just that—"

"Never mind," he interrupted. "Go to your room at once. We will discuss this later."

Seizing the opportunity to escape, she turned and fled up the stairs to her room and slammed the door behind her, collapsing on her bed in tears. She knew it was wrong to have lurked outside the study, but something had compelled her to stay and listen. At the time, Jordan wondered if what she overheard had anything to do with why her mother was so quiet when she drove her to school that morning.

As was typical when her father was upset with her, he soon forgot the incident. She vaguely remembered him coming and sitting on the side of her bed to have a talk. He hadn't actually been terribly angry with her after all. He said something about having lost his temper because he was star-

tled to see her on the stairs when she should have been
in bed.

F orcing her mind back to the work that awaited, Jordan
tossed the newspaper aside and wondered exactly what
Julius might have meant so long ago, when he told her father
he thought "it had all been taken care of."

Chapter Five

As usual, Jordan was in the office long before the majority of the other reporters and staff. She could always count on the reporting pool's assistant, Dorothea, to pick her up a second strong Americano on her way in. A substantial black woman in her forties, Dorothea had admonished Jordan that her eighty-hour-plus workweeks would lead her to self-destruct before she hit thirty. Good naturedly, Jordan had shot back, "And who are you to call the kettle black?"

The words had no sooner left her lips, than she covered her mouth in horror. Dorothea played Jordan's embarrassment to the hilt, eyeing her slowly up and down. After allowing the novice reporter to sweat for a few seconds, she bent over in hysterical laughter while Jordan let out her breath. Afterward, it became an ongoing joke when on her way into the coffee room Jordan would offer to fetch Dorothea a cup of coffee. "White or black?" she'd ask, to which Dorothea always replied, "Don't think I have much of a choice, darlin'."

Their easy banter led to a deep and trusting relationship, which flourished over time. Before starting work at the paper,

Jordan had planned to complete her master's degree at Emerson Collage in Boston, and then go to work for a US broadcasting company. However, shortly after finishing her bachelor's, she was presented with an extraordinary opportunity to return to Vancouver and join one of the province's two leading regional newspapers. Her arrival at the bustling city desk was received with mixed reviews. The female reporters, who numbered a scant six, scrutinized her and left her largely to fend for herself. Time would either expose or promote her, and they weren't going to help with the latter. The men—well —they were the men. Dorothea, having worked her way up from a receptionist over the past twenty years, often told Jordan she could well imagine the locker-room talk fueled by their newest reporter's stunning good looks and intelligence. Jordan laughed off the compliment, but she loved Dorothea for watching her back.

The rest of the clerical staff and reporters simultaneously respected and feared their boss, Ernie McDougall, a curmudgeonly man Jordan estimated to be in his late fifties. As a junior reporter, she knew if she could earn her chops under him, she could work for just about any editor out there. She had come home and joined the newspaper with the ultimate goal of crime reporting, but first she had to prove herself on run-of-the-mill local stories. Ernie seemed to demand a higher level of performance from her than his other journalists. Even on the most mundane stories, the two of them constantly engaged in verbal tugs of war, as he demanded rewrite after rewrite. Although Jordan was aware she often tested his patience, she had proven she always came through for him.

It was going on eight-thirty when Dorothea walked into Jordan's work area to bring her up to speed on the demands of the day. She flinched when she handed her a thick stack of files requiring her immediate attention. Jordan sighed into her coffee cup. "Thanks, Dorothea. Unless it's something urgent, I'm going to lock myself in an empty office for an hour and try to get on top of this stuff before I have to go over it with Ernie by phone." She put her hand on her stomach and winced. Dorothea's eagle eyes caught the gesture.

"Is your ulcer bothering you again? I keep telling you that you need to avoid caffeine. You drink too much coffee on an empty stomach, and I'm guilty of aiding and abetting by getting it for you every morning," she wagged her finger.

"I don't have an ulcer," Jordan reminded Dorothea. "And I love you for being my enabler." She chuckled despite the pain twisting in her gut. "Can you run interference for me and keep the hounds at bay for an hour?"

"You got it, my dear. Go do what you have to do. Don't you worry—I'll throw them some raw meat if I have to."

"You're the best." Jordan winked at Dorothea as she juggled the stack of files with her coffee and maneuvered herself into a nearby vacant office. She raised a high heel behind her and lightly kicked the door closed behind her.

Since discovering the body at her father's home, Jordan's gut aches had become relentless. Having ruled out an ulcer or Crohn's disease, her doctor had placed her name on the wait list for an MRI but said it might take as long as six months to get the procedure. In the meantime, she had prescribed a preventive medication Jordan was to use daily. As was often the case, she had forgotten to take it. She had already checked her desk drawer only to find the bottle was empty and she needed to make an appointment with her physician before she could get more. *Damn, one more thing I've neglected to do.* Hopeful, she scrounged through her purse, which she'd brought down the hall with her. She gave a small sigh of relief as her fingers clasped the familiar plastic container. At

23

least there were enough to get her through until she could see the doctor. Slugging back a couple of pills with a swig of water, she hoped she'd caught it in time. With the assignments Ernie had left, the last thing she needed was to be sick as a dog again.

When the stomachaches had started in eleventh grade, her family doctor attributed them to hormonal changes exacerbated by her father leaving her mother, compounded by the unexpected death of her maternal grandmother, Granny Leighton. Dr. Willis told Jordan's mother her daughter would likely outgrow them in time. Although she did have a few years of respite, they came back with a vengeance when she was in Boston. Since then, rarely a month went by when she didn't suffer at least one debilitating episode.

Judging by the thickness of the files on her desk, she didn't have time to be out of commission, even for a day. She had come to dread Ernie's frequent absences from the office, in part because they always increased her workload. She had little more than an hour before their teleconference to get a handle on the assignment file, to which he'd attached an urgent sticky note. After that, he would be airborne and then in and out of meetings for the balance of the day. Jordan kicked off her shoes beneath her desk, took a gulp of cold coffee, and dug in.

The name of the development first caught her attention. Curiously, she opened the top folder labeled "Whispering Palms." Within seconds, she realized she was reading a précis of her father's real estate project on the big island of Hawaii. She grabbed the next file. Its label was also familiar—the name of another of his projects she knew he'd started in the early eighties. Frantically, she flipped through each folder in succession. They all referenced Gavin Stone or one of his many real estate developments. She inhaled sharply when she got to the last one.

The typewritten notes were on the letterhead of the Deputy Director of Compliance with the B.C. Securities Commission. Her vision blurred, and the words wavered on the page. Her queasy stomach reminded her, as Dorothea said, that she'd ingested nothing other than coffee.

Although Inspector Hunter had filled her in on her father's apparent impropriety, these new facts put it all into stunning context. In disbelief, she speed-read through pages of allegations her father and his company were responsible for hundreds of investors seeing their retirement plans go up in smoke. One man in his sixties reportedly had committed suicide, leaving a note that he was unable to face his wife after losing their life savings in one of Gavin Stone's projects. The notes ended with the deputy director's comment that he would be talking to Mr. Stone about the missing funds the following day. Jordan flipped back to the first page. The date was February 10—one day after Manny Smith's death and her father's subsequent disappearance.

Dorothea looked up in alarm as Jordan bolted from the office toward the restroom. She barely slammed the louvered cubicle door behind her before the acid contents of her stomach heaved violently into the toilet. On her knees, she retched until there was nothing left and her ribs ached. She knew without checking, Dorothea would be outside the stall waiting her out. When she felt well enough, she opened the door and padded to the sink in her stocking feet. Sure enough, the older woman was outside, holding a glass of water.

"Poor baby, what do you think set it off this time?" she asked.

"I don't know. I guess you were right, I probably had too

much coffee without eating anything this morning," Jordan lied.

"Sweetie, why do you keep doing that? And how much sleep have you had?"

"Probably not enough."

"Can I get your pills for you? Will that help?"

Jordan looked at her sheepishly. "No, I just wasted two of the few I had left. I don't think I kept them down long enough to do any good."

"Why don't you go home hon, and I'll cover for you with Ernie. I'm worried about you, Jordan. You can't keep going like this or you'll be no good to anyone," she said, this time more gently.

"You know what? I'm actually feeling a little better now. Maybe it was getting all that coffee out of my stomach. Can you just give me a few minutes to clean up? I need to be on that conference call." Her eyes pleaded with Dorothea.

She sighed loudly. "Girl, you can talk me into anything. Lock the door behind me so you're not disturbed, and I'll text Mr. Grumpy-Pants that you're just filing a story before deadline."

Jordan gave the older woman a tired smile. "Thanks, Dorothea, I don't know what I'd do without you."

"I know, honey, I know," she clucked, shaking her head as she left the ladies' room.

Chapter Six

By the time she got off the phone with Ernie, Jordan knew she was already in over her head. She should have told him immediately about her connection to Gavin Stone, and request the piece be assigned to another journalist. However, he had been in a rush to get through his agenda prior to catching his flight, barking out orders at break-neck speed. Plus, it was as if old Ernie was finally giving her an opportunity to take a shot at investigative reporting, something she'd been pleading for relentlessly. Maybe dangling this carrot was another of his tests—one she was determined to pass. At the expense of her own father, she thought guiltily.

She spent the balance of the morning reading everything she could find on the Internet regarding her father's most recent project, an Arizona development called Desert Springs. According to information posted on the project's website, Stone planned to market in excess of $300 million in commercial and multi-family properties throughout 2011 and 2012, by way of tax-favored limited partnerships.

Referring back to the background files on her desk, she discovered her father had landed in court in 2008 after the

Barclay Group, a high-end financial planning firm in the city, launched a lawsuit against him. The suit was subsequently dropped, with the company president, John Barclay, saying the matter had been resolved privately. In a brief comment, the aging CEO stated, "It (the lawsuit against Stone) was a misunderstanding. He is actually a very decent fellow with whom our firm has dealt since 1985 and we've never had anything of this nature arise before."

The contents of the bulging files that covered Jordan's desk contrasted sharply with Barclay's remarks four years earlier. Each file contained stunning allegations of impropriety and millions of dollars of missing funds, which were to have been held in trust on behalf of Stone's investors. In the latest development, the Supreme Court of British Columbia had ordered Stone's company, Sweetwater Properties, to post a $50 million bond to protect investors' interests. In her ruling, Madam Justice Eunice Brightman said there were substantial questions remaining, with regard to the nature and extent of participation in Stone's alleged fraudulent scheme. Authorities were still trying to track down approximately $30 million of investors' missing funds.

This time, John Barclay's remarks were not nearly as magnanimous, and it was clear that since many of his clients had been Stone's investors, he was looking for someone to blame. His statement to the press was: "This is a complete shock and I can only hope the securities commission will get to the bottom of it quickly. My wife and I knew Gavin Stone extremely well personally and trusted him. This has been devastating, not only for us but for our clients." The elusive $30 million was to have been the focus of discussion at the meeting scheduled with the B.C. Securities Commission on February 10, the date that would forever be etched into Jordan's consciousness.

. . .

After telling Dorothea she was going home to try to sleep off her stomach episode, Jordan headed to her mother's house in the British Properties. It confounded her why Cynthia insisted on hanging on to the six thousand-square-foot house Jordan had lived in as a child. Her mother's stubborn refusal to part with it originally stemmed from her desire to exact revenge on Gavin Stone. Ten years later, Jordan wasn't sure what made her want to live in what now felt like a museum, haunted by memories of a distant past.

When the doorbell went unanswered, Jordan used her key to let herself in. She picked a small pile of mail off the floor inside the door and deposited the various envelopes and flyers on the foyer table. Grabbing the latest edition of the North Shore News, she trudged down the hall to the kitchen. "Mom, are you home?' Glancing at the kitchen clock, she realized Cynthia was probably at the club, imbibing in her usual Wednesday afternoon post-tennis gin and tonic. Undoubtedly, she was commiserating with the other vengeful socialites, whose sole ambition in life was to get even with their nefarious ex-husbands.

She filled the kettle, plugged it in, and perched on a kitchen barstool. Thumbing through the paper, she checked Catherine Barr's "Bright Lights" section, always on the lookout for people she knew. She was in the habit of sending handwritten notes to congratulate them when they appeared in the North Shore's equivalent of the society pages. Always aware she might someday need one of them to grant her an interview, name recognition wouldn't hurt. Not seeing anyone she recognized, she flipped to the next page.

The headline read, "Murder or Suicide: Investigation of PI's Death Ongoing." Instead of the same regurgitated facts the regional and national papers ran, the article went into the sordid details of Gavin Stone's alleged embezzlement scheme. The well-known crime reporter, who appeared to have a personal vendetta against Stone, spun the sensational details into a made-for-television narrative. Comparing Jordan's father to a Bernie Madoff-type swindler, the article intimated Stone was single-handedly responsible for the decimation of hundreds of seniors' bank accounts. The reporter surmised Stone's misdeeds caused at least one poor soul to commit suicide.

Feeling sick again, Jordan unplugged the kettle that whistled for her attention and shoved the newspaper into her bag. Although Cynthia was obviously aware of Smith's demise and the embezzlement allegations against her ex-husband, Jordan hoped her mother hadn't already seen the article. It would only further fuel her bitterness.

Aware of the pain returning to her abdomen, Jordan let herself out of the house and headed for home while she could still safely drive.

Chapter Seven

"God damnit, Julius, how could you have let this happen? I paid you a bloody fortune to handle this. You told me all the papers were in order and there was nothing to worry about. Jesus Christ," Gavin railed as he frantically paced the floor of his study. "Not only will my personal life be a shambles, but I can virtually kiss my business goodbye. And remember, if I go down, you won't be far behind me. I'm sure the Bar Association would take a dim view of some of the 'deals' you've put together over the years. Remember that, Julius!"

As Julius pondered the ill-omened conversation with Gavin all those years ago, he considered his next course of action. Accustomed to doing his best strategizing in the early part of the day, he sat alone in his office trying to come to terms with the events of the past forty-eight hours. Each time he thought back to Jordan's grisly discovery at Gavin's, he found himself reaching into the recesses of his mind, attempting to make some sense of it all. He had put some feelers out about Manny Smith but came up with nothing other than he was the go-to PI for suspicious wives wanting to get the goods on their cheating husbands. But what the hell was he doing in Gavin's house, deceased? And why the drug paraphernalia?

Still pondering the possibilities, Julius heard his cell phone ringing and struggled to determine its whereabouts. By the time he located it in his jacket, hanging on the door, the call had gone to voice mail. However, the caller ID left no doubt who was trying to reach him. There had been three missed calls from Inspector Dave Hunter, and try as he might, Julius knew he couldn't avoid him much longer. Nor could he avoid the conversation with Jordan he knew he must have.

For his part, Inspector Hunter seemed to have savored his task of filling Jordan in on the gory details of her father's insalubrious past. Indeed, Gavin had the distinction of being caught in a raid on a Kitsilano party house in 1970. At the time, the bust was the largest seizure of marijuana and LSD tablets in Vancouver's history. It occurred to Julius that Gavin and the other man involved had gotten off pretty easy. They were, after all, only soft drugs. Compared to the crack cocaine, ecstasy, and the meth labs of today, Gavin's brush with the law seemed almost insignificant.

Julius tried repeatedly to convince Jordan that whatever her father had done in the past, he most certainly had not used, or dealt drugs since Julius had known him. Gavin Stone was far too driven and disciplined, to be involved with drugs. In fact, as he pointed out to Jordan, Stone was to be honored for funding a desperately needed rehab facility on Vancouver's downtown eastside. Julius knew how it would look if Gavin weren't present to receive the award, and had already begun to broach the subject with Jordan of her attending in her father's absence.

A lot had transpired in the many years father and daughter were estranged, and Julius agonized whether he would ever be able to tell Jordan a fraction of what had ensued during that period. The salacious facts the police laid out about Gavin's past with drugs and, more recently, his financial woes, seemed more than Jordan could bear. As fervently as he tried, Julius could not get her to see Gavin's drug dealing and subsequent jail term as the actions of a foolhardy twenty-one-year old. Jordan would have none of it, even though she agreed six months in jail and a fine of $2,500 hardly made him a hardened criminal.

The timing of the event to honor Gavin for funding the drug rehab facility couldn't have been worse. Just days after Smith's death and with all the newspaper headlines which followed, it had taken an inordinate amount of cajoling to convince Jordan to attend the reception on her father's behalf. At the last minute, she reluctantly agreed. As Julius tried desperately to keep it under wraps that Gavin was missing, he thought it critical he and Jordan make an appearance in his absence. He tried every avenue he could think of to reach Gavin but to no avail. In the end, Jordan agreed to attend the dedication of the drug addiction and rehabilitation center, although she adamantly refused to speak for her father. Not wanting to push the issue, and reluctant a public speaker though he was, Julius cobbled together some words to honor his friend, in the hope he could hold the news hounds at bay a little longer.

· · ·

He and Jordan agreed to meet in the lobby of the Deer Ridge Country Club and enter the reception together. The large banquet room was filling up and as drinks flowed, conversations became more animated. Making distracted small talk with Jordan and sensing her desire to depart, Julius hoped the Executive Director of the Gavin Stone Treatment Center would soon take the podium, say a few brief words about his friend, and invite him up to say his piece.

As if reading his mind, the director made her way through the crowd. Tapping a glass to garner the guests' attention, she began her remarks. She spoke eloquently about Gavin's continued dedication to addicts, the most downtrodden of Vancouver's society, and described how they would use his sizable donation. Mercifully, her remarks were brief, and in short order she turned the podium over to Julius. As he took a few moments to collect his thoughts and calm his nerves, Julius noticed Jordan had retreated to a back corner to observe the proceedings. He wondered if she might be planning a quick getaway.

Just as Julius began his speech, a ruckus started somewhere in the room. The crowd parted and suddenly, standing directly in front of the stage, was a man, obviously drunk, glaring up at him.

"Hey, Pinsette, you gonna tell us where the old bastard is? The Gavin Stone I know is a swindler, and is probably traveling the world on everybody else's money. That's why he isn't here!" he bellowed.

Julius tore his eyes from the buffoon before him. Jordan's face had gone ashen. Like a cornered animal, she looked desperately for a way to escape. Horrified, Julius realized the man had mounted the steps and was crossing the stage toward the podium. Even with some extra pounds and the florid complexion, Julius recognized Kroch. His real name was Tommy Krochinski, but with a reputation for being a swine with the women, the pejorative name had stuck. Tommy had been Gavin's partner since the days of his first real estate development company, but they had parted ways acrimoniously. Julius had witnessed enough drunken outbursts from Tommy that he knew he needed to get him outside as quickly as possible.

He quickly intercepted Kroch's attempt to grab the microphone from his hand. "Tommy," Julius said quietly, taking the man's arm with one hand and covering the mic with the other, "let's go for a walk. You don't want to do this here, please."

Yanking his arm away, Tommy sang, "Hey everybody! The snitch is gone, the snitch is gone…the wicked snitch of the west is gone." Leaving no misunderstanding he was addressing Jordan across the room, he slurred, "Who you looking at, missy? Didn't your daddy ever take you to see the Wizard of Oz? Remember the Cowardly Lion? Well, that's Gavin Stone. No wonder he's MIA. Ha, ha, ha!"

Nobody laughed. The guests stood as if frozen. To Julius's relief, one of the security people from the club appeared, took Tommy's arm, and quietly but firmly steered him through the crowd and out of the banquet room. Tommy continued yelling epithets as the rest of the guests slowly returned their attention to the stage.

Julius followed the security guard and Kroch out the door and then went to retrieve Jordan, who stood stunned in her corner. "Jordan, I'm so sorry you had to hear that." He was vaguely aware the Executive Director had re-taken the stage, and was doing her best to control the damage. Although he felt sorry for her predicament, his sole attention was on Jordan. "Come with me, dear," he said, trying to draw her out from where she stood, rigid, her face drained of any hint of color. "Can I get you a glass of water?"

"Julius, who was that dreadful man? What did he mean?"

"My dear," Julius replied, "that was very unfortunate. Tommy Krochinski used to be a partner of your father's. He's a boor. Please don't give him another thought. Come, let's get you out of here," he added, gently taking her arm.

A hard look crossed her face, one he'd seen many times on Gavin's. "Julius, if you don't mind I'm going to go. I just can't be here anymore. I hope you understand."

"Of course I do, but I'm worried about you driving. I would willingly take you home, but I'm afraid I might be needed here a while longer." Seeing the press swarming the director at the front of the room, he realized that was probably a gross understatement. "Let me at least walk you down to the concierge and ask them to call you a cab."

Jordan put a hand up to stop him. Her eyes nervously swept the crowd that had become animated to the point of deafening. "Julius, I have to get out of here. Now. I'm fine to drive."

"All right, but I'll give you a call when this is all over. Are you going back to your mother's?"

"No, I have a place of my own now, a condo up on Deer Ridge. I think I'm just going to go home and unwind. These last few days have all been a bit overwhelming."

Julius nodded. "I understand. I'll check in on you as soon as I can break free."

"Don't worry about me, Julius. Anytime is fine."

She obviously couldn't get away fast enough. Julius felt guilty he had coerced her into attending when she had been vehemently against it.

· · ·

I t was dark when Jordan left the club. *What on earth possessed me to go?* At the time, she'd reluctantly agreed that Julius was right—it would look even worse for her father if there was no one there to represent him. Now she wondered why covering for him had become her responsibility. She reached in her purse for her car keys, and checked her cell phone for any missed calls or texts. There was a light drizzle coming down, and she pulled her coat tighter around her weary body. Clicking the remote to unlock her car, she quickly got in and placed her phone in the console's holder. She'd had nothing but a coffee at the reception and still reeling from shock, she was looking forward to getting into a hot bath with a glass of wine. Although she wasn't hungry, she couldn't remember when she had last eaten. Dorothea was right; she needed to take better care of herself.

She swung her car out of the members-only upper parking lot, coming to a stop before turning left onto the driveway that would take her out to the street. Judging by the number of cars exiting the club's lower lot, Jordan assumed a number of guests had left shortly after the disturbing commotion caused by that horrible man. She let the cars go ahead of her before she made her exit onto Crosscreek Road.

By the time she reached the entrance to merge onto the Upper Levels Highway, the inclement weather had gone from a light mist to pelting rain. It was typical weather for February on the "wet-coast," as many of the locals referred to the North Shore of Vancouver. She was used to driving in such weather but was glad she only had one exit to go before reaching her place on Deer Ridge Drive. A hot bath was starting to sound more appealing by the minute.

Jordan drove the familiar route, lost in thought of the scene she'd just witnessed. Hopefully, a glass of wine and her growing fatigue would help put the debacle out of her mind so she could get some sleep.

Just prior to signaling her right turn onto Exit 8 and Cypress Bowl Road, the headlights of a car in the rear-view mirror blinded her. It hadn't been there a minute ago—where the hell had it come from? She wondered if inadvertently, she'd cut the driver off but she couldn't have; there had been no other vehicles in sight. She hit her signal indicator. To her disbelief, she felt the car ram her back bumper.

Trying desperately to keep a level head, her heart thumped in her chest as she realized she'd missed her exit. She sped up, hoping to make it to the next turnoff, then turn around and come back. But the car behind stayed on her tail. It was hard to believe anyone could possibly follow that close. All she could make out was the silhouette of a lone occupant in the car. She'd heard of road rage, but what was the driver thinking?

She jumped when her cell phone rang. Julius's name and number came up on the hands-free speaker. Heart pounding, she pushed the button to answer the call. "Julius, someone is following me, they're right behind me riding my bumper!"

"Jordan?" Julius said. "Calm down...I can't make out what you're saying. Where are you?"

She peered through the darkness and pelting rain, frantically searching for a sign. Terrified, she'd lost track of whether she'd passed another exit. "I don't know. I'm on the Upper Levels. I couldn't get off at my exit. He rammed my car and now I don't know where I am..."

There was a loud bang and she screamed.

"Jordan, where on the Upper Levels are you? You have to tell me where you are."

She was frantic now. "I don't know. Oh my god!"

"What happened? Stay with me. Look for a sign. Tell me where you are."

"He's trying to run me into the median. I'm looking for where I can get off and turn around…"

"No, Jordan—don't do that! Don't get off the main highway. If you can tell me…"

"I'm coming up to Westmount!"

She sounded dangerously close to hysteria. Julius checked his watch. The gas station would still be open. "Jordan, take the Westmount exit. Can you do that? Don't signal, just do it!"

"All right, I'm almost there. I can't see anything, he's so close behind me, and his headlights are blinding."

"You're doing great. You know the area like the back of your hand. Tell me when you're there." He heard the squeal of tires and silently prayed she'd managed to exit. Alone. "Talk to me, Jordan. Have you turned off at Westmount yet? Keep going straight down to the gas station. Do not stop, do you hear me?"

Silence.

"Jordan?" he yelled.

"I'm here," she quietly replied. "I'm in the gas station, and the car that was behind me is gone. I must have lost him at the last exit."

He could hear the overwhelming relief in her voice. Jesus, if they're seriously out to do her harm, whoever it was will just double back at the Caulfeild exit. "Jordan, do not get out of your car, promise me. Pull right up in front of the gas station where it's well lit. Lock your doors and if the car comes back, lean on your horn. I'm getting into my car now.

I'll be there in ten minutes. I'm going to see if I can get the police to meet us there. Are you all right?"

"Yes, I guess so. I…I don't know," her voice trailed off.

"I'll be right there. I have to get off the line now, so I can call the police. I promise I'll get there just as soon as I can. Just stay where you are."

A s Julius pulled his Jag into one of the gas station's parking spaces, he saw Jordan inside, her fingers laced around a steaming hot cup. The station attendant fussed over her while a West Vancouver police officer earnestly took notes. Two police cars, lights still flashing, sat outside. The officer taking notes turned around. "Sorry sir, we're closed—"

"I'm the one who called you, Officer," Julius interrupted. "Miss Leighton is a client of mine, I'm Julius Pinsette."

I n the ensuing thirty minutes, Julius listened while Jordan gave the police officer the details of what happened. If it were possible, she looked even worse than the night she discovered the body in her father's bedroom. Her long hair, which she had pinned up elegantly for the reception, was a mess, with several loose strands hanging down around her face. Smudged mascara framed her tired and reddened eyes. She perched stiffly on the edge of a grubby, yellow plastic chair.

Undulating red and blue from the police cars outside pulsed across her face like strobe lights. With too many people vying for her attention, Julius thought if he didn't get her out of there soon, she would snap like a twig.

At last, the officer wrapped up. Addressing Jordan, he

said, "I don't know that there's too much more we can do here tonight. The tow truck is on its way and we'll do a forensic examination on the paint chips from the other vehicle. I don't want to get your hopes up but it is possible we can get some vital leads from the evidence on your bumper." He looked at Julius. "If you want to take her home now, you can."

"Thanks, Officer, I appreciate it. I'd actually like to take Miss Leighton to her mother's for the night. Jordan, would that be all right?"

Clearly agitated, and her bravado waning, she pleaded, "Julius, please, I just want to go home and sleep in my own bed. I'm so tired. Please."

Julius's and the police officer's eyes met. He handed both Jordan and Julius his card. "Feel free to call me if anything else occurs to you," he said. "Otherwise, you'll be hearing from us in the next day or two."

Julius opened the car door for Jordan and hoped she was indeed so tired she wouldn't press him for details of her father's possible whereabouts. He couldn't recall going through such angst since Gavin spent the summer of '85 in Italy. The string of events set in motion during those few short months, had irrevocably altered Gavin's and many others' fates.

Even with Jordan safely seated in the car beside him, Julius couldn't shake the haunting feeling the other shoe was about to drop.

Chapter Eight

In the weeks following the death of private investigator Manny Smith, Jordan juggled her feelings about her father's disappearance with those of her mother's ongoing resentment. Reliving the heartache Jordan had felt over the ten years she and her father were estranged was difficult enough. She had bitterly blamed him for leaving her mother and remarrying so soon. But watching her mother struggling with her own range of painful emotions felt infinitely worse.

Though Cynthia had reluctantly agreed to a divorce over a decade ago, she had not remarried. She had been involved in countless relationships over the years but Jordan suspected each one failed hopelessly because of her mother's perception of being a victim. She watched helplessly as the warm and loving mother she'd known, evolved into a cynical divorcée. By comparison, Jordan's assessment was generous. It pained her to overhear others refer to her mother as a spiteful old lush.

Forced to grow up quickly after her father's departure, Jordan recalled the time her mother had referred to herself as weak and milquetoast—the reason, she thought, her husband had left her for someone more exciting. In retrospect, it was probably the beginning of Cynthia's unraveling. Up until then, Jordan remembered her mother as being fun and caring toward everyone. But once it was just the two of them rambling around in that huge house, Cynthia became a shell of her former self.

For a short time following Jordan's grisly discovery at Gavin's home, her mother appeared to put her own emotions aside and rallied in support of her daughter. However, as the weeks stretched on, Jordan observed Cynthia had become distant to the point of avoiding any mention of Gavin Stone. When several newspaper articles named her as Gavin's "ex-wife," it only fueled her hatred for her former husband. As a result, Jordan procrastinated on updating her about the results of the investigation into Smith's death.

After it was revealed Manny Smith had died with a needle in his arm, at Stone's mansion, the PI's family spokesperson expressed shock and disbelief that Smith had ever been involved in the use of illicit drugs. Several of Smith's cohorts, who reported they'd often witnessed him snorting cocaine at a well-known after-hours nightclub, quickly refuted that comment.

Three weeks later, West Vancouver police released the coroner's toxicology findings. Jordan was relieved when informed Smith's death was the result of a lethal overdose of cocaine and heroin. However, her heart sank when Inspector Hunter advised her that although he was still in charge of the case, the West Vancouver Police were now consulting with the Lower Mainland's Integrated Homicide Investigation Team.

"But I thought you said he gave himself an overdose," Jordan said, once again confronting Inspector Hunter.

"No, Miss Leighton, I said his death was a result of an overdose, but we no longer believe it was self-inflicted."

Jordan shook her head. "I don't understand. The coroner's report said he had other needle marks on his body."

"That's true. Smith definitely had been a user in the past, but he covered it well. The coroner discovered a scar track that formed from repeated injection into the same site. In Smith's line of work, he obviously couldn't risk track marks being seen on his arms."

She was almost afraid to ask. "If they weren't on his arms, where were they?"

The inspector cleared his throat. "Ah—." He broke eye contact. "He had one single track on the left side of his groin."

She shuddered at the mere thought of it. "But if he was obviously a user, I still don't understand why you consider this a murder."

Hunter nodded thoughtfully. This time his eyes never left Jordan's face. "Well, judging by all accounts, Smith was right-handed."

"So?"

"It's possible, but highly unlikely that one—he would have injected himself in the arm, and two—that he would have done it in his right arm rather than his left."

The certain knowledge of what that meant languished silently between them. When Jordan could stand it no longer, she said, "So what you're saying is my father is officially a murder suspect, is that correct?

"Yes ma'am...Miss Leighton, I would have to say at this point, we consider Mr. Stone to be our primary suspect. I don't suppose you've heard anything regarding his whereabouts?"

"No, I haven't." In response to his unasked question, she

added, "I would tell you the truth if I'd heard from him, Inspector. But I haven't."

She didn't know which was more sobering, the fact her father was now a confirmed murder suspect, or that she faced the real possibility she might never see him again. All the years she had relished the pain she caused him by refusing to reconcile, it never once occurred to her she wouldn't eventually be able to change her mind.

Chapter Nine

Tropea–Calabria, ITALY
June 1985

S omeone once said a rut is a shallow grave open at both
ends. What a depressing thought, but that was exactly
how Gavin Stone felt. Alone on the terrazzo, he sipped a
perfect espresso, which he'd made in what was to be their
kitchen for the next three months. Why was he feeling so
damned depressed as he surveyed this marvelous little slice of
paradise? Unlike most of his and Cynthia's friends, he had no
interest in seeing the typical tourist destinations of Italy. Not
that he wasn't intrigued by the tour they'd taken of the Vatican, but as soon as he'd laid eyes on the tiny seaside village
of Tropea, he'd felt at peace.

Situated on a reef in the toe of the boot known as the
Calabria region, the travel brochures referred to Tropea as
"La Costa degli Dei"— the Coast of the Gods. The apartment

he and Cynthia had leased for the summer was once a castle. Built in 1721 and renovated in 1921, it perched at the edge of a natural rock formation, overlooking Tropea's charming town. From this fortress-like cliff, fifty meters above sea level, Gavin gazed out over the shimmering azure water of the Tyrrhenian Sea. White sands and spectacular views overlooking the Aeolian Islands provided an inspiring place to perfect one's tan. The few sun worshipers on the beach below seemed ant-like in relation to the huge cliffs that towered above them. He found himself utterly taken with the picturesque, ancient Mediterranean town and its unspoiled beauty.

In contrast, his wife was already restless and bored. After being there just a few days, Cynthia had contacted their travel agent back in Vancouver in the hopes of getting away from what she referred to as "this god-forsaken part of the country full of coarse and vulgar people." From one of the bedrooms in the spacious flat, Gavin could hear her frustration escalate as she tried to make an outside telephone connection. In the last few days, the phone had worked only intermittently. Under normal circumstances, this would have irritated him to no end as it meant he was totally out of touch with his business back in Canada. He smiled with the realization that at that moment, he didn't care.

He was surprised she'd actually made a successful call out. From what he could hear of the one-way conversation, Cynthia was trying to get their travel agent to book her into a "civilized" place on Capri. A popular tourist destination for both Italians and foreigners, Gavin cynically wondered if his wife realized she might be surrounded by still more coarse and vulgar people. As it was June and well into summer, the island was likely to be teeming with tourists, especially locals from Naples and Sorrento, looking for a quick day trip out of the blistering heat of the city.

Ironically, Cynthia had talked him into coming to Italy to celebrate their tenth wedding anniversary. Reluctant to take more than a week away from his business, particularly if it meant leaving the country, it took a fair amount of coercion on her part before he'd agreed to come. In retrospect, she'd simply worn him down, and the truth was he and his business partner, Tommy Krochinski, had been toying with the idea of doing a project in La Thuile, in the Val d'Aosta Valley of Italy. Never one to be accused of being romantic, Gavin appeared to reluctantly acquiesce to Cynthia's nagging, knowing he could combine the trip with business and make it fully deductible.

Earlier the same year, 1985, the French ski area, La Rosière, became the only resort in Savoie offering an international skiing experience thanks to the ski lifts linked with La Thuile via two long draglifts through Little St. Bernard Pass. Although there were already several resorts in the valley, Gavin knew a number of them weren't doing well. As the new decade of the 1980s began, the global economy shifted dramatically from inflation to recession. When the US federal government tightened its money supply, interest rates had shot up sharply, hitting twenty percent.

American developers had built a couple of the La Thuile resorts. When the money-crunch hit, they found themselves unable to build to the high-end specifications they'd promised. As a result, shoddy workmanship and long building delays discouraged many of the wealthier Europeans from buying into these apartment-style resorts. Gavin and Tommy saw it as an ideal time to invest in an existing development they could pick up at a highly motivating price and turn it into a condominium development.

The trouble was, once Gavin arrived in Tropea, he had no desire to leave for even a short time to meet with the contacts Tommy had lined up. He would though, after he'd finished his coffee, at least venture into the little business center round the corner to pick up Tommy's fax. Having run out of milk earlier in the morning, he had made an impromptu stop for pastries at the bakery next door to Ottavio's Little Business Shop, where he'd run into the friendly proprietor who possessed one of the few fax machines in town.

Gavin had no sooner stepped inside the bustling bakery, than he heard his name. "Signor Stone," Ottavio shouted above the hiss of the espresso machine. "How *magnifico* to see you." Everything with Ottavio was magnifico. In his heavy Italian accent, he exclaimed that another fax had come in for Gavin.

"You wait here and I will run and get it," Octavio declared as he waited for his own thick, syrupy espresso.

"No, no, Ottavio, thank you, but I actually have some documents back at the apartment for you to fax back." Nodding his thanks to the barista for his pastries, Gavin continued, "I'll come and get it from you. You enjoy your coffee. I'll see you in a bit."

He realized that was well over an hour ago. It mystified him how he could lose himself in the down-to-earth tranquility of life in the village so soon after arriving. As Cynthia was still on the phone with their travel agent, he quietly let himself out of the apartment. He felt guilty leaving, but he didn't want to deal with another of her tantrums or listen to her disparage any more of the locals. He was happy to escape unnoticed.

When he arrived at Ottavio's shop, Gavin noticed that as always, the ambiance inside was one of controlled chaos. As it was approaching noon, and the hottest part of the day, the hubbub of simultaneous conversations competed with the buzz of the ceiling fans. Adding to the mix was the old-fashioned European ringing of god knows how many telephones. The noise combined to create a cacophony of almost deafening proportions.

In the short time he'd been in Italy, whether in big cities or small villages, gregarious Italians belted out conversations, rather than just speaking them. Old Italian mamas shouted to their families, their neighbors, and sometimes it appeared, even to themselves. Tourists often wondered aloud where the silence was in the charming little getaway as the shops, cafés, and even the streets could turn into pandemonium in a heartbeat. Everyone seemed to know everyone else and nothing seemed odd or offensive about honking one's horn, yelling out the window, or stopping traffic to chat with a *paesano* while crossing the street.

He was in the middle of trying, unsuccessfully, to explain to Ottavio's wife, Pilar, where he'd like her to send the reply to Tommy's fax, when the noise level in the shop suddenly ratcheted up a notch. Now impossible to hear the bell that tinkled when the shop door opened or closed, Gavin was unaware that yet another poor soul had joined the fray.

Seeing Ottavio wholly enraptured with whoever had arrived, Gavin looked over his shoulder to see the latest recipient to be told he or she was *magnifico*. It was as if the waters had parted for Moses. Without exaggeration, the most exquisite woman he had ever laid eyes on made her way through the parted little mob, and toward the front of the shop. Ottavio virtually leapt over the chipped tile counter, reached out to kiss both her cheeks, and exclaimed how *squisita* she was. Pilar, one eyebrow raised, recommenced her perplexed conversation with Gavin regarding his fax. "Vancouver, you say, Signor, but not same area code?"

After quickly acknowledging Ottavio, the woman who had just arrived moved down the counter, making eye contact with Pilar. She smiled at Gavin, and the scent of her musky perfume wafted over him. Ottavio looked crestfallen that his latest object of affection had turned her attention toward Gavin.

"Can I be of any help? I couldn't help overhearing you're trying to fax to Vancouver. I'm from there originally." Smiling at Pilar, the woman said something to her in Italian. Pilar nodded, as if suddenly the penny had dropped. With a quick, "*Mi scusi Signor Stone. Saro solo un attimo,*" she hastened to the back to fax Gavin's documents.

"Wow, thank you! What did you say to her?" Gavin gazed into her emerald green eyes, rimmed by impossibly long, thick black lashes. Her mischievous twinkling eyes and full lips combined to illuminate a resplendent face.

"Ah." Her smile widened to expose flawless white teeth. "If I told you that, you wouldn't need my help." She extended an elegant hand. "I'm Kathryn. Are you new to town? I haven't seen you before."

Accepting her hand, he was just about to say, "My wife and I…" but for some reason he caught himself and said, "Yes, I just came in from Rome a few days ago. I guess I'm still trying to figure out the lay of the land, so to speak."

"Are you here on business, or are you visiting simply for pleasure?"

"Uh, business actually," he replied, already feeling guilty for not confessing he was here for his anniversary—with his wife. "But I find I'm enjoying the relaxation more than doing any business. You sound like you're a native of Tropea, but you mentioned being from Vancouver?"

"Well, I don't know that I can profess to be a true native, but after all these years, I certainly feel like one of the locals.

I have a small house just on the outskirts of town, and I come back every summer. I know, it's the worst time of year for the heat and the tourists but I love it, pandemonium and all," she said, getting jostled against him.

Gavin found himself ducking around another person who had somehow managed to wedge himself between them. To keep up their conversation, he and Kathryn engaged in a somewhat comical dance, like geese straining their necks this way and that. Pilar returned with his documents, and before he'd had a chance to thank her, the man who had interjected himself took his place at the counter. Kathryn hooked her arm through Gavin's and steered him out the shop's entrance, leaving the bedlam behind.

"I hope you were finished with your business," Kathryn laughed, "but I figured we'd better get out of there quickly before we got trampled to death. As you might have noticed, Ottavio squeezes every square inch he can out of that place. The regulars keep telling him he should expand but he's too cheap. He and Pilar are sweet, and they always pay their rent on time so I shouldn't complain."

"You own the place?

"Well yes, but don't be too impressed. It's been in my family for as long as I can remember. I inherited it from my parents."

Sizing her up somewhat differently, Gavin said, "Tell me more about Vancouver. Is that where you live when you're not here?"

"Not anymore. It's a long story." She clutched his forearm to stop him from stepping off the curb, narrowly missing a taxi that careened around the corner.

Wide-eyed, he turned to her. "God, you take your life in your hands as a pedestrian in Italy. Does everyone drive like that?"

She let out an unabashed, throaty laugh. "Yes, pretty much. You'll get used to it," she assured him.

"I guess—if I don't die first." They both laughed.

They had safely reached the other side of the street, and he desperately wanted to continue their conversation. He thought about inviting her for a coffee at the only place he knew of, but it was back across the street and right next door to Ottavio's. Although he doubted Cynthia would step out into the great unwashed, he was nervous all the same. Still standing on the street corner, Gavin wracked his brain for what to say next.

Kathryn glanced at her watch and gasped. "Oh my goodness, I'd better get going. I'm supposed to be at a friend's for a late lunch. Forgive me, but I must run."

"Wait. Will I see you again? You must let me buy you a coffee for helping me out today." His heart was hammering like a schoolboy's. He couldn't remember the last time he felt this exhilarated, if ever.

"Well, I'm certainly not going anywhere. I'm sure we'll run into each other again. Have a wonderful afternoon—and put some sunscreen on or you'll be mistaken for one of our famous red onions! But they are very sweet," she added impishly.

He watched her graceful gait as she made her way down the narrow street. Not having had the courage to study her more closely when they were jammed together in the shop, he saw she was wearing a strappy yellow sundress. Her mane of chestnut hair fell in thick layers down her back, showing off toasted olive-hued arms and shoulders. Her legs were long and tanned, and her Roman sandal-clad feet easily negotiated the uneven cobblestone walk. Willing himself not to go after her, he watched her disappear around a corner.

What an idiot! He remembered shaking her hand but

couldn't remember if he'd even said his name. Not that it would make any difference if she wanted to find him. Why would she? Well, at least they had a connection through Ottavio.

As his pulse returned to normal, he turned and walked back to the apartment. And Cynthia.

Chapter Ten

Simultaneously, Gavin felt a combination of guilt and relief when he finally saw Cynthia off to Capri. Appalled at the prospect of taking a train to Solerno and then catching a ferry to the island, she hounded her husband to find someone who would fly or sail her there privately. Ottavio, of course, had come to the rescue. It seemed no sooner had Gavin mentioned his predicament to his new friend, than the man found someone willing to take not only Cynthia, but also her sizable quantity of luggage. Gavin wondered when his wife had become so spoiled and demanding. Perhaps it had happened during his frequent absences from home, and he'd simply been oblivious. Once his business started doing well, he had found it easier to throw money at their relationship than to invest any real emotional time. He wondered briefly if it would have been any different if they'd had children.

Content with the knowledge that Cynthia would be gone until the beginning of September, Gavin formulated a plan to meet with the investors Tommy had lined up. In the meantime, there was much to do.

. . .

The July noon heat was unrelenting, and the sun worshipers on the beach below were mostly in the water, staying cool. Gavin found himself staring into the apartment's open refrigerator, which contained nothing palatable enough to sustain his suddenly ravenous appetite. Prior to their arrival, Paolo, the gregarious building manager, had stocked the kitchen with some basics until he and Cynthia could get out and fend for themselves. But that was almost a week ago and except for picking up bread and milk, they had yet to go grocery shopping, choosing instead to eat most of their meals out. None of which, it seemed, had been up to Cynthia's standards.

Gavin looked at his watch and suspected there wasn't much to be accomplished during *riposo,* Italy's version of siesta, which charmingly, the locals still observed. *Might as well grab something to eat and then get some advice on where to shop.* Fortunately, during the high tourist season, many of the little restaurants and cafés remained open during the afternoon break. From his brief time in Tropea, Gavin had discovered a multitude of eateries as he wandered through the lanes, ducking into interesting little nooks and crannies. It would be perfect to enjoy lunch in the shade of a parasol before a ten-minute trek down to the beach, followed by shopping.

He stepped out of the cool stone apartment building into the blinding midday sun and headed down the Corso Vittorio Emmanuale, the long street that was a favorite with both locals and tourists, until he found a suitable café. Lucky to snag one of the two remaining tables, he was grateful for the reprieve of the shade. A waiter—probably the owner—brought a menu, which Gavin perused and quickly made a choice of a draft *Nastro Azzura*, antipasto, and *calamari partan*, a deliciously refreshing concoction of calamari marinated in olive oil, lemon, white wine, and parsley. While he waited for his food to come, he sipped his beer and watched tourists wander lazily up and down the street as they headed to or from the dead-end vista. From there, one could revel in breathtaking views of the sea.

After lunch, feeling satisfied and relaxed, Gavin ventured back out to the cobblestone road and the sizzling heat. It was still only one thirty and the beer had made him sleepy. As most of the shops, with the exception of a few touristy ones, would be closed until about three o'clock, there wasn't much he could do in the way of grocery shopping. While tempted to go back to the apartment to take a nap, he knew he would feel more refreshed if he went for a swim. He surmised that making his way down the roughly two hundred steps to the beach wouldn't be what would do him in—it would be the two hundred coming back up. But at least it would be marginally cooler on the ascent.

Gavin quickly stopped by the apartment to put on swim trunks under his shorts and grab a towel and a book. He descended the long flight of stairs and at last, stepped onto the warm velvety sand of Tropea Beach. He wasn't prepared for how many people were there but reminded himself he was in the thick of tourist season, particularly for Italians and Germans. As he looked for a place to lay his towel, he heard squeals of laughter from children jumping off an old boat anchored close to shore. Bobbing lazily on the water, the wooden vessel appeared encrusted with coat upon coat of red, white, and green paint. Though the clearness of the turquoise water made it look shallow, he had experienced first-hand that the sandy shelf dropped off quickly.

After a refreshing swim, he lay propped up on his elbows,

facing the sea. He'd been looking forward to cracking the latest book by Ken Follett, one of his favorite writers, but quickly found he was unable to concentrate. Instead, he watched people walking along the shoreline, catching snippets of various accented conversations over the haunting cries of the gulls. As he watched lovers stroll hand-in-hand, he found himself thinking of Kathryn and wondering where she lived. Would it be too obvious to ask Ottavio? He definitely wouldn't ask Pilar, as he recalled her cynically rolling her eyes at Ottavio's uncurbed enthusiasm when Kathryn had come into the shop. He suspected she had that effect on everyone.

Then it struck him. He had never even looked to see if she was married. But then again, although he was married, he seldom wore his wedding ring. It had long been a source of irritation for Cynthia, especially on this trip, where they were supposed to be celebrating their anniversary. He had no reason for not wearing it other than the wide, snug band caused an outbreak of eczema if he wore it for more than a few days. Though not wearing it had started innocently enough, he had to admit the absence of a wedding band proved quite convenient on a number of occasions.

His guilty thoughts were interrupted by a blond, mid-sized dog tearing past him, showering his book with sand, and then jumping headlong into a family of picnickers sitting close by. A tanned woman in a white bathing suit—presumably the wayward canine's mistress—quickly followed. Ignoring Gavin completely, the woman rushed over to the family who had become the dog's new best friends. After apologizing profusely to them, she turned to Gavin.

"I'm very sorry, did she…Gavin?" she gasped.

He looked up and saw it was Kathryn. *Thank you God*, he said silently. "Kathryn, what are you doing here?" From his vantage point, he was acutely aware of her toned, brown legs. Flustered, he stood up and brushed himself off.

"We were just walking over from my beach. Jezebel usually swims all the way. Normally, I can't get her out of the water but apparently, something caught her attention and…" She looked over to see the kids feeding the dog bits of their sandwiches. "Today, she decided to come ashore and wage destruction." Raising her sunglasses from her face, she perched them on top of her tousled chestnut hair. Looking down at his book, now mostly buried by sand, she said, "I'm so sorry. Did she do that?"

Gavin smiled in spite of himself. Kathryn actually seemed more disconcerted than he was. "Yes, I'd have to say she did but hey, I'm grateful to her. What a surprise, it's lovely to see you again. Do you come here often?" He instantly felt like an idiot, regurgitating what was surely the world's oldest and worst pickup line.

Not missing the irony, she laughed. "Yes, actually I do, just not usually with such a badly behaved dog." Seeing the family packing up to go, she turned her attention from Gavin. "I hope my dog didn't cause you to leave. I feel just terrible," Kathryn said to the parents. The husband assured her they were not leaving for any reason other than the time.

"No, no, we have to get back. We love dogs, don't worry. Our kids have been watching her swim every day and are thrilled to meet her." His wife nodded in agreement as they smiled, waved, and walked toward the steps that wound up to town.

"Jezebel, come here. I want you to meet someone, and you need to apologize," Kathryn said, beckoning to the dog.

Gavin reached down to pat the blond head. "Jezebel. That's quite the name but it rather suits you. You look like a she-devil, and now we know you behave like one," he chuckled. The dog sniffed him gently and then drew back to check him out more thoroughly. Satisfied, she regally offered a paw.

Kathryn laughed. "No, Gavin has no treats for you Jez— don't beg." Looking at Gavin she said, "I'd better get back, or they'll wonder if we've drowned."

He wasn't going to miss another opportunity. He bent down to retrieve his book and towel. "I'm pretty well done for the day myself. Do you mind if I walk back with you?" He looked at Kathryn's toned figure, and hoped he wouldn't embarrass himself walking back up the two hundred stone steps. Usually in good shape, he realized he hadn't been for a run since he'd been in Tropea. It had been just too hot.

"I'd love that, but you'd have to come this way," she said with a tilt of her head in the direction of the opposite end of the long beach. Puzzled, Gavin looked toward the protruding outcrop of rocks.

"We came over from the beach in front of my house. I know you can't see it at the moment, but just beyond those rocks there's a small inlet you can wade to when the tide is out."

"You're kidding, you live on the beach? You're right, I didn't know there was anything beyond the rocks." He walked down that way when he'd been on Tropea Beach earlier in the week, and assuming he'd reached a dead-end, turned around to make his way back. He had been just around the corner from her.

Crestfallen, he tried not to show his disappointment that once again they were parting ways too quickly. "It's been much too short, but I'm glad Jezebel was misbehaving or I wouldn't have run into you," Gavin said with a wistful smile. The sun illuminated the golden streaks in her chestnut hair. Sunglasses still on her head, she squinted, weaving her black lashes closer together. Looking into her eyes it was impossible not to compare them to the color of the aquamarine sea.

"Do you have to get back?" Kathryn asked. "I have houseguests, but we're having a simple dinner at my place tonight. I can't guarantee what you'll get, but there will be plenty of it."

Not sure if she was just being polite, Gavin hesitated.

"I'm sorry," she apologized, "I didn't mean to put you on the spot. I understand if it's a bit short notice."

"No, no…it's not that at all. I'm just not sure I'm dressed for the occasion."

She looked down at his legs. "Do you have any pants?" she asked with a laugh.

"Yes of course, I wore my shorts and a shirt down here," Gavin said, a little self-consciously.

"Perfect, then that's all you need. You'll find everyone is pretty casual here, if you haven't noticed already."

Gavin, don't blow it. You have an invitation from a beautiful woman you've been fantasizing about since you met and now she's invited you for dinner. Go, you imbecile!

"In that case, I'd love to, thank you. I feel very ungentlemanly though. I can't even contribute any wine to the occasion."

"Um." She appeared to ponder her words. "Well, I could be persuaded to let you do the dishes if it would make you feel better."

"Deal," said Gavin.

With Jezebel leading the way, they walked until they rounded the mammoth outcrop of rocks, arriving upon a picturesque little cove with its own sandy beach. They passed several stone staircases that disappeared into lush foliage. Near the end of the small beach, Jezebel bounded up the steps which obviously led to her home.

"All right, Jez, you lead the way," Kathryn laughed. Noticing Gavin trying to brush the sand off his feet, she said, "Oh, don't worry, you can rinse off in the outdoor shower at the top. Follow us."

Walking behind her up the steps, he was even more appreciative of her physique. Her tan was stunning against the white fabric of her one-piece. In a land of bikini-clad women, she carried herself with sensuality and elegance. Admiring how low her swimsuit plunged at the back, Gavin found it nearly impossible not to rest his eyes on the two dimples on top of what he imagined to be an exquisite bottom.

They rinsed themselves under the outdoor shower and followed Jezebel up to the next level. As they walked through a small orchard of lemon trees, a citrusy, sweet scent wafted past his nose. Finally reaching the top, they had to go single-file to navigate a cobblestone path bordered on one side by an aging concrete wall, crowned with ornate wrought iron work. One of the most beautiful gardens he'd ever seen opened like an oasis onto a shaded patio.

He looked around the property in amazement. Lush plants and shrubs of all shapes and sizes encircled him. But it was the symphony of color that assailed his senses. Immensely tall, scented clusters of white oleander and magenta bougainvillea hugged the walls surrounding the garden. Intoxicating jasmine carpeted the pergola overhead, providing a lacey awning from the late afternoon sun. Various varieties of cacti, ranging in color from soft, dove grey to yellow and pink, filled every nook and cranny of the property. Gavin was astounded to see plump, mauve-tinged figs lying carelessly on the ground—fruit he loved and had to pay handsomely for during their short import season at home.

"Oh my god, Kathryn, you live here? It's spectacular," Gavin said, drinking it in with all of his senses.

She stood so close he could feel the warmth of her shoulder brush his arm. "Turn around," she replied. "The truth is the house is falling down around my knees, but the view makes up for it." She pointed out toward the sea. "Over there is the volcanic island of Stromboli. And no, just in case you're wondering, I never take this view for granted."

Gavin could see all the way along the sandy coastline, including Tropea Beach where they had come from. Directly across the cerulean water, where gentle waves glimmered like fairies skipping across sun-kissed peaks, were the Aeolian Islands. Mesmerized, he stood still, breathing in all the scents and sounds.

"Hello darling. We wondered where you'd gone," a female voice sang from the house above. "John was just preparing drinks, so you're back in the nick of time."

Gavin turned to see an attractive woman he estimated to be in her early fifties, descending from the upper level of the house, carrying a drink.

Kathryn waved to her. "Caroline, come here. I want you to meet someone."

Caroline's white-blond hair was tied back in a low pony-tail. She was much shorter than Kathryn but she was toned and fit. Her friendly blue eyes looked directly into Gavin's. With an affable smile, she held out her hand.

"Gavin, this is my dear friend, Caroline. She and her husband, John, are here on their way to the UK. Caroline, this is Gavin. He's from Vancouver."

"Hello," Caroline said with a decidedly English accent. "It's a pleasure to meet you. Where in Vancouver are you from?"

"Hello," Gavin replied, shaking her hand. "West Vancouver actually, on the North Shore."

"You're kidding—we are too. Where in West Van?"

About to say "we," Gavin swallowed and said, "I'm up in the British Properties. Quite near the golf course. I'm sure you know it."

"Oh, for heaven's sake, we're almost neighbors. We're just down on Deep Dene."

"Yes, of course. I know exactly where you are. It's lovely down there."

"It is, but I must confess, we're escaping to the continent to get away from a massive renovation we have going on. What started as a bit of updating became the renovation from hell, as John refers to it. I'm praying it will all be done by the time we return from the UK."

"Darling, where *are* you?" a man's voice with an upper-crust English accent called from the deck. "Oh, there you are, and you found our wandering hostess. Jolly good, we thought you'd run away from home, Kathryn. Are Caroline and I driving you mad, love? Don't worry, we'll be gone soon."

Carrying his drink down the stairs, John joined them on the patio. Kathryn gave him a peck on the cheek. "I would never get tired of you, John. Your bar service is exceptional, my love. No, you can stay as long as you like," she said, winking at Caroline.

"Darling, meet Gavin, a friend of Kathryn's. Gavin, this is the one and only John Barclay," Caroline said.

A handsome man, about five foot ten and of slender build, John had a full head of white hair and impish blue eyes to match his wife's. Taking Gavin's hand in a warm handshake he said, "It's a pleasure to meet you, Gavin. I hope you're staying for dinner. Caroline and I picked up some lovely swordfish, and I could use some help with this barbecuing nonsense. Even after all our years in Canada, I've yet to master that manly duty," he said with a boisterous laugh.

Gavin instantly liked them both. "Well, I'm not sure

Kathryn meant to invite me to stay for dinner. I think I have Jezebel to thank for that. But I'd be happy to work for my keep and help you with the cooking."

"And the dishes, don't forget." Kathryn interjected.

"And the dishes, of course." Gavin replied.

"Why are we all standing here?" Kathryn said. "Let's go and sit on the patio. John, you and Gavin get to know each other and Caroline and I will whip up something for appetizers. Do you mind helping me, Caro?"

"Of course not, darling. Toodle-oo, you two. And don't talk about us while we're gone," she said, winking cheekily at Gavin over her shoulder.

Prior to sitting down with their drinks, John had directed Gavin in through the French doors to the living room, so he could use the facilities. On his return from the bathroom, he could hear the girls chatting in the kitchen. Caroline was peppering Kathryn with questions.

"Where did you find him, ducky? He's absolutely gorgeous!"

He heard Kathryn laugh. "Caro, slow down; I only just met him in town the other day and then bumped into him on the beach today when Jezebel half buried him in sand. I don't actually know much about him."

"What's to know?" Caroline asked. "You exasperate me, you do. Can you not see he's absolutely smitten with you?"

"Caro, you are a shameless romantic! When are you ever going to give up matchmaking?"

"Not until we've thawed that frozen heart of yours and found you someone who is truly worthy of you. That's when I'll stop, my darling."

"Chop chop, my little matchmaker," he heard Kathryn reply. "I need a ton of parsley to balance out the garlic and sundried tomatoes for the brie."

"All right, but you absolutely must tell me more about him."

Worried John would wonder what was taking him so long, Gavin sneaked past the kitchen but not before he heard Kathryn laugh and say, "I'm not sure I know enough about him to tell. For all I know, he could be an axe murderer. I'm glad you and John are here to keep me safe."

D ining al fresco was like a scene out of a movie. Kathryn's modest home had two terraces. They had their drinks and appetizers on the lower red-tiled patio, surrounded by Birds of Paradise, some other tall plants that looked like orange irises, as well as lavender, and eucalyptus. As they enjoyed the simple but scrumptious pre-dinner goodies the girls had put together, conversation flowed easily as if the two couples had known each other forever. It felt wonderful to be included in the camaraderie and not feel like an outsider. John and Caroline were obviously well educated and vastly traveled but at the same time, tremendously funny and self-effacing.

Engrossed in lively conversation, they eventually moved to the upper terrace for dinner. It housed a weathered and well-worn dining suite under a covered portico, with close access to the barbecue. Gavin marveled at an even grander view, if that were possible, while he cheerfully took over the task of cooking from a somewhat befuddled John. He had no idea what time it was, but they had long since watched the sun sink quickly into the Tyrrhenian Sea, and Kathryn had lit dozens of candles on both the upper and lower decks. The evening was nothing short of spectacular.

After accepting a multitude of compliments about the fish he had cooked to absolute perfection, Gavin chatted comfortably with John as if they were old friends. The ladies took the plates into the kitchen with promises of a dessert to die for.

"Kathryn, I don't think I can eat another thing. I have had an elegant sufficiency, my girl. No more food, please," John begged, rubbing his slightly protruding belly.

"John, thou doth protest too much," Kathryn admonished. "No self-respecting Brit would consider dinner complete without something sweet. We'll give you some time to digest, and I promise it will be worth the wait." She kissed the top of John's head as she and Caroline disappeared into the kitchen.

Gavin was half-listening to the women's muted conversation from inside when John turned to him. "Tell me more about this development you're looking at doing here, Gavin. I'm fascinated."

Over drinks, they had mostly talked about what John did professionally. Gavin learned he was a broker who had a clientele consisting of many of the who's who of Vancouver, a number of them well known in the entertainment industry. A significant portion of John's financial practice included selling limited partnerships. He and his organization apparently were always on the lookout for ground-floor opportunities that used tax-efficient strategies to add to their clients' sizable holdings. Upon learning the name of Gavin's company, it turned out John had one of his staff currently looking into his Hawaiian project to see if it would be a suitable investment for his clients.

"Six degrees of separation, eh what?" John said with a chuckle. It was indeed a small world. "Just out of interest, what kind of capital would you need to raise to do the project in La Thuile?"

"Somewhere in the region of ten to fifty million," Gavin replied.

John whistled and took a long sip of his wine. He slowly

twirled his wineglass and the mellow *Rosso Reserva* rippled lazily around the bowl. "That's quite a spread," he said, looking at Gavin across the table.

"Yes, it is," Gavin, agreed.

"So from what you've said, your company picks up apartment developments for a song, freshens them up a bit, and then turns them into condos. You then sell individual units to investors via shares in limited partnerships. Do I have that right?"

"You have it exactly, John. We'd like to convert the La Thuile project into a three-hundred-unit condominium development and put in some high-end retail space on the street level."

"Sounds ambitious to a mere financial planner like me, but you've obviously had experience with your other projects, which I understand have been quite successful. This would be your first one in Europe though, yes?"

"That's correct. It's my main reason for being over here," Gavin agreed. "To see if it's feasible and if we can make the numbers work based on how extensive the renovations would be. My sources tell me the original developers essentially ran out of money and had to start cutting corners. I need to get some surveyors and inspectors in there to tell me if what is needed is mostly cosmetic, or if it would be more on the structural side."

"And that's why the spread in the amount of capital you'd need to raise," John said.

"Precisely."

"All right you two, no more business talk," Caroline said, preceding Kathryn from the kitchen. "We have here the pièce de résistance and if you wolf it down without due appreciation, Kathryn will be most offended."

"Point well taken, love. But Gavin, I'm quite serious—I

want to explore this more with you. Let's get together if we can before Caroline and I go over to the UK, because we'll be flying directly back to Vancouver from there. Can you spare some time in the next few days, my good man?"

"Absolutely, John, it would be my pleasure," Gavin replied, grateful John's interest seemed genuine.

"All right then ladies, how much longer are you going to keep us waiting then? Come on, let's see it," John bellowed. "What is this subversive creation you've whipped up, Kathryn, tiramisu?"

"Oh, John, you are so pedestrian," admonished Caroline. "Kathryn is much more adventurous than that, aren't you darling?"

"Well I don't know about adventurous, but I do want to give you a totally authentic culinary experience while you're here in Tropea." Kathryn replied.

Suddenly, Gavin forgot everything around him. His dinner companions, the sublime setting—they all blurred into the background. Kathryn had changed earlier in the evening to a simple mid-calf, black skirt, and strapless red linen top that showed off her tiny waist. She had put on some lip-gloss and brushed her hair so it fell loosely around her shoulders. Carrying her dessert concoction in both hands, her face glowed in the warm light of the birthday candles. She took his breath away.

"Happy birthday to you, happy birthday to you," she and Caroline sang, "happy birthday, dear John...happy birthday to you." As Gavin joined in, all three added, "and many more," to their hearty refrain.

"Darlings, you shouldn't have. I wanted to keep this one a

secret. I'd hoped you'd forgotten," John protested, clearly thrilled they hadn't.

"Blow out the candles, John," Kathryn said, looking over at Gavin and smiling. "And don't forget to make a wish."

When Kathryn put the cake on the table in front of John, Gavin was surprised to see the candles were in the shape of the number sixty. He would have pegged both Caroline and John to be in their early fifties at most. They both looked marvelous. Obviously, life was good. After blowing out the candles, John took the knife Kathryn handed him. "And what pray tell is this divine creation, my love?"

"Dolce di Taglierini. I used to make it with my Nona. It's made with egg noodles, tons of eggs, raisins and ricotta, with an orange marmalade and honey sauce," Kathryn said, pointing to an antique silver sauceboat. "I hope you like it."

"Like it? As satisfied as I am, you were right, lovey, this is worth the wait. Ladies first," John said as he cut the cake and handed a plate to his wife.

A drink called Sgropino, made with Proseco, vodka, and lemon sorbet, followed Kathryn's exquisitely decadent dessert. It was so named, she informed them all, because it can cause you sneeze like a mare shaking flies from her nostrils.

"Darling, our stay with you has been the ultimate," Caroline said. "We feel like we've experienced the authentic south of Italy from you, don't we, John?"

"Indeed," John was quick to agree. "But my darling, I think it's time for this old codger to turn in for the night."

The two men stood to shake hands. "Gavin," John said, "I look forward to our get-together before Caroline and I leave." He took Kathryn by both shoulders and gently kissed her forehead. "Another beautiful meal, my sweet. You've been much too good to us. Enjoy the rest of the evening you two. I hope we're not leaving you with too much of a mess in the kitchen, but I'm afraid I must go up to bed. Goodnight."

Giving Kathryn a wink, Caroline also rose. "And I'm going to join my beloved. It's been a perfect day, but I must turn in as well. It was a pleasure meeting you, Gavin."

"The pleasure's been all mine," Gavin said, extending his hand. "I hope you both have a good night's sleep."

"Thank you, old chap." John hooked his arm through his wife's. "I'm sure I shall sleep like a baby. Give me a call in the morning and we can set a time to meet. In the meantime, cheerio you lovebirds."

"John!" Caroline admonished. "You're embarrassing them, darling. You're cut off. Come to bed this instant," she chided, gently pushing him into the house.

W ithout a watch, Gavin had completely lost track of time. After the Barclays went to bed, he and Kathryn sat for at least another hour, nursing their Sgropinos. He hated to leave but knew he must. She was so easy to be with, and like him, seemed unaware of the time. But he thought it the gentlemanly thing to let her get to bed as well.

"I don't know what time it is, Kathryn, but I think I'd better make good on my offer to help you with the dishes, and then I should probably find my way home." He wasn't entirely sure how he was going to do that.

"You're sweet, but Caroline and I cleaned up as we went along. You and John seemed to be having such a good chat, we didn't want to disturb you," Kathryn replied. "But if you wouldn't mind helping me put all the candles out, I'll drive you back to town."

"I'd be happy to do that but please, I can just walk back or perhaps you can call me a cab?"

"I'm afraid you won't find a taxi at night, and you'd most certainly get lost walking. I won't hear of it. Please let me drive you, it'll only take a few minutes."

"All right then, if it's no trouble, I'd appreciate that."

After snuffing out all the candles, he helped her bring in the last of the glasses. He'd been in the house once during the evening to use the bathroom, but as she and Caroline were busily chatting in the kitchen, he hadn't wanted to intrude. He hadn't been surprised the inside of the house was elegant, but at the same time, warm and welcoming. At the time, he had noticed Kathryn had some truly stunning paintings on many of the walls, indicating quite an eclectic taste.

"Come, let's go through the house. I'll just grab my keys and we can go out the front," Kathryn said.

She led him to a quaint outside terrace, covered in large rough stone tiles. In the understated outside lighting, he saw what appeared to be a new, white-bricked wall covered with fuchsia bougainvillea. As he passed through the arch that led out to the street, he looked back at the house. It was almost completely obscured by the lush vegetation that clung to the wall, most of which was dwarfed by an enormous pineapple palm. A few cars lined both sides of the street, and Kathryn led him to a little red Alfa Romeo convertible. Jezebel appeared from the darkness, wagging her tail in anticipation of a car ride.

"No Jez, I can't take you with me. Go back inside, I won't be long." They both laughed as her sad little face with one flopped over ear made it clear she didn't understand why she couldn't go with her mistress. But she dutifully padded back through the archway heading toward the house.

In the close quarters of the car, with the top up, Gavin was aware of Kathryn's subtle perfume, which he remembered from their first encounter in Ottavio's shop. He was surprised how soon they reached the outer limits of Tropea's historical area. Kathryn shut off the engine as they turned to each other in the moonlit evening. They both starting speaking at the same time and laughed. "You go first," she said.

"No, no, what were you going to say?"

"I just wanted to tell you how much I enjoyed this evening. I know Caroline and John enjoyed your company as well. John has extremely good connections, not just in Vancouver, and I think he could be very helpful to you. I hope you'll have time to meet with him before he leaves."

"I absolutely will. I liked him very much, and I think we might have some common ground we can explore. Your friend Caroline is lovely as well. They both obviously care very deeply for you."

"Yes, they've been like a cross between good friends and parents for me. I love them to pieces," Kathryn said. "Oh, I'd better give you my number so you can call John in the morning. We're all early risers, so call anytime." She pulled a pen and paper out of the little glove compartment, wrote down her number, and handed it to him. They were so close he could feel her warm breath. Unexpectedly, he was tongue-tied. He had so much he wanted to say to her. Neither spoke for a moment until Kathryn broke the silence.

"You look so sad, what's the matter?"

He cleared his throat. "There's something I need to tell you, and I feel like an absolute shit," Gavin said. Not knowing any other way to say it, he looked into her eyes and said, "Kathryn, I'm married."

"Yes, I know," she murmured in the dark.

"You know?"

"Gavin, Tropea is a small town. My Tropea is even smaller. Everybody knows everybody here."

"I guess. I should have told you sooner, but there just didn't seem to be a good time. I'm sorry."

Kathryn laughed. "There really wasn't, was there? Our meetings were both quite fortuitous. I understand your wife has gone over to Capri."

Surprised again, he briefly wondered how she knew. "Ah...Ottavio, right?"

"Yes." He could see her smile in the dark.

"Gavin?"

"Yes," he said, his heart threatening to burst out of his chest.

"Thank you for telling me."

"I'd like to see you again." He held up the slip of paper she'd given him. "Would it be all right to use this number to reach you and not just for John? Perhaps we could have lunch and I could explain."

"I'd like that. Yes, of course you may call. And you only need to explain what you want to."

Neither of them spoke. Should he kiss her? He didn't want to ruin a magical evening, but he couldn't get out of the car without doing something. As if to answer his unspoken question, she leaned into him and kissed him slowly and tenderly.

When she pulled away, she said, "Why don't we have that lunch you talked about and see how things go from there?"

"Deal," he said. He held her chin in his hand, kissed her again and got out of the car while he still could.

Chapter Eleven

S itting in the tiny café hidden among a maze of picture-perfect lanes just off the main palazzo, Gavin sipped an espresso and looked forward to his meeting with John Barclay. Having arrived a few minutes early, he watched the summer tourists milling about exploring the shops and restaurants. He marveled at his good fortune for ending up here. Not just in this part of Italy, but that he was experiencing the fruits of a pretty successful run in his business. Based on the heydays of his misspent youth, it was a wonder his life hadn't taken a very different path. The past fifteen years had gone astonishingly fast.

As a young realtor in 1970, he was frustrated trying to break into the cliques of the established real estate sales-people in Vancouver. After several false starts in the business, he set his sights on the sleepy little town of Whistler, where a few visionary planners had decided to build a ski resort, and set about creating a carefully planned playground for the rich and famous—and all ilk in between.

Gifted with a knack for making friends quickly and easily,

Gavin soon found himself at the tender age of twenty-one making more money than he knew what to do with. Actually, he *had* known what to do with it. He hesitated to calculate how much money he had spent on women, parties, and cocaine. Thankfully, the latter was just a distant memory.

He started his career right out of high school, at a little-known real estate office in what was then the Whistler town center. Over the next three years, that company developed into his biggest competitor when he later got his brokerage license and opened his first enterprise, Brandywine Realty. Along the way, he met another badass young realtor at the same firm, Tommy Krochinski. The two of them combined what remained of their drug-addled brains and planned how they would ride the wave they were convinced was about to take Whistler by storm.

Tommy had a few ragged edges, but man—nobody could score with the ladies like he did. Using his street-boy charm, Tommy had somehow collected a veritable Rolodex of well-heeled older women who were looking to exact revenge on the ex-husbands who had left them for more recent models. Tommy made it his personal mission to take them under his wing—not to mention the sheets—and help them find properties in which to sink their hard-earned divorce proceeds.

He and Gavin had worked fiendishly to build their real estate business and they played even harder. Life became one twenty-four-hour party after another, after another. Literally, everything they touched turned to gold, and at the respective ages of twenty-one and twenty-three, they had become major players on the Whistler scene. That was, until they took a well-earned trip down to Vancouver. Simply by being in the wrong place at the right time—for the cops, that is—he and Tommy found themselves in the middle of a late-night drug raid at a party house in Kitsilano.

Back then, "Kits," a community just over the bridge from downtown Vancouver, was known as a funky place, largely inhabited by hippies, yippies and fledgling Green Peace members. West Fourth Avenue was the place to hang out and be seen. One-time splendid heritage-style houses had been split up into apartments, and young people who couldn't see themselves living in characterless cement jungles rented there. And partied.

Neither Tommy nor Gavin knew whose house they were in that night. Via the grapevine, dozens of other like-minded partiers heard about the revelry and crowded into the dingy, run-down flophouse. Gavin was so blasted from snorting cocaine and smoking pot that when the cops broke down the door yelling, "This is a raid—nobody move!" Gavin thought it was all a big joke. The joke turned out to be on him and Tommy, as everyone else scattered, and the two of them were among the few left standing. Technically, both of them had enough LSD and marijuana on them to be charged with trafficking. Along with a few other unlucky reprobates, they were loaded into a Vancouver Police paddy wagon, taken to the Main Street station, booked, and thrown in a holding cell for the night.

That night in jail turned into four months in prison, along with a $2,500 fine. In retrospect, it was a ridiculously lenient sentence. Fortunately, he and Tommy were housed in the same medium-security correctional facility, and by the end of their prison terms, they had hatched a plan for the second phase of their real estate career. Only trouble was, they had criminal records.

He was jolted from his daydream by a familiar English accent. "Gavin, good to see you! I hope I haven't kept you waiting." John squeezed his way between crowded tables and was about to sit down.

Gavin stood to shake his hand. "No worries, John, I got here a little early by choice." Looking at his half-empty cup he added, "I'm having an espresso. What can I get for you?"

John motioned him to sit down. "All is taken care of, my good man. In the short time I've been here, Antonio knows exactly what I like and it's on its way. I told him you might need a topper-upper yourself.

"Before we talk business," John continued, "I must pass on a message from the ladies. Caroline made me promise faithfully not to bore you with too many tales of my business prowess. And, Kathryn...well, Kathryn said to tell you that you left your book at the house, and therefore you must come back for dinner to retrieve it. All good stuff, wouldn't you say?" He winked at Gavin.

"I don't need to be asked twice to have another dinner with Kathryn. But we agreed next time we meet, I'd take her to lunch." Gavin chuckled, scarcely hiding his delight in hearing from Kathryn.

"A brilliant idea, old boy," John volleyed back. "You can count on us to encourage her to take you up on that. I think she's quite taken with you."

Gavin wondered what, if anything, Kathryn said to the Barclays after he had confessed to being married. He suspected she hadn't mentioned it, or John would likely not be as magnanimous. Once their coffees came, the two men spent almost an hour discussing the details of the ski development Gavin had in mind.

Eventually, John closed his worn, leather-bound book in which he'd rapidly been making notes. "Gavin, this sounds very exciting. Let's meet when we're both back in Vancouver. In the meantime, let me work on getting some more information on selling this project as a limited partnership to our clients. I have a few in mind who I think would be interested."

"I look forward to that, John. I'll get my partner working on things at his end. Here's one of my cards. I'll fill Tommy in on our meeting. If you have any questions, just call."

John tucked the card into his polo shirt pocket and then folded his hands on top of his journal. He leaned forward, fixing Gavin with an earnest gaze. "Old boy, I hope you won't think me presumptuous, but please take good care of whatever relationship you have with Kathryn. She's had a tough go of it. I'm afraid Caroline and I are quite protective of her. I'm sure she'll tell you about it if she hasn't already."

"She hasn't said anything," Gavin said, a bit lost for words. "But I can assure you, John, I think she's a very special lady. I wouldn't knowingly do anything to hurt her." John didn't appear to be warning him, but the older man's fatherly concern gave him pause for thought.

Grinning, John said, "I don't doubt that. Caroline and I didn't give you much time to yourselves the other evening. No doubt you two have a lot to discover about one another, when we old fogeys aren't there to intrude."

Pulling more than enough out of his wallet to cover their beverages, Gavin extended his hand. "John, I'm grateful for your time and I very much appreciate the advice—both business and personal. You've been very kind, and I promise you I will take good care of Kathryn."

G avin assumed Kathryn would be celebrating her last dinner with the Barclays before they left the next day, so he didn't call that evening. He remembered John saying they'd be departing for the airport the following day around noon. It was all he could do to wait that long to call her.

His heart leapt when she answered the telephone on the second ring, and that she sounded so warm when he identified himself.

"I'm so glad you called. John said he enjoyed his meeting with you. How are you?"

"Yes, we had a very good meeting. Am I catching you at a good time?"

"Absolutely. I just came back from a walk with Jez. What are you up to?"

"Not much…" he hesitated, feeling like a nervous schoolboy. "Kathryn, I know it's short notice but I wondered if you'd be open to changing lunch to dinner, and if you might be free this evening?" There, he'd gotten it out. He simply couldn't sit around another night unable to concentrate on anything other than her.

To his enormous relief she replied, "I'd love that. The truth is I'm already lonely, and John and Caroline have only just left. What did you have in mind?"

"Well, I feel a little awkward, but would you mind choosing the restaurant? I'm still finding my way around, and I trust your judgment better than mine." He wanted to ask her to make sure it was quiet and romantic but thought better of it.

"I know just the place. It's quiet and boasts one of Tropea's finest views. But I have one request."

Agreeable to just about anything this exquisite woman asked of him, Gavin said, "Of course, what's that?"

"There's a place on the way where I'd like to stop for just a few minutes. Would that be all right?"

"Yes, but now you've got my curiosity piqued."

"Ah, you'll find out soon enough," she said, laughing. "Why don't I pick you up at your place at say, seven?"

"I'll agree to everything, except I will pick you up. I'm afraid I'm not secure enough in my masculinity to let a lady pick me up for a date. I do have a car, you know—albeit a rented one— but I think I can find my way back to your house."

Chapter Twelve

P roud of himself for finding Kathryn's house, Gavin pulled his rented Mercedes 380 SL out front. Jezebel, no doubt hearing the scrunch of the tires on crushed stone, bounded through the arched wall, tail wagging, sniffing optimistically for treats.

"Sorry, Jez, I have nothing for you," Gavin said. Refusing to take his word for it, she pushed her nose into his hand as she escorted him to the open front door.

"Is that you, Gavin?" Kathryn called from somewhere in the house. "I'll be down in a minute. Make yourself comfortable."

The interior of the house, which he had observed on his brief visit the other night, was indeed in need of some repair. However, the overall look of distressed woodwork and walls added a patina that exuded an earthy charm. Kathryn's living room was tastefully furnished with various antique pieces. An overstuffed cream-colored loveseat and a colossal easy chair with ottoman that would easily seat two people side-by-side formed a cozy conversation area. Colorful paintings covered almost every wall. He was scrutinizing the signature on the large canvas above the couch when he heard Kathryn's voice behind him.

"I see Jezebel showed you in. Did you have any trouble finding us?"

Turning around, the sight of her nearly made his jaw drop. Trying to find his words, he swallowed self-consciously. "No, actually I'm amazed I remembered my way back. I hope you don't mind that Jezebel let me in."

"No, I asked her to, and she obviously remembers you. Believe it or not she's quite selective about who she lets onto the property," Kathryn replied.

She had on a simple black jersey top, sleeveless on one side and cut away on the other, leaving one sun-kissed shoulder bare. Low on her hips she wore a wide leather belt over a long, paisley skirt. A deep slit up the front showed off her perfectly tanned legs. Flat, leather sandals fastened around her ankles. She had brushed her hair back from her face, elegantly securing it with a barrette, leaving the rest of her sun-streaked mane to flow over one shoulder.

"Really? I thought she'd let just about anybody in if she thought they had treats in their pocket, which unfortunately I didn't bring." Gavin laughed and reached down to scratch Jezebel's ears.

Unsure of what to wear, Gavin originally had donned a long-sleeved white linen shirt and slacks. Although white highlighted his rugged dark looks, he felt somehow he resembled the Man from Glad, and at the last minute, changed his trousers to beige linen. It was unlike him to be so insecure. She moved toward him, kissing him on both cheeks. There was that perfume again; it had an unmistakable but subtle muskiness that he would remain always in his memory.

"All right Jezzie, you guard the house. We'll see you later," Kathryn said, gathering her keys and purse.

Looking at Jezebel's disappointed little face, Gavin said, "I thought you said she loves car rides. Couldn't she come with us?"

"Are you serious? You don't mind?"

"No, not at all. If she doesn't mind being squished in the back seat."

"Well, you heard the man, Jez, you can come. I hope you know how lucky you are. You can be our chaperone," Kathryn said, beaming at Gavin.

Though he initially found the drive nerve-wracking, he began to enjoy navigating the twists and turns of the road, which kept steadily ascending. Each time he shifted gears, he was aware of Kathryn's bronzed knees, and he felt an intimacy he'd long forgotten. The warmth of the low setting sun and the light breeze blowing through his hair was exhilarating, and they chatted easily as she pointed out the sights. He couldn't remember when he had last felt this comfortable with another person—certainly he never had with Cynthia. Although the tingle of new excitement was there, he also felt as if he'd known Kathryn forever.

"Just beyond this bend, there will be a hidden drive," she said, pointing to the right. "You'll need to slow down a bit or you'll miss it. There, can you see that open gate? Just go straight through it and up the driveway."

He followed her instructions and turned up a long winding lane, the car's tires bumping roughly over old stone and sun-scorched grass. The driveway came to a circle around a chipped and weathered fountain long ago run dry, in front of an ivy-covered stone building. Scattered about were a few children's toys and what looked like a paint easel.

Puzzled, Gavin looked over at Kathryn. "Is this where you wanted to stop?"

Before she could answer, Jezebel jumped out of the back

seat, over the side of the convertible. She whined and wagged her tail furiously. Evidently, she had been there before.

Gavin came around to Kathryn's side and opened the door, offering his hand as she gracefully stepped from the car.

"Yes, I promise we won't stay long, but with John and Caroline with me for the past two weeks, I haven't gotten up here once, and I wanted to look in on the children. Do you mind?"

Unsure if they were at a private home or perhaps an orphanage, he looked around at the largely overgrown property. "No, of course not, but where are we?"

"Well, it was a converted private school, but now it houses children with emotional problems who come from nearby cities. Some are autistic, but many of them are coping with severe trauma. A nun who's formerly from the Vatican runs the house. That's a whole story in itself. She's nothing short of amazing with the children, and of course she has help, but not enough."

Kathryn looped her arm through Gavin's, and led him to the front door, which Jezebel was already pawing excitedly. Kathryn reached for the rusted iron doorknocker and pumped it up and down several times. A grey-haired woman opened the door and beamed at her unexpected guests.

"Jezebel!" she said in thickly accented English. "*Katarina, mia cara*, I didn't know you were coming." The nun opened the door wide and ushered them in.

"Sister Serafina, I hope we're not intruding at the children's dinner time. I'd like you to meet my friend, Gavin Stone."

"Welcome, Signor Stone," she said, taking his hand in both of hers. The sister looked at Kathryn and said, "No, no. Supper is over and bath time has not yet begun. The children will be most happy to see you. Can you stay for tea?" she asked hopefully.

"No, we mustn't, but I'd love to see how they're coming along from their last session. Would that be all right?"

"Of course, cara." She waved them forward. "Come... come with me to the art room."

They followed her along a narrow stone corridor. As the sister opened a squeaky wooden door, Gavin could hear shrieks of children's laughter coming from inside. When they saw Kathryn, several of the smaller ones leapt up and ran to her, nearly knocking her over with their enthusiasm.

"Katarina, Katarina," they all yelled at once. Gavin couldn't understand the rest of what they said or Kathryn's responses back to them in Italian, but they obviously adored her.

Only one little girl remained on her cushion in the middle of the floor. She looked to be about four or five years of age, and unlike the other children, she never looked up from her crayoning, completely undistracted by the mayhem. While Sister Serafina tried to quiet the little ones, who thankfully were lost in the fun of climbing all over Jezebel, Kathryn walked over to the little girl and knelt beside her. Gavin stood in the doorway and watched.

"*Thula, Ciao come stai?* Hello, Thula, how are you?" Kathryn asked.

The little girl showed no sign of hearing and didn't look up.

"Thula," Kathryn said again. Still, no response. Kathryn cupped one hand under the little girl's chin and gently lifted her face to look at her. Her liquid brown eyes looked pitiful as Kathryn softly brushed a dark curl from the child's face.

"Do you have anything you want to show me today, Thula?" Kathryn asked quietly. Again, there was no reply.

Sister Serafina stopped fussing with the other children and watched intently.

"I'll come again soon, Thula. Perhaps you can show me your painting then," Kathryn said. She slowly got up from the floor and walked over to join Serafina and Gavin. She looked back at the child and asked the sister, "Has she made any progress at all since I was last here?"

"Sadly not, my dear, but give it time. The therapists are working with her every day that they can. It's at God's mercy, we must be patient, yes?" the nun said, putting her hand gently on Kathryn's arm.

"Yes," agreed Kathryn, although she seemed reluctant to accept the sister's prognosis. "I'll be back at my usual time next week, Sister. Is there anything I can pick up in town that the children need for their classes?"

"I will look forward to that cara, but no, I think we are quite well off for supplies. I hope you know how grateful the children are for all the things you've sent from America. Before you arrived for the summer, one of their biggest treats was opening the boxes of art supplies. You have made such a difference in these little ones' lives, Katarina. I know it seems slow, but they are progressing, with your help." The squat little woman reached up to embrace Kathryn. Gavin was moved to see tears in Kathryn's eyes as she reciprocated.

The sun made its majestic dip into the sea just as they were shown to their table at Cucina Nascosto. Meaning "hidden kitchen," the multi-tiered restaurant, tucked into the mountainside, was surrounded by lush vegetation that offered up a delicious mixture of scents for its guests. Unsure if they were original or well-replicated props, Gavin marveled at the Corinthian pillars that framed an azure pool at the edge of the furthest tier of the restaurant. All the tables sat parallel to the sea, ensuring no guest had their back to the million-dollar view.

After many two-cheeked kisses and Kathryn asking after the proprietor's family, he insisted on seating them personally. Looking around, Gavin noticed that almost everyone in the place appeared to be locals. Accustomed to the establishments in town that catered more to the tourists, he was nervous that he might not know what to order. To his enormous relief, no sooner were they seated than two Prosecos arrived as if by magic.

Perhaps reading his thoughts, Kathryn raised her glass and said, "I hope you don't mind, but Lorenzo won't even let us look at a menu. He just orders whatever he thinks you'll like. But I can vouch for his choices, and I promise you the bill will be very reasonable."

"Cheers." Gavin raised his champagne flute to hers and let out a little sigh of relief. "To be perfectly honest, I feel a little out of my league. So, instead of worrying about what to order I can focus on you and all the questions I've been dying to ask," he said, smiling at her across the table.

"And what questions would those be?" Kathryn asked, with mock innocence.

"Well to start with, tell me about your relationship to the children. It sounds like you are very involved with their progress, sending them art supplies even when you're not here."

Kathryn took another sip, put her glass down, and waited a few seconds. "I do. You asked me at Ottavio's if I still live in Vancouver. I moved to Carmel, California when I was in my twenties, and with Caroline and John's help, I was able to build a small art gallery there. It's actually a combination of a gallery and a workshop where art therapists work with emotionally disturbed children."

"So, is that what you do? You're an art therapist?" he asked.

"No, I thought about trying to get my credentials at one point, but my first love is painting. Once I got established in Carmel, I decided to donate the back part of the gallery, and some of my time, for a couple of the therapists in town to carry on their work with the children."

"That's marvelous," Gavin said. "What a selfless thing to do—but you're an artist?"

"Yes, it's a frugal way to decorate my house," Kathryn said, laughing.

"Those beautiful paintings I saw are yours?" he gasped. "They're magnificent. I was trying to see the name of the artist when you came downstairs."

"You're very kind. Yes, they're pretty well all mine except for a few I have scattered around of my students' work—done by some of the children you saw today with Sister Serafina."

"So that's what you meant when you told Thula that maybe you could see her painting when you go back. You've been working with her?"

"Yes, in tandem with a qualified therapist, of course. The children are very vulnerable and I would never try to do it without a professional. My grandfather left the house to me, and it sat in disrepair for years. My parents immigrated to Canada and had very little interest in coming back here." Gavin nodded in rapt attention.

"About three summers ago, I brought one of our Carmel therapists with me, and together we got the house into decent shape and connected with the few others we could find in the local area. Mostly, we get young people from the bigger cities who are doing their apprenticeships. They volunteer their time as part of their practicum. It works well, but unfortunately, it isn't steady. The children need more consistency to move forward. We desperately need two full-time therapists, but the cost is something that's impossible right now." She looked down and toyed with her wine glass.

Reaching for her hand, Gavin looked at her downcast eyes and realized he was falling hopelessly in love with each new aspect of this woman. When she looked up, her eyes were moist and she looked away, embarrassed.

"Our visit there today brings up some deep emotions for you, doesn't it?" Gavin asked gently. "But remember what the sister said, you need to have patience." She nodded, not removing her hand from his.

"You mentioned Caroline and John. Is that where you met them—in Carmel? They're obviously very fond of you. John speaks of you like a daughter," he added.

"No, I met John in Vancouver. The bank that was administering my trust fund referred me to his firm." She hesitated. "After my parents died."

"I'm so sorry, Kathryn, you must have been awfully young to have lost both your parents. Was it a car accident?" He wasn't sure he should be asking.

She rubbed her bare arms as if chilled; her eyes still glistened with tears. "They were gunned down in front of a restaurant called Thomasina's on the east side of Vancouver. It was never proven, but it was widely believed to have been a targeted execution."

"Execution. You mean by the Mafia?" He felt as if they were talking about an Al Pacino movie. "You mentioned your grandparents, but your last name is Bell," he said, puzzled.

"Yes, my father changed our family name from Belisario when he and my mother immigrated to Canada. At the time, I didn't understand why other members of the family went to Montreal when they left here and we went to Vancouver. I learned much later that my father was desperate to get away from his ties in the old country and wanted to start fresh. New country, new name. But their happiness only lasted eight years."

Stunned, Gavin didn't know what to say. He knew the restaurant Kathryn referred to; it had been a well-known eatery in Vancouver until it closed maybe ten years ago. There were always rumors about the comings and goings being Mafia-related, but no one really knew for sure if it was true or just titillating gossip.

"Kathryn, we don't have to talk about this if you don't want to…"

"No, it's all right. It was a long time ago now." She brushed away her tears and smiled at him reassuringly. "I was only six when it happened. We'd been out for a big family celebration and I'd fallen asleep in the restaurant. When it was time to go, my father carried me to our car, which was parked out front, and then he went back in to get my mother, who was still saying her goodbyes. I saw my parents come outside onto the sidewalk. Then I heard a couple of pops and both my parents were on the ground, covered in blood."

"Oh my god, Kathryn, you saw it happen?"

"Yes, I must have awakened after my father put me in the car, and I was sitting up looking out the window."

Gavin was nonplussed. He had absolutely no words that wouldn't sound trite. Kathryn had wrapped both hands around the stem of her glass and he reached out to touch them.

"What happened after their deaths? Who looked after you?" Gavin asked, his heart breaking at how suddenly small and vulnerable she looked.

"My mother's sister, who lived in Vancouver, fought to keep me from being sent to live with family in Italy, and she was so good to me. I didn't speak for a year after it happened. I had what's called selective mutism. A child psychologist suggested to my aunt that art therapy might be helpful. Apparently, I had been quite the budding little artist even at a young age, and the doctors hoped it would help bring me out of my self-imposed silence."

"So that's why helping the children Sister Serafina looks after is so important to you," Gavin said quietly.

"Yes, I hate to think about what might have happened to me had I not received help. Several of the kids who I went through therapy with ended up going down some very bleak roads. I know of at least two who committed suicide in their teens."

Kathryn paused awkwardly as the waiter, with a flourish of hands and a brief explanation in Italian, placed a plate of antipasti on their table. When he left, she continued, "Gavin, I'm so sorry. The last thing I wanted to do was to put a damper on our evening. Please tell me I haven't."

"No, of course you haven't. I asked, and I hope I haven't made you feel uncomfortable by bringing it up. It's just that I realized after our evening together with the Barclays that I had no idea what you do."

Kathryn took another sip from her almost empty champagne flute. "Well now you know." She smiled hesitantly. "Probably a lot more than you wanted to."

He drank in her beauty, softly illuminated by candlelight. "I find myself wanting to know everything about you. Thank you for telling me."

Her face brightened. "You must be starving." She looked at the large platter before them. "I know I am. Let me tell you what some of this is so you don't feel as if you're taking your life in your hands."

Red wine arrived, and they chatted comfortably while exquisitely tasty dishes came and went until they both had to plead with the waiter to cut them off.

"But you must have dessert. And special drinks are coming for you," the waiter exclaimed, in barely understandable English.

Kathryn took the lead. "All right, but just one, *solo uno*, and two forks please." She looked at Gavin, shaking her head and laughing.

"I'd better not have any more drinks if I'm going to drive that windy road back. Can you tell him no to the drinks?" he asked Kathryn.

"I could but it'll hurt Lorenzo's feelings. Just smile and accept them."

Kathryn was right; he couldn't believe their bill, considering all they had heartily consumed over the past two and a half hours. They said their goodbyes to the proprietor and staff, with more cheek kissing, and made their way out to the gravel parking lot. He had forgotten all about Jezebel, but there she was, sleepily rising from the backseat, as she heard their voices.

"Hello girl," Gavin said. "I bet your mouth was watering with all those yummy food smells." She wagged her tail, curled up and went back to sleep.

In spite of all they'd had to drink, with Kathryn's navigation skills and Gavin's driving, they arrived safely in front of her house. He had been thinking all the way back from the restaurant what he should do if she invited him in. He knew without a doubt what he wanted to do, but he was uncharacteristically concerned that he should not move too fast. He was also painfully aware that although they had talked a lot about his business and his future, they hadn't talked about the one thing that loomed in the background: his marriage.

He and Jezebel came around to see Kathryn from the car. Having put a shawl over her shoulders during the ride home, she pulled it tighter around her in the cool evening air. "Are you tired?" she asked. "Would you like to come in?"

"No, I'm not tired and yes, I'd love to come in." He looked directly into her eyes. "Are you sure?"

"Of course I'm sure. Jezebel, what do you think, can he come in?" she asked the dog playfully. As if to answer, Jez wagged her tail furiously and led the way to the front door.

"What can I do to help?" Gavin asked as she tampered with the electric coffee grinder.

"I don't know, it just seems to have stopped working," Kathryn said.

Catching her intoxicating scent, he gently took the appliance from her hands, placing it on the kitchen counter. "Do you really think we need another coffee?" he asked, pulling her closer. He could feel the heat of her body as she leaned into him. Brushing the hair from her upturned face, he kissed her full lips. As their tongues explored each other's mouths, his hand trembled as he flicked his thumb over one erect nipple and then the other. She shivered under his touch.

"Are you sure?" he asked breathlessly, as he slipped her halter-top from one breast.

She laughed that deep throaty laugh, as she hungrily returned his kisses. "No, but it's too late to turn back now."

He bent over to take her hard nipple in his mouth, at the

same time reaching for the front slit of her skirt. She moaned as he slid his hand lightly up the inside of her legs, stopping just short of her panties. Playfully, she moved his hand away.

"You tease," he said, his breath hot in her ear.

"Me? Look who's talking—you're driving me mad!"

"That's the idea," he whispered, covering her mouth again with his, and darting his tongue inside. She moaned as he effortlessly slid her lithe body onto the granite counter and reached under her skirt.

G avin had no idea how many times they made love after finally going to bed that night. But it was enough that Kathryn protested when he became aroused again as the sun came up.

"You are insatiable," she laughed. "I won't walk for a week."

"Only a week? I must not have been very good then."

She kissed him tenderly. "You were exquisite. But I'm starving. Can we eat something and

go for a swim?"

"Only if we can go in without a swimsuit. I didn't bring one, remember?" He reached for her.

"I know just the place," she said, wrapping herself in a sheet, escaping his attempt to pull her back into bed. "The salt water will be good for my wounds."

Chapter Thirteen

North Vancouver, British Columbia
August 1985

K rochinski's absence from yet another meeting had Julius trudging up the worn stairs of Tommy's three-floor walkup, as breathless as he was livid. At the top floor, he rounded the corner and hammered on the battered wooden door. After several banging sessions, the door finally opened.

Naked but for a frayed and torn pair of sweat pants, Tommy squinted and rubbed his head, no doubt nursing a headache caused by another night of hard partying. Julius pushed past him, his eyes doing a quick sweep of the apartment. The living room looked like a bomb had hit it and he could see into the bedroom, which wasn't in much better shape. Judging by the tousled blonde sprawled on the bed, Julius surmised Kroch must have had a good time.

"Jesus, Tommy, this is the third meeting you've missed this week. I told you Gavin said it was critical you be there this morning," Julius said, his temper ratcheting up a notch. "John Barclay's people were understandably pissed, but I managed to convince them you must be ill, or had gotten into an accident." If only we should be so lucky, he thought.

Julius wasn't entirely sure anything he said was permeating Tommy's thick brain. "They had some things to attend to so I let them use the boardroom, and we've rescheduled to meet in my office in less than an hour. Get some coffee and take a shower. I am not leaving here without you, understand?"

Tommy nodded but unhurriedly lit a cigarette. Julius watched as he took a few drags and then stubbed it out in an ashtray overflowing with ashes and a partially smoked joint. He could see the residue of where someone had sniffed several lines of cocaine off the mirrored coffee table. Not wanting to remain in Tommy's pigpen longer than necessary, he made an exaggerated gesture of consulting his watch.

Disgusted though Julius was, he had to give Tommy his due; within ten minutes, he was showered and changed, and with the girl still passed out in his bedroom, he slammed the door behind them. Steering his Porsche Carrera over the Lions Gate Bridge into downtown Vancouver, he led the way back to Julius's office, arriving just minutes before Barclay's people emerged from the boardroom.

Although Kroch tried valiantly to focus on his presentation, it was clear to Julius that he was hurting from the night before. He heard Krochinksi had thrown the party of all parties at Vancouver's au courant oyster bar. According to Julius's sources, the booze and broads had been laid on liberally. Potential investors had their every whim catered to, from private lap dances to "happy endings" in the semi-privacy of the rooms downstairs.

When Tommy had thrown these kinds of bashes in the past, Julius knew there wasn't much his hired harem wouldn't do. The girls were paid enough for one night to take the next few weeks off. Tommy might have lived in a crappy apartment, but when it came to flashy clothes, his wheels, and parties, he spared no expense. Once again, Julius wondered why Gavin stayed with a partner who was as different from him as chalk and cheese.

No doubt, the infamous restaurant's roof deck would have been at its finest in August, a month that was usually spectacular on the west coast. However, Julius knew the real reason for the timing of this particular shindig was that Gavin Stone was out of the country. Burying the cost of "client appreciation" evenings wasn't that big a challenge for Tommy, but getting Gavin's approval would never have flown. Instead, Gavin would have opted for what Tommy referred to as "an elegant snoozer" at his snotty country club.

"Everything we do says something about us, Tommy," was Julius's admonishment in Gavin's absence. As usual, when Julius issued the familiar refrain, Tommy looked like he was listening to a scratched record. And as usual, he paid Julius no mind.

"Yeah, no kidding. It says we're fucking boring, is what it says," Tommy sneered. "And that's why we're not getting the investors we need to keep the Hawaii project running." He lit another cigarette even though Julius had asked him repeatedly not to smoke in the office. "Shit, Julius," Krochinski said to Gavin's best friend and lawyer. "I'm beginning to feel like a one-armed paperhanger juggling funds and accounts while my holier-than-thou partner is flitting around fucking Europe."

The mere thought of Kroch juggling funds made Julius exceedingly nervous.

.   .   .

K rochinski had concluded his dog and pony show for the Barclay group and Julius's attention snapped back to the business at hand. In spite of himself, Kroch seemed to have done an adequate job outlining the upside potential of the La Thuile project, and John Barclay's lawyer had asked questions that showed their team had a high level of interest. They scheduled a second meeting for the following week.

Relieved the meeting was over, Julius walked to the underground garage with Krochinski. He watched as Tommy threw his briefcase into the passenger seat and backed the Porsche out of one of their company's designated parking spaces. With a quick "see ya," he gunned the sports car, screeched up the ramp and was quickly out of sight.

Arrogant little prick, thought Julius.

R eflecting on the meeting as he drove home, Julius was still annoyed at personally having to roust Krochinski from his tawdry morning-after no show. He had to hand it to him though; he had an uncanny ability to adapt to the situation at hand. Julius had argued with Gavin numerous times that Tommy was not a good choice in partners, particularly as their developments were now attracting more upscale investors. But as was usually the case, there was no reasoning with him. One of the qualities Julius most admired in Gavin was his unwavering sense of loyalty.

It wasn't just that Gavin and Kroch went back to their partying and prison days. Although he was rough around the edges, Julius had to admit Tommy had been carrying the ball while Gavin remained in Italy. In fact, if not for him, Julius suspected they would not have had the opportunity to pitch their ski development project to the Barclay Group. Gavin was responsible for bringing John Barclay to the table, but it was Kroch who had done all the research for Barclay's team. At their meeting, he had answered each question or objection without hesitation, having committed every fact and figure about their proposed Italian project to memory. Despite looking like hell and not showing up on time, Gavin's renegade partner held his audience in the palm of his hand. Julius suspected the Barclay Group assumed he'd been up all night preparing for their meeting.

With that said about Krochinski's surprising competence, Julius would have to inform Gavin of his partner's proclivity for schmoozing with Vancouver's financial bottom-feeders of Howe Street. But that discussion could wait until Gavin's return in two weeks. When Gavin had unsuccessfully tried connecting with his partner by telephone, Julius had assured him the meeting with John Barclay's people had gone exceptionally well.

As the firm's in-house lawyer, Julius had one more meeting with Barclay's counsel to go over a few of the finer points of their agreement, after which he was assured they would move ahead quickly with a number of Barclay's affluent clients. By all accounts, they were anxious to get in on a ground-floor opportunity to own significant shares in the La Thuile resort. Highly motivated by the commission structure they had hammered out, John Barclay's firm would be rewarded handsomely. Not to mention they'd given him a ninety-day head start to offer shares exclusively to his clients before opening up the limited partnerships to other brokers in Vancouver.

It was a brilliant plan. Kroch certainly had Barclay's team believing he had a waiting list of interested investors who were chomping at the bit to sink millions into their project. Whether or not he actually did, Julius didn't know. There were many things about Tommy Krochinski, that Julius didn't know, and it worried him to no end. But the possibility that other investors were ready to pounce at the opportunity certainly escalated the Barclay Group's sense of urgency.

So, for the time being, Julius put his ever-present qualms about Kroch out of mind.

Chapter Fourteen

Annoyed there was no answer at Tommy's by nine a.m. Vancouver time, Gavin hung up the phone. He had wanted to brief his partner on a few critical points prior to the meeting with John Barclay's junior partner and their lawyer. At least he could count on Julius, so he probably needn't worry. Gavin had tried to reach Kroch on and off for the past two days but could never raise him. In the past, that had not been a good sign.

It was a little past eight o'clock in the evening, in Tropea. He shook off his nervousness and focused on coaxing the somewhat spartan apartment into a suitable ambience before Kathryn's arrival for drinks. Afterward, they were heading to a charming little restaurant within walking distance, in the heart of the historical area for dinner. As power outages were a regular occurrence, the flat was well stocked with dozens of candles, and he had managed to score a case of rare wine from a local vintner. When he heard Kathryn crank the old doorbell downstairs, he took one last look around the apartment and ran down to let her in.

As usual, they had a marvelous dinner. The only thing

that could mar such a perfect time was the realization their evening together was ending. They talked nonstop over drinks, on the walk over to the restaurant, and now as they made their way back to his apartment. Gavin hung on to every minute detail of their conversation and banter. He found himself completely lost in the private world he and Kathryn had created for themselves over the past few weeks. It was as if no one else existed. But someone else did—Cynthia. He was painfully aware that as quickly as he had become obsessed with Kathryn, the time to return to Canada with his wife was drawing near.

Since spending that first magical night at Kathryn's house after dinner up the mountain, he had put thoughts of Cynthia and his life in Vancouver to the back of his mind. He had taken Kathryn with him when Tommy urged him to go to La Thuile to meet with an architect, and then a second time to meet with a group of potential local investors. She had fit in effortlessly as she entertained, flattered, and generally capti-vated everyone connected with the project. Kathryn worried she was overstepping her bounds, but Gavin assured her he couldn't have been more delighted with how well she related with those who he needed in his camp. Her considerable knowledge of the area, as well as her fluency in Italian, was invaluable. Typically, his wife had never taken an interest in his work—only the lifestyle it created.

"What are you thinking about?" Kathryn asked, wrapping both arms around one of his as they walked back to the apartment.

Unsure of what to say, he opted for the truth. "I'm just wondering how I can possibly live without you when I go back to Vancouver and you to Carmel. I can't imagine being apart from you."

They stopped under the soft illumination of an old-fashioned carriage light and faced each other. He put his arms around her slender frame and smelled her perfume, felt her hair brush his neck. After a time, he gently pulled her away, searching her eyes. They welled with tears and he felt a warm droplet on his arm. He thought his heart would rip from his chest. "Kathryn, I don't know how I'm going to do this, but if you will have me, I'm going to find a way for us to be together. Can you wait for me?" He felt his throat tighten as he choked out his last words.

"Gavin, you don't owe me anything. I'm a big girl. I knew what I was getting into—a beautiful summer romance. I don't have any expectations of you."

Her words pierced his heart. "Is that all this has been to you? For me, this isn't just a summer romance, Kathryn…I love you." He couldn't quite believe he'd finally said it aloud. He felt her shiver, although the mid-August night was still balmy. Looking deeply into her eyes, he searched for her reaction to what he had just blurted out. "I'm sorry. I shouldn't have sprung it on you like this. Are you shocked?"

She touched the side of his face tenderly and another tear spilled on her pashmina. "No, I'm not shocked. I think I've just galvanized myself not to expect too much from our relationship, given your situation."

"Cynthia, you mean?"

"Well yes, but it's obviously more complicated than that," she replied. "You have an entire life in Vancouver, and I have mine in California. And your business—things are so complicated, Gavin." She looked upward to keep more tears from overflowing.

Gavin felt awkward standing in the middle of the street having such an intimate conversation. But they had made a pact—it was Kathryn's suggestion—that they never spend the night together at his apartment. He respected her for that but knew he couldn't be without her tonight, of all nights. Surprisingly, he and Cynthia had only spoken on the telephone a handful of occasions, as he was more often out of the apartment than in. Without an answering machine, he had no idea how often she might have called, but he made a point of telling her he'd been back and forth to La Thuile a lot. If Cynthia suspected anything, she didn't let on.

"Would it be all right if we collect your car and go back to your place tonight? I don't want to leave things like this," he murmured, stroking her hair. "I know we've been avoiding this subject, but we need to talk about it. We can't ignore it any longer." He held his breath for her response.

"Of course," she said quietly. Somewhat more lightheartedly, she added, "How about if I make us my special Italian coffees? We can sit outside around the fire pit and talk."

His chest ached, trying to hold in his emotions. Gavin would have agreed to anything at that moment, just as long as he didn't have to leave her like this.

I t had been an all-night discussion back at Kathryn's house. True to her promise, she made them her special Italian Nudges. Gavin ground and brewed the coffee while Kathryn concocted her house specialty. He watched in amazement as she poured into each pottery goblet an ounce of Kahlúa, an ounce of crème de cacao, and an ounce of Grand Marnier. Leaving him little room to fill the rest of the cup with coffee, she added a generous dollop of whipped cream and on top of that, an ounce of Benedictine brandy.

As they sat in front of the fire pit of her upper dining portico sipping their coffees, it was easy to see why she referred to them as "nudges." Gavin generally had a high tolerance for alcohol, but whether it was the effort of trying to hold his emotions at bay, or the late hour, he definitely felt the effect. Eventually draining the pot of just coffee without the accoutrements, they talked long into the night about their future together. He wanted to pinch himself in disbelief they were even having such a discussion.

"Kathryn, I can't possibly live without you now that I've found you. I had no idea I could ever feel this way about anyone," Gavin confessed.

"You must have felt that way once, before you married your wife, didn't you?"

Sadly, he hadn't. "Honestly, I don't think Cynthia would be that surprised if I suggested a divorce, and fortunately I'm now in a position to be able to handle the fallout financially." "Fallout" was probably an understatement; it would be more likely to rival Mt. Saint Helen's 1980 eruption in the Pacific Northwest. Although he would once have described his wife as milquetoast, the last few years of reveling in the success of his business and the lifestyle it bought, definitely had an effect on her previously reticent personality. In spite of the unflattering suggestion by outsiders, Gavin sensed part of what had contributed to Cynthia's hard exterior was her frustration over her inability to have a child. After multiple miscarriages, it was something they never discussed anymore.

As he gazed at Kathryn's face, illuminated by the dying flames of the fire, he was acutely aware of the contrast between the two women in his life.

"Gavin, I want you to be sure about this. Once you talk to Cynthia, I doubt there will be any going back. Are you positive this is what you want?"

He turned, taking her hands in his. "Perhaps I should be asking you that," he replied. "Do you love me enough to wait? Things might take longer than we've planned." Apprehension washed over him as he waited for her reply.

"I'd be lying if I said I haven't felt guilty about getting involved with a married man."

He nodded, determined not to interrupt.

"But I love you and I can be patient."

He breathed a sigh of relief.

"I just need to know when we leave here and go back to real life, that our relationship can withstand the obvious stresses. I promise I'm not going anywhere."

Gavin remembered her saying those very same words the first time they met, after they had crossed the street and she was running off to her lunch with friends. At the time, he was afraid he'd never see her again. They had come such a long way in just a few months.

"Then we need to start making a plan and I promise you I will be honest and upfront with you every step of the way. Will that be enough for the next little while?" Gavin asked.

"Of course. The reality is I will have a lot to do as well when I get back to Carmel. But how long will it be before I see you after we leave here?"

Conscious of the dichotomy of promising to be upfront and honest with Kathryn while being deceitful with Cynthia, he assured her that traveling to see her regularly would not be a problem. But he wondered how he would survive without seeing her every day. In the past, his business had been enough to keep him preoccupied. At least he knew he could talk to her daily by telephone. However, the days ahead threatened to be dismal, regardless of how busy he would be when he returned home.

Chapter Fifteen

Tropea, ITALY
September 1985

G avin moved slowly as he packed up the last of his and Cynthia's personal belongings from their rented apartment. After meeting Kathryn just a few short months ago, he felt as though he had been cast in a dream. Now, he felt caught in a nightmare as he contemplated the seemingly endless list of what had to be done.

Kathryn convinced him it would be better not to ask Cynthia for a divorce until they returned to Vancouver. Given his wife's flair for the dramatic and her recent penchant for making scenes, Gavin tended to agree. Rather than picking her up at the train station in town, he had arranged to meet her at the Lamezia Terme, where they would depart for Vancouver. He had but an hour before Ottavio would arrive to drive him the 55 kilometers from Tropea to the airport.

His slow pace was also the result of exhaustion from being awake most of the previous night. He and Kathryn had made love with an urgency rooted in fear and doubt as to when they would next see each other. They'd whispered and cried in each other's arms, until he had finally left her bed in the early hours of the morning. As he took one last look around the apartment, it took every ounce of willpower he possessed not to telephone her. He longed to hear her voice one more time, but last night he had promised her he wouldn't call. They both knew that to drag out their goodbyes one more time would break each other's hearts.

On the plane, Gavin settled into his first-class seat beside his wife. He was surprised when he'd first seen her in the Elite Passenger Lounge prior to boarding. In the midst of fixing himself a Scotch, he had heard Cynthia's voice behind him.

"Hello, Gavin," she said, offering her cheek. "I wasn't sure if you were here yet, so I went into the ladies lounge, and freshened up a bit. It was such a long, hot trip back from Capri. Have you been here long?"

Dutifully kissing her, he noticed she had lost some weight and was dressed exceptionally well. Though she no doubt was wearing designer clothes, for the first time he noticed how she lacked a sense of her own style. He couldn't have told you what labels Kathryn frequented, if any, but she wore her clothes with a sense of casual elegance that appeared effortlessly put together. Tanned and with a new hairstyle, Cynthia looked—well, brittle. She had a tendency to wear too much makeup and that hadn't changed. She often complained about the nondescript mousiness of her hair. Now, she sported a severely angled cut, lightened by blonde streaks.

Thankfully, he had very little time with her before the lounge concierge discreetly reminded them of their impending flight and encouraged them to ready themselves for priority boarding. They made small talk as they walked down the gangway, and once their hand luggage was stowed, Cynthia pulled a sleep-mask from her Prada bag and moved over in her seat as far away from Gavin as possible. Tired, he knew he wouldn't sleep, and fished in his briefcase for the latest faxes from Kroch that Ottavio had given him en route to the airport.

"Signor Stone," Ottavio had said as he dropped him at Lamezia Terme. "I shall miss you. Do you think you will be back soon?"

"I don't know, Ottavio. I must return to my business in Canada, although I'd certainly love to come back here some-day. It is one of the most beautiful places I could ever have imagined."

"I'm sure the beautiful Miss Kathryn will be wanting you to come back as well, yes?" he asked with a conspiratorial wink.

Nothing more needed to be said. Both men knew what they were discussing. Gavin wondered if it was simply a matter of course for Italians to have both a wife and a mistress.

He tried to force thoughts of Kathryn and his predicament about Cynthia from his mind, at least temporarily, while he read Kroch's fax. His partner had outlined the deal put on the table by the Italian investor Gavin and Kathryn had met with the previous week. Gavin had to admit it was an attractive offer, and Kroch was urging him to accept it. John Barclay's group had agreed to move ahead and was already introducing the La Thuile project to their clients. But Gavin and Tommy were going to have to move quickly and raise a lot more money than they had originally anticipated if they wanted to get their first European development off the ground.

Kathryn had given Gavin a crash course on how Italians did business in the area. She pointed out early on that no construction or renovations could start without the appropriate "non-Mafia" certificate. However, in that particular region of Italy, one could not get a non-Mafia certificate without the assistance of the Mafia. It presented an intriguing irony.

For weeks before departing Tropea, Gavin had continued to stew about this new reality of doing business in a foreign country. Noting his frustration, Kathryn introduced him to an old family friend whom she had known since childhood and suggested Gavin and he meet further to discuss La Thuile. They enjoyed a glorious evening at Vittorio Constantine's Mediterranean estate, combining business with pleasure, and their conversation ran long into the night. Insistent that Kathryn come along, Constantine charmed them both with tales from his boyhood with Kathryn's father, Enrico. He even hinted that had her father not beaten him to the punch, he would have asked Kathryn's mother, Francesca, to marry him. It was with a twinkle in his eye that he often addressed Kathryn as *mia dolce figlia*—my sweet daughter. Gavin couldn't help but feel a lump in his throat when Vittorio described the despair he still felt over the murder of Kathryn's parents.

In exchange for ten percent of La Thuile, Constantine was prepared to handle the logistics of permits and other Italian bureaucratic necessities, virtually ensuring the conversion from resort-type apartments to condos would be approved, and the project would come in on time. That meant Gavin, Kroch, and their investors could start reaping their rewards sooner, and they would have something tangible to show the high-end retailers with whom they hoped to partner.

As Gavin finished reading the brief, for the first time in the past twenty-four hours, he felt a glimmer of hope for a future that included Kathryn and Tropea. Although ten percent was a sizable cut, he intended to give Kroch the go ahead just as soon as they landed. All they needed was for Julius to work his magic and prepare the agreements.

Chapter Sixteen

West Vancouver, British Columbia
September 1985

G avin briefly considered taking Cynthia out to dinner. But at the last minute, he thought better of it. Given what he had to tell her, he could only imagine being in a restaurant and the scene that might ensue, depending on how she took the news. He had tried to get a handle on his wife's feelings for him after they had vacationed separately in Italy for three months, but he simply could not read her. Though somewhat cool toward him when they first returned home, she quickly jumped right back into her social scene with friends, and insisted he join her.

By the end of their second week back in Vancouver, he knew what he had to do. Kathryn hadn't pressured him once. In fact, when they talked daily by telephone she cautioned him to plan his approach carefully and not to rush. Gavin was the one who could not live with the sham of his marriage any longer. He had scheduled his discussion with Cynthia for that evening.

As usual, she was late getting home so he made himself a drink. He had tossed and turned in their bed the previous night, replaying over and over what he intended to say. Tired and anxious, he wanted to get it over with. He heard the garage door open as he dropped some ice into his Scotch. Her keys jangled as she dropped them on the marble table in the foyer.

"Gavin, I'm sorry I'm late," she called out. "You wouldn't believe the traffic. It took me an hour just to get through the Stanley Park Causeway."

Her voice was getting closer and his heart beat faster as she approached the den. "I'm afraid the time just got away from me. Millie and I tried that divine new restaurant on Robson, and you'll never guess who we ran into. Oh, you're in here," she said, stopping in the entrance to the den. "Why aren't you sitting outside? It's such a gorgeous day for September. Did you hear they're forecasting an Indian summer? You know, I don't for the life of me understand why you stayed as long as you did in that godforsaken town in Italy, but I, for one…"

He cut her off. "Cyn, could you please sit down? I have something I need to talk to you about."

"Of course, but I need to get out of these sticky clothes. You know, I thought it was going to stay overcast today so I wore my—"

"This can't wait, Cynthia. I need to talk to you now."

She looked at him and scowled. "Oh, all right then," she said impatiently. "But make it quick. I've invited the Lauriers over for dinner tonight."

"You did what? I told you this morning we needed to talk. How could you have invited company for dinner?"

"Oh for god's sake, Gavin, Ted and Lois aren't company.

It's just a casual barbecue outside. Ted wants to talk to you about his new venture and Lois…"

"Cyn, sit down!"

Startled, she dropped hastily into a leather chair. This was starting badly.

Impatiently, she drummed her long, artificial fingernails on the end table. All at once, the movie in his head started rolling in rapid motion. Frame by frame, he saw their empty, childless life, complete with one social engagement after another which Cynthia dragged him to, screech haltingly to a precipice. The abyss he saw on the other side made his mouth go dry.

"Gavin, I haven't got all day, you know. What is it you wanted to talk to me about?"

His well-rehearsed speech flew out the window. "I want a divorce."

The thin smile never left her face. "You what?" she asked.

"I want a divorce. I'm sure you must see we've been living entirely separate lives for some time now and…"

"You can't be serious," she said, the smile fading somewhat. "Whatever are you talking about? You just took me to Italy to celebrate our tenth wedding anniversary. Gavin, what's wrong with you, are you feeling all right?"

"I'm feeling fine, Cynthia. We lived apart in Italy for almost three months. I would hardly call that celebrating our anniversary."

"But I thought you were happy attending to all that business stuff you had going on in Latill."

"La Thuile," Gavin replied, exasperated. "And that's not the point. We both know we had no connection long before we went to Italy."

"Oh, *really*?" she replied, drawing out the last word. Her tone became curt. "I'm surprised you noticed—you were never here. I don't know where the hell you were most of the time, but it certainly wasn't with me." Her voice changed from steely cold and took on a high-pitched cadence.

"Cyn," Gavin said tiredly, "let's not do this. I will make sure you are well provided for and…"

"Well provided for. Are you kidding me?" she hissed at him as she rose from her chair. "I have given you ten years of my life, and you're telling me I'll be well provided for? If you think for one minute—"

The doorbell rang. They both froze and stared at each other. Cynthia looked at her watch. "Shit, it must be Ted and Lois. I can't deal with this—*you* let them in!"

"Me?" shouted Gavin. "I didn't invite them over, why should I handle this?" he said to her back.

She stopped cold in her tracks, turned slowly and deliberately toward him, and fixed her eyes on him like a laser. In a voice so quiet he had to strain to hear her, she said, "Because you need to explain to our best friends why after ten years of marriage, you have decided to leave me." Her face had completely drained of color. "And," she added, "you'd better ask Ted if he knows a good divorce lawyer, because I will take you for everything you have, everything you ever hoped to have, and everything you might have in the future."

She turned on her heels and marched out of the room.

Chapter Seventeen

Carmel, California
Mid-September 1985

With the convertible's top down, the late September afternoon sun warmed Gavin's neck and forearms as he navigated the fifteen-minute drive along Highway 1 from the Monterey airport to Carmel-by-the-Sea. The breathtaking view of the stunning Pacific coastline to Kathryn's home afforded him time to get his thoughts in order.

In almost daily telephone conversations with Kathryn, Gavin had avoided bringing up his discussion with Cynthia regarding the divorce. To her credit, Kathryn didn't ask; it was one of the qualities he admired about her. Unlike his wife, she never pressured or made demands of him. However, he had detected a certain urgency in Kathryn's voice when she asked when he'd be able to make it down to see her. As this was his first visit to Carmel since they had both returned from Italy, he felt a twinge of nervousness reminiscent of their first date in Tropea. The tingle he felt in his gut quickly put to rest the fleeting thought he'd had about ending their relationship and staying put in his marriage. Although it was a practical solution, particularly given Cynthia's current state of mind, he knew a future without Kathryn would be impossible.

Though Cynthia steadfastly refused even to discuss the subject of divorce, the reality was Gavin had already asked Julius to find him an aggressive divorce lawyer and start proceedings. One way or the other it would eventually become a done deal. The only question was how much it would cost.

Such ominous thoughts quickly vanished as he took a right turn onto Ocean Avenue. From Kathryn's instructions, he surmised he was on the main drag that went all the way through the quaint little village of Carmel, finally ending up at the sea. Before long, the white sand beach Kathryn had described came into view and he hung a left onto Scenic Road, which ran parallel to the beach. True to its name, the street boasted expensive-looking homes, designed to take full advantage of the superlative beachfront views. Gavin consulted the handwritten directions lying on the passenger seat. By his calculation, he had reached Kathryn's address. He slowed the car but hesitated to turn into the driveway that ran from the street to the back of a massive property. Checking the number on the open gate again, and confirming it did indeed match the address in his notes, he stopped the car.

"Why is it you appear utterly and hopelessly lost, each time I see you?" asked a familiar voice.

He turned to see Kathryn standing beside the car, behind his left shoulder. She looked even more beautiful than when he'd last seen her. Recognizing him, Jezebel strained at her leash and Kathryn had to hold her back from jumping on the car.

"Jezebel and I thought you'd be here about now, so we kept an eye out for you from the beach." She looked intently into his eyes. "It's so good to see you," she beamed. "Come, let me just grab the mail and then you can follow us up the driveway."

He wanted to jump from the car and throw his arms around her but he resisted the temptation. "You live here?" he asked incredulously.

"I know, it's pretty grand, isn't it? But don't be deceived, I rent a little carriage house in the back. I wish I could say I owned this whole place but sadly, I don't," she said, walking slowly alongside Gavin's car. "Just park over there," she said, pointing toward a closed garage door.

Gavin put his vehicle in park and leapt from the car, leaving the door open. Wrapping her in his arms he said, "Oh my god, I've missed you so much." He hadn't realized just how much until that moment. They shared a long, passionate kiss. Eventually pulling himself away, he held her at arm's length. She gently touched his cheek. Although she was smiling, he detected something in her eyes that inextricably made him nervous. He hoped against hope she hadn't asked him to come to Carmel just to break it off. But why would she? She could easily have done that by phone.

"You look so serious, my love," Kathryn said. "What are you thinking about?" She looked at him questioningly. "Come, I have a lovely bottle of Pinot Grigio chilling in the fridge. And we can still catch the last of the sun on the deck." Beckoning him to follow her into the coach house, she followed Jezebel.

"Shall I bring my bag?" Gavin asked, looking back at the open car door.

"Well, of course. That is, if you're planning on staying," she said, teasingly. "Do you need any help?"

"None," Gavin said, retrieving his leather bag from the back seat. "And yes, I was planning on staying, if you'll have me," he laughed. Maybe it was just his imagination that something was different with her.

He followed her through the front door and into an attractive entryway. The floor, made of rose-hued Travertine marble, contrasted sharply with charcoal-tinted walls, which provided a gallery-like backdrop for several large paintings. Kathryn started up two flights of ebony-colored, open-backed stairs. Jezebel bounded ahead of her and Gavin followed.

As he reached the landing on the way to the first floor, a painting that covered the wall from floor to ceiling captivated him. Gazing upward as one would view a majestic tree in an old growth forest, he felt as though he was standing under a waterfall lit from beneath like a rainbow projecting upward. Framed against an azure sky and modestly draped in mist, a mythical nude woman lay across the waterfall looking knowingly into the watery basin below. Even with her long hair painted in shades of mauve and purple, cascading seamlessly into the catchment pool just above Gavin's head, there was little doubt it was Kathryn. Off to one side, as if sliding off the canvas, was a ghostly black shadow, which repeated briefly on the opposite side. Though beautifully lit, he could feel the iciness of the frothy water above him.

"Is this one of your student's pieces?" Gavin asked dubiously.

"No, that's mine. It's called Healing Mist," Kathryn looked down from the second-floor landing.

"It's magnificent, Kathryn," Gavin said. "How long would this have taken to paint?"

"You don't want to know," she said, laughing. "That piece was literally a labor of love and salvation. I started it when I was sixteen and going through a rebellious patch, still dealing with the loss of my parents. Then it sort of evolved over a period of several years. That's why I love working with oils. There are many layers under what you see now. It was shrouded in black in the beginning, but over time, it's become lighter and more colorful. I don't think it will ever be finished." She smiled ruefully. His heart lurched, seeing the pensive look in her eyes.

Looking away, Kathryn said, "Come on up. I don't want you to miss the sunset." She led him into a spacious, open-plan living room and then rounded the granite counter, which separated the living area from the kitchen.

As Kathryn busied herself opening a bottle of wine, Gavin looked around. The ebony-colored floors continued throughout, with several areas covered with elegant Persian rugs. The entire length of the living room and kitchen consisted of wall-to-wall glass that opened out to a sea-view deck, which was almost as large as the inside entertaining space.

"You call this a coach house?" Gavin asked in disbelief.

"I know," she said, handing him a glass of chilled wine. "I'm pretty lucky. The owners are almost never here and I'm free to use their pool when they're gone. I hardly ever do though. I much prefer swimming in the ocean."

"But your view is amazing." Gavin said. "The design of the property is brilliant. I thought when you said you had a small coach house in the back, you wouldn't be able to see the water. This is exceptional, Kathryn, and it doesn't look very small to me," he added.

Leading him out to the stone patio, Kathryn raised her

glass. "Cheers," she said. "I'm so glad you're here. I've missed you."

"I've missed you more than you know," Gavin responded, clinking her glass with his. She smiled warmly before taking a small sip of her wine. But again, he thought he saw something in her eyes he couldn't quite fathom. *I must take things slowly*, he thought. Perhaps it was just his business, as well as the challenges with Cynthia, that were making him imagine things.

They sat and watched the sun go down, slowly dipping into the Pacific, before their thoughts turned to food. Gavin offered to take her out for dinner, but Kathryn said she had put a little something together for them and he happily agreed to stay in.

"Okay, put me to work. What can I do?" Gavin asked, as Kathryn made her way to the kitchen.

"Nothing, it's all done. But you could light the candles on the deck for me. I've noticed the evenings getting a little cool already. If you want, you could light the propane fire as well." She handed him a lighter. In the center of the patio was a fire pit, encircled by a round ceramic-tiled tabletop.

"Consider it done," said Gavin.

Kathryn first brought out martini glasses filled with a delicious seafood ceviche. They dawdled over their appetizers, chatting, and generally catching up on each other's lives. Eventually, she cleared their empty dishes in preparation for the next course. Gavin refilled his wine glass and sat back to watch the flames licking at the artificial logs. Next on the menu was a refreshing and colorful salad that tasted as divine as it looked. He detected the flavor of pears and Stilton cheese—two things for which he and Kathryn shared a passion. Dipping freshly baked focaccia in olive oil and balsamic vinegar, he appreciated that Kathryn had recreated much of the cuisine they'd enjoyed in Italy.

"Could I talk you into opening a bottle of red before our next course?" Kathryn called through from the kitchen.

As Gavin came in from the deck to open the wine, he could smell the unmistakable scent of fresh sage. Kathryn was sautéing several leaves, which she placed on squares of butternut squash ravioli, each topped with a bright pink prawn. Her face glowed from the heat of the gas stove and a few strands of her chestnut-colored hair escaped, framing her face. He'd never seen her look so beautiful.

"Hmm," Gavin said, coming into the kitchen and putting his arms around her. "I didn't realize how hungry I was until you started feeding me." He brushed his lips against her neck.

"Well, when I was a little girl," Kathryn said, leaning back against him while stirring the sage, "my father told me he'd married my mother for her cooking. I loved spending time with her in the kitchen and watching how she did things. Her cooking seemed so effortless." She took the sauté pan off the stove and turned to him.

"You miss them, don't you?" Gavin asked.

"I do, even after all these years. Isn't that crazy?"

"Not crazy at all," Gavin replied, looking at her tenderly. "But your mother didn't teach you how to cook like this. You were too young, right?"

"Yes, it was actually Caroline who taught me how to cook. She was like a mother to me." Kathryn put the finishing touches on their plates. "Let's eat this now, while it's still warm," she urged. Gavin followed her back outside with the open bottle of Cabernet.

They finished their meal with coffee and Gavin had a liqueur. Despite his best attempts to hide it, he was getting sleepy and stifled a yawn.

"I saw that," Kathryn teased. "You must be exhausted after your flight and drive down. Let's take these into the kitchen and I'll show you the bedroom where you can put your things. I'm just going to take Jez across to the beach for her last outing and I'll be right back. Would you like to take a shower?"

"You read my mind. I know it's not that late, but after that amazing meal and the wine, I'm feeling a little tired," he admitted. "But I'll come and take Jez out with you."

"You're so chivalrous, but I'm fine. You go and have yourself a nice hot shower."

They put their glasses in the sink and Kathryn led the way down the hall. Like the rest of the house, her master bedroom was spacious and looked out to the ocean through more floor-to ceiling-windows. There was a small patio off the bedroom, and at some point during their meal she must have come in and lit the candles. She showed him to an ensuite bathroom complete with soaker tub, separate glass-enclosed shower, and bidet. Although Kathryn said the upstairs living area was only about 1500 square feet, the design of the coach house made it appear much more spacious. No doubt, the main patio added another 600 square feet or so to her living space. Rented or not, Kathryn lived as elegantly here as she did in Tropea.

Gavin was drying himself off when he heard her come back into the bedroom. "Did you find everything you need?" she called.

"Yes, and I'm glad you and Jezebel are back safe and sound." Wrapping a thick white towel around his waist, he emerged from the bathroom to see Kathryn turning down the bed. She had pulled her hair loose, and still in her light summer dress and bare feet, she walked around the bed, tossing extra pillows on a nearby chair. As she walked past him, Gavin reached for her. She shivered as he held her in his arms and their lips met. As his towel slipped from his waist and fell to the floor, it was clear Kathryn would have to forgo her turn in the bathroom for the time being.

They made love until the candles had long since extinguished themselves and slept happily in each other's arms.

Chapter Eighteen

Gavin looked at the bedside clock and couldn't believe it was 9 a.m. Kathryn's side of the bed was empty, but he could still smell her muskiness on the rumpled sheets. Judging by the cloudless blue sky, it was another perfect day in paradise, and he wondered if she was on the beach with Jezebel. The gate she assured him she'd closed the night before was open. Parked cars already lined the street that gave visitors easy access to the beach.

Most of the parked vehicles were convertibles, open-air Jeeps, or run-of-the-mill cars with their windows fully rolled down to combat the expected heat. About to turn and head to the bathroom, a quick glint in one of the cars caught Gavin's eye. Someone in a nondescript white sedan lit a cigarette and a tendril of smoke snaked out the barely cracked front driver-side window. He wondered if Kathryn was about to have a visitor and hurried into the bathroom, brushed his teeth and ran wet fingers through his hair. Digging a pair of faded jeans and a black tee shirt from his bag, he padded barefoot into the living room.

Kathryn was in the kitchen. "Hey, sleepyhead, how did you sleep?" she asked, smiling at him from the sink.

"I slept like a baby, thank you, but why didn't you wake me? I can't believe it's so late."

"I thought you needed it. And besides, there's nothing more important on my schedule today than going for a good coffee and a walk on the beach. Did you have anything you need to do?"

"No, I am completely in your hands," Gavin said, joining her in the kitchen. She was wearing loose-fitting white linen pants, a white tank top, and flip-flops. "And mighty good hands they are too," he added, as he stood behind her and pulled her hair aside to kiss her neck.

She giggled and kissed him back. "Perfect, then get something on your feet, and I will take you to the best coffee place on the planet, then a walk with Jez on the beach. How does that sound?" Jezebel's ears perked up at the sound of her name.

"That sounds splendid. Then I'll take you out for breakfast. It's the least I can do after the incredible meal you cooked last night."

Kathryn hesitated and gently pulled away. "Why don't we get something to go at the café and we'll just take it with us on our walk. There's something I need to talk to you about." She turned back to busying herself at the counter.

"Okay," Gavin said slowly. Something niggled at him from within. Again. But he decided not to push it and instead, went to find his shoes.

Jezebel was out the door well before Gavin reached the bottom of the stairs. He and Kathryn followed, closing the door behind them. The white car was gone, leaving a conspicuously empty parking spot across the street, on the beach side.

"Don't you lock it?" he asked.

"No," she laughed. "You need to leave your big city attitude behind, my love. I've lived in Carmel for years and most of us never lock our doors."

Gavin didn't say anything more but noticed she left the iron gate at the entrance to the driveway open as well. Perhaps it was because he lived in a prestigious area of West Vancouver, that he was hyper-conscious about security. He had a secured gate with an intercom and alarm system in the house he still shared with Cynthia.

As they entered the bustling coffee bar just off Ocean Avenue, the ambience reminded Gavin of the café next door to Ottavio's shop in Tropea. The front door stayed permanently open, through which a steady stream of java-seeking aficionados came and went, greeting each other by name. The smell of fresh-roasted coffee and various pastries enticed his senses.

"Here, take my wallet," he said to Kathryn. "I insist on this being my treat and I'll stay out here with Jezebel."

"Oh, Jez can come in. Most of the merchants and restaurants are dog-friendly," Kathryn answered.

Sure enough, there was a big bowl of water on the floor inside the café, as well as another on the sidewalk. They ordered large cups of steaming dark-roasted coffee to go and walked out onto the street clutching two warm cinnamon rolls in a paper bag. Making the three short blocks back downhill to the beach, Kathryn let Jezebel off her leash and they began their walk. Even with the cool air of autumn approaching, there was a handful of local children building sandcastles and playing along the water's edge.

They walked a good distance, passing Kathryn's recessed water-view house. She knew many of the passersby and stopped to say hello and introduce Gavin. Eventually, they stopped at an outcropping of rock at the end of the beach. Again, Gavin thought of Tropea's central beach and the rocks that separated it from Kathryn's home. Jezebel went in to swim while he and Kathryn settled on a smooth rock to finish their coffee and eat their breakfast.

"This is pure heaven, Kathryn. I can see why you love it here. In a different way it is as beautiful as Tropea."

"I do love it here," she agreed. "Every fall I get anxious about leaving Italy and coming back to the States. And then when I'm back, I think how incredibly lucky I am to live in two such gorgeous places." She looked pensively toward the ocean. "I only wish you were here with me."

"Kathryn, there is nothing I want more than to live here with you. That's something I wanted to talk to you about. But you said you had something you wanted to tell me." Apprehensively, he added, "You go first."

She had barely touched her cinnamon roll and put it aside. As she wrapped both hands around her coffee cup, he noticed they were trembling. "You know I love you more than anything. I never thought I'd find…" She looked over at him, her eyes brimming with tears.

Oh god, no. He knew it. He sensed something even when she had given herself to him freely and passionately the night before. The feeling she was holding something back.

"Kathryn," he said, taking her coffee cup and putting it down between them. He took her hands in his. "I was praying this wasn't what you were going to tell me but I'll be okay if you say it's over." He knew he was lying.

"Gavin, that's not what I want. Not at all, but…" She started to cry.

"Whatever it is sweetheart, just tell me," he implored.

She gazed out to the sea for several seconds and then took a deep breath. "I'm just wondering if we should take a break to make sure this is what we both want. I didn't want to tell you over the phone, but it's been weighing on my mind. You have so much on your plate with Cynthia, and your business. I'm thinking of going back to Italy, it might give us both some…"

"Italy? But you just got back," he said incredulously. In slow motion, his mind wandered back through the magical times they had shared there. He didn't think he could ever lose himself so deeply. Now, he couldn't conceive of losing her.

He snapped out of his thoughts and realized Kathryn was looking at him intently, tears coursing down her cheeks, waiting for a response. "I don't know what to say," he said, feeling his own eyes burning. "I thought you wanted a future with me. What happened?" He held his breath.

"I do—more than you know. It's just that everything has happened so fast, and you'd be throwing away years, in both your marriage and everything you've worked so hard to build. I don't want to be responsible for that."

"I'm still young, I can rebuild. *We* can rebuild." He smiled at her and wiped away the single tear running down her cheek. "Sweetheart, I won't lie to you, it didn't go well with Cynthia when I asked her for a divorce, but being with you makes me more determined than ever to get it over and done with her as soon as possible." He swiveled on their rock perch so he could look directly in her eyes. "Is there someone else? If so, please just tell me." He thought he'd choke on the lump that ached in his throat.

"No, of course not. Gavin, that's not what this is about," she said, looking back at the ocean.

For the first time in two decades, he cared nothing about his business and even less about the ruin that threatened to befall him from his divorce. In that moment, he only cared about this woman, whom he loved beyond reason.

Seconds passed, seconds that seemed like minutes, until Kathryn finally said, "Gavin, if a life together is truly what you want there is nothing that would make me happier. But I need to know I'm not the reason you're divorcing your wife. If we're meant to be, I'll still be here after you and she have gone your separate ways. I don't want you resenting later what you gave up for me."

"I am absolutely sure, my darling. I've never been surer about anything in my life. But I told you it wasn't going to be easy. I thought you understood that. If you go back to Italy, perhaps I can relocate." Apprehension washed over him, thinking of Kroch and Julius's reaction. "It might actually be a better place to manage the La Thuile project." Who was he fooling? "You've made up your mind, haven't you?" he asked.

She didn't look at him. "Yes, I have. I'm not going immediately. I have a couple of exhibits coming up and some work to do with the kids but yes, I know this is something I have to do—for us."

"Could we consider it a trial separation?" He held only a glimmer of hope. "Kathryn, I don't think I can go on not knowing if I'll ever be with you again."

When she didn't reply, he choked on his words. "I guess I'd better try to book the next flight I can back to Vancouver."

At last, she spoke. "I don't want you to go back yet. Can't we savor the last few days we have together?"

He wanted desperately to stay. Could he endure the torture of wondering if each special moment might be their last? But he knew he was too weak to say no.

Chapter Nineteen

The precious four days they had together flew by. Their mornings started with coffees on the beach and ended with late nights on the deck, talking and often dining around the fire pit. Though they both felt the heaviness of what was to come, Kathryn delighted in taking Gavin down Carmel's tiny cobblestoned streets and alleys that led to charming shops and out of the way restaurants only the locals knew. Plants like geraniums, which were annuals in Vancouver, formed perennial hedges and sculpted trees. Everywhere they went in the seaside town, the scents and sights of flowers threatened to riot in the streets. It was a place where Gavin could see himself living or eventually retiring. If only.

Later the same day Kathryn told Gavin of her decision to return to Italy, he begged her to show him her gallery. Faced with the possibility their affair would end, he was trying to pack a lifetime into the mere days they had left.

She had arranged to take four days off while he was in town and asked the artist who rented space next to her gallery to cover for her. From the first moment Gavin laid eyes on the Yellow Dog Gallery, he knew how extraordinarily talented and dedicated to her art Kathryn was. Named for Jezebel, the small shop exuded a casual elegance, warmed by brightly colored canvasses and whimsical ironwork.

A life-sized bronze of Marmaduke, the Great Dane that became popular in the 1954 comic strip, caught his eye. Kathryn explained she bought the statue from the sculptor and placed it inside the front entrance to draw people in. Gavin watched enthralled as tourists and locals alike came into the gallery and marveled at Kathryn's paintings. She spoke to each visitor as if he or she was the most important person she'd ever met. They seemed in awe of meeting the gallery owner and artist in person.

After seeing the last of her visitors to the door, several with small paintings in hand, Kathryn motioned for Gavin to follow her to the back of the shop. They passed through a secluded brick courtyard that led to a diminutive outbuilding. She looked at Gavin and put her finger to her lips as she silently opened the door. Inside were four young people who Gavin thought to be in their early teens, standing before their canvases, painting. Quiet music played in the background, and an adult was deep in conversation with one of the youngsters. Though he couldn't make out exactly what the woman was saying, she was obviously praising the student's work, and he was shyly nodding in agreement. Without interrupting, Kathryn closed the door and they moved back into the court-yard before she spoke.

"That was one of the therapists who works with the kids," Kathryn said. "Julia is amazing. I wish I could take her to Italy with me to work with Thula."

Gavin thought back to the sweet but silent little girl he encountered on his first visit to Sister Serafina and the children. He remembered how despondent Kathryn was at Thula's apparent lack of progress.

"The boy you saw the therapist talking to?" Kathryn continued. "He saw his father kill his mother and then shoot himself in their family home. After that, he was in and out of juvenile facilities for troubled youth. Thankfully, one of the psychologists saw his sketches and she referred him to our program. He's been studying with us for a year now, and hasn't reoffended once. In fact, I'm putting several of his pieces into the gallery."

In awe of the deep satisfaction Kathryn derived from not only her own art, but also the work she did with children, Gavin wondered what he'd done to deserve the love of this remarkable woman. And how cruel was God to put her in his path, only to take her from him.

Chapter Twenty

G avin tried unsuccessfully to read on the plane during the last leg of his return flight from Carmel to Vancouver. Realizing he was simply reading the same page repeatedly, he closed his book and dropped it into his briefcase. Unable to focus on anything other than Kathryn's proposal that they should have some time apart while she went back to Italy, it became patently obvious he needed to move out of the home he shared with Cynthia. Upon his return, he would push the lawyer, whom Julius had retained on his behalf, to move quickly on divorce proceedings. Perhaps then, Kathryn would see how deadly serious he was about putting his marriage behind him and being with her.

If it seemed tense living in the same house with Cynthia before he left for California, he knew the situation would be untenable upon his return. Although his wife could drag the divorce proceedings out with unrealistic financial demands, even she knew once Gavin met her price, their marriage would be a thing of the past. It already was; all that remained was to make it official.

As he drove up the driveway just after midnight, Gavin's heart plummeted when he saw lights on in the house. Knowing it meant Cynthia was still up, he parked in the four-car garage and grabbed his bag. He hoped he could go quietly through the kitchen and up the back stairs to one of the guestrooms without running into her. Upon entering the house though, all hopes of that were dashed.

Cynthia was standing by their massive granite kitchen island, draining the last drops of a bottle of wine into a lipstick-smeared glass. Still dressed from a night out, her eye makeup was smudged and she was missing an earring.

"Well, well," she slurred, "my wandering husband has returned. Where 'ya been, Gavin? Off with one of your little whores again?"

"Cyn, you're drunk, and I'm not about to have this conversation with you." He started up the stairs. "I'm exhausted. I'm going to bed."

"I'm sure you *are* exhausted," she said with a snicker. "How was your business trip? Come on, I'll open another bottle of wine, and you can tell me all about it."

Halfway up the stairs and against his better judgment, he stopped and turned. He had never known Cynthia to be much of a drinker, but that had changed in the last few weeks as she alternated between passive behavior and aggressive outbursts. Disgusted, he thought better of making a retort and continued climbing the stairs.

"Gavin, come on…Gavin!" she yelled after him. "Can't we just talk about this?"

He heard her slam a cupboard door as he fell into bed. He prayed he would be able to catch a few hours of uninterrupted sleep.

. . .

B y mid-morning the next day, Gavin had viewed and leased a furnished penthouse apartment in Vancouver's west end, close to his office. Waiting until he knew Cynthia would be at the club for her afternoon tennis game, he left the office early, packed a minimum of his clothes, and left her a note to the effect that anything else she had to say to him should be addressed to his lawyer. Grateful he had been given permission to use the previous tenant's phone line as long as he paid the long distance charges, he cracked open a beer that had conveniently been left in the fridge, and spent the remainder of the evening willing himself not to call Kathryn. As excruciatingly painful though it was, he had given her his word he would respect her wishes not to contact her for the next few months. He exhaled heavily. The only thing that would get him through the time ahead would be to laser focus on what he needed to do.

E ventually, the dozens of daily messages from Cynthia stopped. Gavin had instructed his secretary, Lauren, not to put his wife's calls through, but he felt guilty at the abuse Cyn heaped on his devoted assistant. Handling it with her usual aplomb, Lauren laughed and said although it was all part of the job, she was grateful Mrs. Stone had stopped calling.

It had been two weeks since Gavin's return from Carmel. The evenings were the worst, as he did everything he could to distract himself from calling Kathryn when his long days at the office finally ended. He and Kroch worked day and night to keep up with John Barclay's people as they met with each of the clients they'd earmarked as potential investors for the

La Thuile project. True to his word, Kathryn's friend and his now business partner, Vittorio Constantine, continued to forge ahead getting all the necessary permits in place to begin the rebuild.

He wished he could share the progress with Kathryn. He wondered if she was still in Carmel or if she'd already gone back to Tropea.

Chapter Twenty-One

Gavin and Kroch were in the middle of yet another heated debate about expenses when Lauren tapped on his office door. Opening it, and tentatively sticking her head in, she said, "Gavin, I'm sorry to interrupt, but there's a woman on the line who sounds quite distraught, but she won't tell me who she is." Picking up on Gavin's unasked question, she shook her head. "It's not Mrs. Stone."

"I'll take it Lauren, thanks. Tommy, don't go away. I want to get this thing finished," he added, exasperated. He rounded his desk and picked up the phone. "Gavin Stone speaking."

"Gavin, I'm so sorry to call you at the office but I didn't know what else to do."

Her name froze on his lips. Putting his hand over the receiver, he looked across the room. "We'll have to finish this later, Tommy. But I want those expense reports on Lauren's desk before the day is out, is that clear?"

"Sure, *boss*," Kroch said, belligerently.

Gavin waited while Tommy took his time gathering up his papers. When the door closed behind him, he said, "Kathryn, what's wrong? Are you all right?"

"I'm fine and I'm so sorry to call you at work…"

"Never mind that," Gavin said impatiently, "what's wrong?"

"When Jezebel and I were out for our beach walk this morning someone broke into the house."

"What? Are you okay?"

"Yes, I'm fine. The strange thing is nothing seems to be missing."

"How did they get in?" Gavin suspected he knew the answer.

"I confess, they didn't exactly break in, I left the door unlocked. I know, I know, please don't lecture me."

"If nothing's missing, then how do you know there was someone in the house?"

Her voice cracked. "Because that large painting on the wall of the landing has been slashed to bits."

"Oh, Kathryn, no!" Gavin's heart sank. He knew how much that painting meant to her. The years of work and all the emotions that had gone into it.

"And that's all?" He caught himself. "I'm sorry, Kathryn, I didn't mean it that way. I know how precious that painting is to you. I just meant was there anything else damaged or disturbed?"

"The police asked me the same thing, and there's nothing I can see. It looks like my filing cabinet might have been rifled through, but I'm not even sure about that," Kathryn replied.

"Well, sweetheart, the main thing is you're safe. But I want you to promise me you will not only lock the front door, but also the gate, even during the day. I'd feel better if you would look into getting an alarm system installed," he continued, knowing she'd be unlikely to agree to that. "Is there someone you can spend the night with? I don't want you there by yourself."

"I'm not moving out of my own home, Gavin. And besides, I'm not alone, Jez is with me."

He mentally beat himself up for not being with her.

"Gavin, are you still there?"

"Yes, I'm still here. I just wish I could be with you, that's all."

"I do too," Kathryn replied. "I shouldn't have called you, but I felt so overwhelmed after the police left."

"Don't ever worry about calling me, Kathryn. I want you to," Gavin assured her. Lauren stuck her head in again, signaling he had another call on line two.

"Sweetheart, I have to go, but may I call you tonight from the apartment?"

"Yes…and Gavin?"

"Yes."

"Please try not to worry. We'll be fine. I love you. I'll talk to you tonight."

T he call on line two was the bank. The manager, with whom Gavin enjoyed a personal as well as a business relationship, was calling to tell him the company's operating account was overdrawn and their line of credit had reached its limit. Stunned, Gavin assured him he'd take care of things and instructed Lauren to find Kroch. Several hours later, Lauren managed to locate him and Gavin was now going up one side of him and down the other.

"Well what the fuck do you think I've been doing, Gavin?" Kroch fired back. "While you were lying around on the beaches of Italy all summer, I've been doing my job, your job, and trying to keep the Hawaii project going."

"That project was finished months before I left for Europe. I wouldn't have gone if it hadn't been. What do you mean you've had to keep it going?"

"Well, there were some special assessments we didn't know about, and a lot of the balconies had to be redone. There were drainage problems," Kroch responded cagily.

"What kind of drainage problems?" Gavin demanded. "And how many balconies are we talking about?" He knew it would be a waste of time pointing out that in Hawaii, balconies were referred to as "lanais."

His partner refused to make eye contact.

"Tommy, how many?"

"About three quarters of them, I think."

"What! Are you kidding me? That's…what, a hundred units?" Gavin asked.

"Yeah, that sounds about right."

"How the hell did we pay for the repairs?" Gavin demanded. "And why didn't you get a hold of me? Shit, Tommy, the bank just called. We're overdrawn on our main account and tapped out on our line of credit. Julius tells me you've been wining and dining all these so-called potential investors at In the Raw, and Lauren says she hasn't had an expense statement from you in months. What the hell is going on?"

"Maybe you should be telling me that, mister hotshot," Kroch yelled back. "You left me holding the bag all summer, and now it looks like your wife is trying to take us to the cleaners. How about your part in all of this? I've just been trying to keep our asses out of the fire."

Gavin stopped short of his next response. His eyes narrowed as he sized up his partner. "How the hell would you know what Cyn is trying to do?" He hadn't told Kroch anything about his wife's demands on his personal or business assets, and he was damned sure Julius hadn't either. He thought he detected a look cross Tommy's face indicating he knew he'd been caught.

"Well, it's just a guess on my part," Kroch, breaking eye contact again. "I know how these things tend to go. Divorces, I mean."

"I can assure you I can handle my settlement with Cynthia," Gavin said, curtly. "I just need you to focus on getting these limited partnerships put to bed with the Barclay Group. And I want a written rundown on the expenses associated with the Palms project. Do I make myself clear?" Gavin paused for emphasis.

"Yeah, yeah, no sweat, I can do that," Kroch said, looking at his watch. "But I gotta be somewhere."

"Tommy, I'm not kidding. Have that information on my desk no later than Friday. Do you understand?"

"Yeah, sure," he replied, already on the way out the door.

Gavin sank into his leather chair and contemplated what he would tell the bank.

Chapter Twenty-Two

G avin literally worked day and night, which helped the days fly by at breakneck speed. While consumed with worry after the break-in at Kathryn's home in Carmel, his spirits were buoyed by the opportunity to reconnect with her. After it happened, they had spoken long into the night, their conversation ending with Kathryn's agreement that although she still planned to go to Italy, she would phone him before she left. Until then, Gavin tried to stay focused on work.

G avin knew, as part of refocusing on things other than Kathryn, he had to make some tough decisions about Tommy Krochinski, and their partnership. Julius had been pushing him to do something before Tommy's undocumented expenses threatened to put them over the edge.

"Dammit, Gavin, why haven't you removed Kroch as a signatory on the corporate account?" Julius demanded. Gavin had promised he'd consider it when Julius had first suggested Kroch might be screwing them, but he'd neglected to take action.

Gavin leaned back in his chair and ran his fingers through his thick black hair. He had been reluctant to rock the boat until he had the full accounting report he had demanded from Kroch. However, maintaining a train wreck as a business partner was exacting an enormous toll. It meant he'd had to transfer a sizable amount from his personal account to cover the shortage at the bank. Somehow, he'd managed to convince his friend and banker to extend their line of credit, based on the brisk business John Barclay's sales team were doing. As luck would have it, the Barclay Group was a long-term client of the bank, a fact that went a long way to putting the manager's mind at ease. The bank held the investors' money in escrow, which gave them the security they needed to advance Gavin's company more credit.

That crisis averted, Gavin was meeting with Julius to discuss the latest settlement proposal from Cynthia's lawyer. They also needed to strategize about what kind of damage control they should do going forward.

He and Julius had decided to get away from the office and meet in the lounge of the Deer Ridge Country Club. After Julius made a point of inquiring how the lounge's hostess was doing, they continued their conversation. Gavin thought he saw Julius wink at her when she offered to send the waitress over with more coffee.

"Gavin," Julius began after settling into the chair opposite him. "I have to tell you again, I have grave concerns about Kroch. Some of the stuff I'm hearing on the street is not good. I know you feel indebted to him," Julius acknowledged with a sigh. "Believe me, I admire your loyalty, but frankly, I'm not surprised. Judging by what has been going on while you were in Europe, you need to seriously consider cutting him loose."

Julius had been the beneficiary of Gavin's loyalty when

he had found himself on the losing end of a malpractice suit, which ultimately resulted in his disbarment. Not only had Gavin gone to bat for his long-time friend, he had also taken the then bankrupt Julius into his company as his key legal advisor. Although everything Julius did behind the scenes for Gavin's company had to be signed off by a licensed junior lawyer, Gavin had single-handedly kept Julius financially afloat, as well as financed his successful appeal to get his license back. The lawyer now worked exclusively for Gavin's development firm. He also owned a significant chunk of shares in the company.

There was very little Gavin didn't share with Julius, but in the interests of keeping his business concerns in the forefront, Gavin chose not to tell him anything about his relationship with Kathryn. He desperately wanted to confide in his old friend and counselor, but he'd have to save that for a later time.

They were preparing to go over the papers Gavin's divorce lawyer, Robert Soules, had faxed over earlier in the day. An old law school chum of Julius's, Robbie asked him to discuss the proposal with Gavin first, as Julius could better grasp the ramifications Cynthia's demands would have on the business. He prepared himself for the bad news.

"Mr. Stone," the hostess murmured quietly into Gavin's ear, "there's an urgent call for you. I can forward it through to the library if you'd like." Gavin noticed Julius appreciating her ample cleavage as she leaned down longer than was necessary.

"Julius, will you excuse me?" Gavin asked. As he left the table to take the call, he heard Julius asking Gloria to bring them each a Scotch.

"Hello, Stone speaking," he said, when the call was transferred through.

"Is this Mr. Gavin Stone?" a female voice asked tentatively. He could barely hear her with the sound of bells ringing in the background.

"Yes, who's this?" he asked.

"My name is Suzy Jacobson, I'm the artist in the gallery next to Kathryn's," she replied. She hesitated. "I'm sorry to call you like this but…"

His heart lurched. "Has something happened to Kathryn?" The air left his lungs.

"Yes, I'm at St. Vincent's Hospital."

Oh dear god, no.

"Kathryn was brought in by ambulance about an hour ago," she continued.

"Is she all right?" A chill crept down his neck.

"They brought her in with stab wounds. Don't worry—she's conscious. She asked me to call your office and your secretary told me where you could be reached."

"Stab wounds?" Gavin repeated, feeling the blood drain from his face. "Where was she? What happened?" He could see Gloria eying him discreetly from her station.

"I…I don't exactly know," the woman answered. "But I do know they brought her from home. She called nine-one-one herself. She's very distraught about Jezebel being left alone in the house so I'm going back there, but I was wondering if you…"

"I will be on the first flight I can get," Gavin answered before she could finish her sentence. "Please tell her I'll be there just as soon as I can."

Chapter Twenty-Three

He felt as if his eyeballs were bleeding as a trauma doctor explained Kathryn's injuries to him. The attending physician happened to be filling out a chart when Gavin skidded into the fourth floor nursing station. The doctor looked up when he heard Gavin asking for Kathryn Bell and quickly came around from behind the counter to introduce himself.

"Are you family?" he asked.

"No...yes," Gavin blurted out. "I'm...a close friend. Is she all right?"

Presumably taking it for granted that he was intimately acquainted with his patient, the physician led him into a nearby waiting room and closed the door.

"Miss Bell has sustained quite a few cuts and lacerations but fortunately, many of them are surface, defensive wounds on her hands. I presume she received them when she fought off her attacker. There was one deep gash though, just above her left shoulder that required surgery."

Gavin couldn't help thinking of Kathryn's elegant hands and wondered if she'd ever hold a paintbrush again.

"I'm happy to tell you she seems to be doing well. We're keeping an eye on her though." The physician paused, as if unsure of his next comment. "Were you aware of any other health issues she's had of late?" he asked Gavin.

"Other issues? No, why do you ask?"

"Ah…no reason. She sustained a concussion when she fell down the stairs, presumably trying to escape."

Gavin was still thinking of the doctor's earlier remark. "She fought off her attacker?" What the hell happened?"

"I'm afraid you'll have to ask the police that, Mr. Stone. I'm not sure she knows what happened herself. She was in shock when they brought her in, and now she's recovering from surgery. She was a very lucky lady. There were no major organs involved."

The doctor's pager buzzed and he looked down at his belt. "I'm sorry, I have to go. You are welcome to go in and sit with her, but she might be asleep for some time," he warned. "A word of caution, please don't overwhelm her with a lot of questions. One of the nurses was present when the police questioned her and she became quite agitated. Right now, we want to keep her calm."

Gavin nodded. "I will be very careful not to upset her, thank you," he said, shaking the doctor's hand.

"Good luck. I'll check in on her a little later. Take it easy. You look like you could use some rest yourself."

G avin was dozing in a chair by Kathryn's bedside when he came to with a start. He heard her weakly call his name.

"I'm right here, sweetheart," he said, standing over her. "How are you feeling?"

He moved to take her hand, forgetting both were wrapped

in gauze. Instead, he put his fingers lightly on her forearm and squeezed gently.

"How did you know?" she asked, groggily.

"Your friend, Suzy, called me."

"Jezebel," she gasped. "I have to…"

"Jezebel is fine. Suzy got her and she's at her apartment over the gallery.

"The doctor says you came through surgery with flying colors. They just need to keep an eye on you over the next forty-eight hours. You need to rest and stay calm," Gavin whispered. "Can you do that for me—for us?"

She nodded silently. He gently wiped the tears from her eyes and she drifted back to sleep.

As the police considered it a crime scene, Gavin couldn't stay at Kathryn's place, but Suzy was able to book him into a small motel near the hospital. Finally convinced by the nurses to take a break while Kathryn slept, he'd gone back to take a shower and grab a couple hours of shuteye.

He left a message for John and Caroline Barclay, after asking Julius to track down their home number. The phone in his hotel room rang as he dressed to go back to the hospital.

"Hello, Gavin?" Caroline's unmistakable accent rang in his ear.

"Hi, Caroline, thank you for calling back so soon. I'm sorry if I disturbed you."

"You didn't disturb us at all, darling. Tell me please, how is she?" Her concern was palpable.

"She's doing well under the circumstances," Gavin said. "The doctor said it could have been much worse."

"Thank God," Caroline let out a long breath. "How long

will you be in Carmel? John isn't back from his workout yet, but I know he'll want us to fly down as soon as possible."

Gavin lowered himself heavily onto the side of the bed. "Caroline, I understand you want to see Kathryn, but you can't get into her house right now. It's taped off and is under investigation by the police." He felt guilty discouraging her from coming, but he wanted whatever precious time he had with Kathryn to be his alone.

"Gavin, what happened? Tell me everything."

"I'm not sure I can tell you much at this point. The police are giving me very little information, and Kathryn isn't strong enough yet to be of much help, I'm afraid."

There was silence on the other end of the phone.

"Caroline, I need to ask you a favor."

"Anything, darling, you know that."

"I know you're anxious to see Kathryn, but she and I have been going through some problems, and I was hoping to have a little time with her here alone, before I have to go back to Vancouver. That's when I think she will really need you," he said more casually than he felt.

"Having a lovers' spat, are we?" Caroline asked. "And John and I would be the third wheels, would we?"

"No, it's just that…"

"I'm teasing you, darling. I'm sorry to hear that, Kathryn hasn't said anything to me about it. You had better not hurt our girl, Gavin," she said more seriously.

"I'm sure everything will be fine, but I think it would be better for me to stay here, and make sure she gets an alarm installed in the house. Put these incidents behind her…" Gavin trailed off as he tried frantically to get his thoughts in order.

"You said incidents, plural. What else has happened? Gavin, what aren't you telling me?" Caroline asked sharply.

Shit! Despite a few hours of sleep, he hadn't eaten and his head was pounding. "What do you mean?"

"You know exactly what I mean. I insist you tell me this instant." She'd lost her friendly tone.

Gavin sighed. "Caroline, it's too complicated to explain over the phone. I'll be back in Vancouver no later than next week, and we can talk about it then." He instantly regretted calling her, but he'd promised Kathryn he would. And he couldn't very well go back to the Barclays in Vancouver and act as if nothing had happened.

"All right then, please tell Kathryn we love her and we'll be there in a few days. But I expect you to tell us everything when we see you," she warned, her tone still curt.

"Yes, okay, Caroline." He breathed a silent sigh of relief. "I promise I will."

A familiar sense of foreboding crept under his skin. He put the phone back in its cradle.

Chapter Twenty-Four

Vancouver, British Columbia
September 1985

Gavin, what have you gotten yourself into now? Troubled, Julius pondered his last telephone conversation with Gavin. The information his friend had shared with him on the drive to the Vancouver International Airport was alarming enough. He was not entirely shocked Gavin had a woman in California. However, it was the urgency and obvious panic surrounding Gavin's trip to Carmel that most disturbed him.

Gavin had been calling from a hospital when he implored Julius to track down the Barclays' unlisted home phone number. He had often suspected Gavin cheated on Cynthia, but assumed they were casual affairs which meant nothing. This was clearly a different matter. Perhaps more troubling was that somehow it involved John Barclay. They were in the thick of things with the Barclay Group bringing their wealthier clients into the La Thuile ski resort. This latest development did not strike Julius as a good omen, particularly as they were deep in negotiations with Cynthia's lawyers to hammer out a divorce settlement.

As Julius tried to put the pieces of Gavin's latest puzzle together, his secretary buzzed him that Cynthia Stone's lawyer was on line two. Speak of the devil.

"Pinsette here."

"Julius, it's Loretta Sterling calling. I'm sorry to spring this on you at the last minute, but I'm afraid we'll have to put off our deposition today, as Mrs. Stone is apparently ill."

"Not a problem, Loretta," Julius replied, relieved he didn't have to tell her his client was out of the country. In the kerfuffle, he'd forgotten all about their appointment.

"I'm reluctant to reschedule until I know the nature of her illness. Would you be agreeable to my assistant getting back to you in the next day or two?" she asked.

"Of course, if you'd be good enough to just give me as much notice as you can. Mr. Stone may need to travel shortly, on business."

"Thanks, Julius. Leave it with me. I appreciate your courtesy."

Thankful for the reprieve, Julius buzzed his secretary and asked her to locate Krochinski. With any luck, she would find him sober and able to bring Julius up to date in Gavin's absence.

"What do you mean Tommy is out of town?" Julius asked Brenda. *Am I the only goddamned person left in this city who gives a hoot about Gavin Stone's business?*

"I'm sorry, Mr. Pinsette, but that's all I know. The woman who answered his home phone said she had no idea when he'd be back and hung up on me." His secretary looked flustered.

"I'm sorry too, Brenda, I didn't mean to take it out on you. Why don't you take an early lunch?" He smiled apologetically.

"Are you sure? Can I pick something up for you on my way back? How about a nice bowl of that Sicilian tomato soup you like from the deli downstairs?"

He was not the least bit hungry but in the interest of appearing more conciliatory, he agreed.

Chapter Twenty-Five

Carmel, California

Once the initial post-surgery grogginess wore off, Kathryn was able to provide a decent account of the attack. At the outset, the police were reluctant to let Gavin stay during their questioning, but Kathryn's insistence that he remain in her hospital room left them few options if they wanted to get the necessary information. Their payback, it seemed, was to question Gavin ad nauseum about his relationship to Kathryn and his whereabouts at the time of her attack. Finally, they conceded that as long as his alibi about being in Vancouver checked out, they would be discreet regarding his marital status. Not that it would matter much at that point.

Apparently, Kathryn had started out on her morning beach walk with Jezebel, only to realize she had forgotten her wallet. Planning to get something from the café up the hill to take with her on her walk, she left Jezebel at the end of the driveway while she ducked back into the house to get some money. Whether she disturbed a burglary in progress or someone may have been out to harm her, was yet unknown. What was clear was that as she headed down the hall to the master bedroom, someone grabbed her from behind and attempted to plunge a knife into her abdomen.

Although Kathryn was fuzzy about some of the details, she recalled breaking loose from her attacker's grip and frantically running along the hall to get away. In her haste to flee down the stairs and out the door, she had felt a sharp pain in her left shoulder. Then she tripped and tumbled to the marble foyer floor. Jezebel, hearing her mistress's screams, bolted through the open front door and lunged at the person who by then was leaping over Kathryn's crumpled body. As Jezebel gave chase, Kathryn recalled crawling to the phone in the little alcove just inside the front door and calling nine-one-one.

The most frustrating part was she never got a glimpse of her attacker and so was not able to give even a vague description of height, weight, or hair color to the police. With no other incidents in the small town of Carmel, they were at a loss to connect Kathryn's attack with any recent crimes. Wondering if the motive was robbery, the lead investigator advised her they would require access to the main house on the property in the owners' absence. Perhaps it was a robbery gone wrong that had been intended for her landlord's mansion. At the moment, the officers said, it was all a matter of supposition.

After an hour of questioning, Kathryn grew noticeably tired. Both detectives appeared satisfied but requested that she remain available in case they needed further information. Breathing a sigh of relief, Gavin walked them to the elevator before returning to Kathryn's room.

She lay back with her head on the pillows, vacantly staring out the window. Although reluctant to tax her further, Gavin knew he must talk to her and pulled up a chair close to her bedside. "How are you feeling?" he asked.

"Honestly? Like I've been run over by a bus," she said, doing her best to give him a cheery smile.

"I understand. You've been through a lot, but you did well with the police. I'm sure what you were able to remember was very helpful."

"I don't know. Without being able to give them any kind of description, I wonder."

Gavin hesitated. "Kathryn, I need to talk to you about something. Are you up to a few more minutes?"

"Of course, what's wrong?"

"Well, you know how you asked me to get a hold of the Barclays?"

"Yes, poor Caroline. Was she terribly worried?"

"Of course she was. They both adore you, you know that."

"Yes, I didn't want to upset them but they're like..." Kathryn choked. "They're like my parents, you know." Tears trickled from the corners of her eyes. Gavin reached out and gently wiped them away.

"I know they are. Of course, Caroline wanted to come down as soon as she and John could get a flight. That's what I want to talk to you about."

Kathryn looked puzzled. "What's wrong?" she asked again.

"Just hear me out, please? I know you want to get back to your house and to Jez, but I want you to think about what I'm going to say." Gavin hesitated.

"I'm not moving out of my own home, if that's what you're going to suggest. I refuse to be intimidated. You heard

158

the police, they thought it was a robbery and they got the wrong house."

"No," he said patiently, "they said they thought it was a *possibility*."

"So, I should let whoever did this intimidate me into moving out?"

"No, I just think that maybe taking Jezebel and going back to Italy would be better for you right now. You said yourself you want some time away from us."

"And you're suddenly all right with that?"

"I've been giving it some more thought," Gavin hedged. "I can't say I'm relishing the idea of being away from you again, but I know you're right. I need to get things finalized with Cynthia and deal with some other pressing issues before I have any business making promises to you."

She searched his face earnestly, as if looking for clues to his sudden turnaround.

"You've had an awfully sudden change of heart," she said warily.

Gavin hadn't wanted to tell her, especially with what she'd been through, but he had to. "Sweetheart, Cynthia is trying to take me to the cleaners with this divorce. And we're right in the midst of selling John's wealthiest clients into the La Thuile development." He felt profoundly guilty about what he was about to say.

"Kathryn, I need this project to go through and to get Cynthia to settle reasonably if I'm to secure any kind of a future for us. Do you understand?"

"That's why I didn't want to be a part of this," she replied. "Our relationship is forcing you to do things that later you may resent me for." There was no mistaking the anguish in her eyes.

He thought for an instant about what he was going to say.

"I know you've had a lot thrown at you all at once, but I could stay on a few more days and arrange to get everything packed up for you. Then once your doctor gives you his approval to travel, I'd breathe easier knowing you were safe." She glared at him in protest.

"Kathryn, you've been violated twice in your own home, what makes you think it won't happen again?"

"I don't know, Gavin. I hate that I'd be letting whoever did this, win."

He was glad he'd had a few hours to swing by the gallery, between talking to Caroline and coming back to hospital. Fortunately, Suzy had known where he could find the therapist Kathryn had pointed out to him on his last visit. He took a deep breath and prayed he could pull this off.

"Sweetheart, if you can go now, the therapist you have working with your troubled teens could go with you to Italy and start working full-time with Thula."

Her face registered disbelief. "How in the world could I do that, Gavin? I'd love to take Julia back with me. You know that. But I can't possibly afford what she's been offered in San Francisco."

"Actually, you can. And it's already a done deal if you just give the go ahead," Gavin replied, with a wide grin.

"But what about the job she's already accepted? She wouldn't go back on that."

"She would and she did, especially when I told her all about little Thula. She's really motivated to work with her, Kathryn, and I can make that happen." He stood up and leaned over her bed, his eyes fixed on her face. "I want to do this for you, sweetheart. Please, would you let me make the arrangements?"

Seconds seemed like minutes before Kathryn let out an exhausted sigh. "Yes, my darling, I'll go. But I don't know how I'm going to get everything done before you leave. I guess the good news is I can get back into my house. And I haven't been home long enough to worry about Jezebel's health certificate to get back into Italy." She tried to stifle a yawn. "I'm sorry, all of a sudden I'm exhausted."

Gavin squeezed her arm. "You get some rest. I'm going to go back to the hotel and get the reservations made for you and Julia to go to Italy, and then I need to make some calls to Vancouver."

"Okay, mister charisma," she laughed. "Now I know how you manage to convince investors to put money into developments they haven't even seen."

Gavin kissed her before she could change her mind, and left with a promise to be back soon.

Chapter Twenty-Six

With Gavin in Carmel for another week, Julius found himself with the unenviable task of meeting with Kroch to get an update on where they were with Barclay's clients. They were making good progress raising the necessary capital through the sale of limited partnerships, but Julius needed to know how many more of John's clients were likely to buy in before they opened the opportunity up to other financial planners in Vancouver.

Initially reticent that Gavin was giving up ten percent of the Italian project to Vittorio Constantine, Julius had to admit the old man had indeed delivered on his promises. In an extra-ordinarily short time, Constantine had the anti-Mafia permits in place, and they'd begun work on the conversion from resort-style apartments to self-owned condominiums. What Julius required was to know how many irons Krochinski had in the fire with other financial planners who could provide them with additional investors. As was always the case, the new project was going to take more money than they'd originally estimated, and the Hawaii development on the Big Island apparently needed more repairs than just the rotting lanais. Julius was not looking forward to crossing swords with Kroch, aware Gavin's last meeting with him had not gone well.

"You called?" Kroch sauntered into Julius's office without knocking.

"Why don't you come in, Tommy?" Julius said sarcastically, not looking up from his paperwork.

"Yeah, so what's up?" He sniffed loudly, helping himself to a Coke off the bar.

"I've been trying to reach you since Friday," Julius said. "Where have you been?"

Kroch eyed Julius up and down. "Grabbed a flight down to Vegas on Thursday with a couple of buddies, what's it to you?"

Julius put his hands up in a sign of surrender and came around from behind his desk. He motioned for him to sit. "Tommy, I don't want to fight with you. I just needed to get some information while Gavin is away, and it would have been helpful if I could have gone over it with you on the weekend, that's all."

"So where's our golden boy this time?" Kroch asked, flipping the top of the soda bottle into the wastebasket.

Ignoring the jibe, Julius replied, "Out of town on business. It's taking him a little longer than expected."

"Yeah, I'm sure," Kroch replied with a sneer. "Well, I'm here now. What do you want to know?" He half-drained the bottle in one slug.

Julius consulted his notes. "Well, to start with I'm wondering how it is we didn't know anything about a hundred lanais that needed to be replaced until it was already a done deal." He took off his glasses and pinched the bridge of his nose.

Kroch glared back at him. "What exactly are you suggesting?"

"I'm not suggesting anything. I'm simply asking you a question, and I'd appreciate a straight answer." He would be damned if he'd let himself be intimidated by this low-life scumbag. "The accountant said you signed for these repairs out of the general account, and he still doesn't have any trade invoices to match them up with." The repairs had put the company's operating account into overdraft and tapped out their line of credit. But he wasn't going to tell the little bastard that.

Krochinski stared at him. "You know, I had this fucking conversation with Gavin before he left for who knows where, and I told him then what I'll tell you now." He pointed a finger at Julius. "The invoices are on the way. Which part of that don't you two understand? There were a number of trades involved, and I'm waiting for them all to come in together," he added.

Julius tried another tactic, deciding the conversation was going nowhere. As convincingly as he could, he said, "Tommy, I know how hard you've been working to connect with other financial planners in town." He paused to allow the compliment to sink in. "The sooner we can fulfill the first dibs we gave the Barclay Group, the sooner we can open it up and get the balance of the capital needed to keep funding the conversion in Italy. How long do you think it will take Barclay's people to finish going through their client list for potential investors?"

Basking in Julius's disingenuous praise, Kroch sat back and lazily put his feet up on the mahogany coffee table. "Well, as a matter of fact, I took a couple of those guys down to Vegas with me, and they're as motivated as hell to bust out of the gate. All we need is to give them the go-ahead and they're prepared to deliver."

Resisting the urge to shove his feet off the table, Julius took a deep breath and smiled tightly. "Excellent. I'll apprise Gavin of that. In the meantime," he said, fixing Kroch with an unwavering gaze, "I assume you'll have those invoices to the accountant no later than two weeks from now, right?"

Krochinski gave Julius a snide smile. "Sure, you go ahead and tell Gavin that, and in the *meantime*," he imitated Julius's tone, "you can assume anything you want."

He tossed his empty soda bottle into the trash and headed for the door.

Chapter Twenty-Seven

West Vancouver, British Columbia
February 2013

It was almost five when Julius pulled into the members-only parking lot of the Deer Ridge Country Club. Initially, he wondered if it would be an appropriate place to meet Jordan, given the horrific scene she'd had to witness with a drunken Krochinski, at the reception honoring Gavin. However, unless they met in his office, which seemed too formal, the club was probably the best place to chat and have dinner. He had just ordered his usual pre-dinner drink of Cardhu when he saw Jordan enter the lounge. He stood to give her a warm embrace, pulling out a chair and waiting until she sat down before sitting himself. The waitress brought his drink and Julius asked, "What would you like, my dear?" Surprised when she asked for a Scotch as well, he sat back in his chair and observed her in an entirely different light.

As if reading his thoughts, Jordan waited for the waitress to leave. "I know it's probably not what you were expecting me to order. You probably think of me as I was before I went off to journalism school, right?"

Blushing, Julius quickly assured her. "Not at all, I'm delighted to see what a self-confident woman you have become. Your father would be exceedingly proud." As soon as he'd said it, he instantly regretted his words. The smile left Jordan's face. "I'm sorry, I didn't mean to upset you."

Recovering quickly, she put her hand over his on the table. "Don't worry, it's okay. I just…I'm unsure of …" The server discreetly interrupted, placing Jordan's drink in front of her. As she took a sip, Julius watched her, lost in thought.

"You seem far away, Julius. What are you thinking?"

"I was actually recalling when you were a little girl, sitting in your pajamas on the stairs outside the study. I sometimes saw you through the open door when I met with your father. In fact, if I thought he might see you, I would try to distract his attention so he'd look the other way."

Her smile widened to a grin, exposing beautifully straight teeth and causing her almond-shaped eyes to curve up at the corners. "I do remember getting busted once, but thank you for not giving me away the rest of the time."

"You're welcome. I think your mother knew, but as far as she was concerned, you could do no wrong."

"Ah, yes…" For a moment, it seemed Jordan had drifted off to her own little world. "You know, Mom and I were so close, but we've gone through a rough patch in the last few years. In a way, I think I blamed her for my father leaving us."

Julius cleared his throat. "Yes, I did hear something about that, but you know your mother was and still is your best supporter. When you were little, her life completely revolved around you. I know it was hard for her when you left for college in the States."

Jordan nodded and took another sip of her Scotch. "I always thought I was so lucky I didn't have a nanny when I was growing up like so many of my friends did."

Julius shook his head. "Your mother would never have allowed someone else to raise you."

"I know. I remember asking her once why she didn't have a career like my friends' mothers, and she said raising me was the only thing she'd ever wanted to do. I remember Gran telling me what a miracle it was for Mom to have me. I loved hearing her stories about me being born in Italy and how difficult it was for Mom to have a baby."

Julius fidgeted uncomfortably in his chair, picked up a menu, and handed one to Jordan.

"I'm sorry, I'm boring you with silly little girl stuff. I know you wanted to talk to me about the investigation." She seemed to be deliberately avoiding asking about her father.

"You could never bore me, dear," Julius replied. "I'm just thinking it might be a good idea to order dinner. Are you hungry?"

As if she had overheard, the waitress came, put their drinks on a tray, and led them from the busy lounge to a quiet corner of the adjoining dining room.

They enjoyed a pleasant dinner, although what was unspoken was obvious. Jordan had no interest in talking about Gavin. Patiently, Julius inquired about her new job. He knew several executives at the newspaper personally and considered it significant the Senior Editor had recruited her from Boston and put her into Ernie McDougall's department. The competition for the junior position would have been fierce and Julius suspected Gavin had pulled some strings behind the scenes. He knew he had kept abreast of Jordan's progress and had been desperate to renew the bond with his daughter. So why had he disappeared without a trace before seeing her?

He waited while she stirred cream and sweetener into her coffee. "Jordan, would you mind if we talked about what happened before that night at Gavin's house? Do you know what he wanted to talk to you about?"

She sat back in her chair and placed her spoon deliberately on the saucer, seemingly resigned to discussing the subject. "As I told the police, Julius, I have no idea why he wanted to see me after so long. I was in my office working late when I got a text asking me to meet him at the address he gave. I didn't even know it was from him except he put his name at the end of the message. He just said it was urgent and he begged me to come and he'd explain it all later."

"What did you think when he hadn't contacted you all these years?" Julius knew full well Gavin had tried many times to reach his daughter but she never returned his calls.

Jordan sighed and toyed with her cup. "You know, I remember thinking I couldn't stay estranged from him forever and I was just…" Tears welled up and she tried to blink them away. "I'm just tired of all the fighting and the blaming, with both him and my mother. I just wanted to come back to Vancouver and get on with my life and get rid of all the bitterness and hatred between us."

Their waitress approached with more coffee to which Julius imperceptibly shook his head.

"I'm twenty-seven and I don't want to live like this anymore. I don't know if I can ever forgive him, but I was willing to at least listen to what he had to say." She wiped her nose and looked at Julius through her tears. "And now he's gone and I may never get that chance. He did a lot of really shitty things to us, but I know he's not a murderer. Or for that matter an embezzler. And yet the police aren't looking at anyone else for the murder, are they?"

Julius leaned in. "I won't lie to you, Jordan. It doesn't look good, especially in light of the B.C. Securities Commission's investigation into millions of dollars of investors' missing money. But you have my word I will do everything possible to find Gavin and to clear him of this. I just don't know where to start, and I was hoping you might."

Slowly, she shook her head. "I truly don't, Julius. I would tell you if I did."

He believed her. But it meant they were no further ahead than they were a few weeks ago.

"You look exhausted, and I'm sorry to put you through this. Is there anything more you'd like or shall we get out of here?" Julius asked.

"No, thank you, nothing more." She had only picked at her meal.

He signaled for their bill but Jordan hesitated.

"Julius, there's something else I need to talk to you about. It's about my work." For the second time he waved away the approaching server.

"Well, I certainly don't have your expertise in the area of journalism, but I do know some of the higher-ups there. What can I do to help?"

Jordan started to speak several times, only to stop and rub her hands together nervously. She took a deep breath and exhaled. "I've been assigned an investigative story to work on, and I know I shouldn't be doing it. But I haven't told my boss yet."

Julius nodded sympathetically. "I remember feeling that same way when I started out as a young lawyer. It wasn't long after I'd been called to the bar that I was handed a case for which I felt totally unqualified. But you must have confidence in yourself, Jordan. You made it through some extremely stiff competition to get that job, and whatever it is I know you're up to the task."

She shook her head. "It's not that."

Julius cocked his head, looking at her expectantly.

"I've been assigned to write an investigative piece on my father's company and the alleged missing funds, not to mention he's the prime suspect in the murder. As you know, my surname is now Leighton, so Ernie, my editor, hasn't put it together yet."

Julius stared at her and his mouth went dry.

Her words came out quickly. "I know I should have told him my family connection, but it's my only chance of finding Gavin and clearing his name. It's also my chance at breaking into crime reporting." A scowl darkened her face.

Julius took a long sip of water. "How long have you known about this? When did you get the assignment?"

"A few days ago. I was going to deal with it right away, but my boss was out of town and I was under huge pressure to go through everything quickly and bring him up to speed. Then I got another of my gastro attacks, and..."

"Jordan," he interrupted, "you must have the story re-assigned. You should have done it immediately," Julius whispered. "If you're caught, you will face serious disciplinary action. You will *never* rise any higher in the ranks. Hell, you'll be lucky to get a job working for a two-bit community paper. Do you understand?"

"I know that, but it's my only hope, Julius, don't you see?"

"What I see is a young woman who has worked incredibly hard to get where she is, and whose journalism career is going to be over before it even gets started. This is insane.

You're already in trouble even if you do fess up, because you haven't done it in a timely manner."

"I know, Julius. I know all that."

"Then how much longer do you plan to work on the story before you say something? You shouldn't even be talking to me—it's a conflict of interest." He hoped she hadn't developed her father's predilection for high-risk behavior.

Instantly, the warmth of her blue-green eyes turned a dark bottle green and an impenetrable wall went up. It struck him how quickly her mood changed. He had seen the same thing with Gavin many times.

"I'm not planning to work any further on it," she answered, curtly.

Julius was getting impatient. "Jordan, I don't understand. You said you've been given the assignment and..."

"I'm planning on taking a leave of absence starting tomorrow."

"You're what?" He stared at her. "I don't know which could possibly be worse for your career—not disqualifying yourself from a story that is a grave conflict of interest—or not giving the paper any notice that you're taking a leave. Jordan, what is *wrong* with you?" He was aware he was losing patience. Other diners turned in their chairs to look.

The wall was still up. "I've been to see my doctor, and she's given me a letter stating that due to stress caused by events of a personal nature, my stomach attacks have worsened to the point of being debilitating. Her orders are for me to be placed on disability leave immediately." There were no signs of tears as she told Julius her decision.

"I'm very sorry to hear about your health, Jordan, but it seems to me you might have concerned yourself a long time ago with contacting Gavin while he was here and desperately wanted a relationship with you." He paused to let his words sink in. "How long do you plan to be off work, and how is any of this going to help your father? You've been assigned a story that is unquestionably a conflict of interest," he grimly reminded her.

"There is nothing that prevents another reporter from working on this case," Jordan said pointedly.

Julius was confounded. She seemed to have worked all this out, and yet he still couldn't follow her logic.

"You asked me if I knew anything that would help find my father and clear him of murder, Julius. I don't, but I know how I can get access to information that might help us."

Frustrated, Julius shook his head. "I'm not following you."

"In my absence, the case will be assigned to another journalist in my department. Our shared assistant, Dorothea, and I have a close relationship, and I know she'll feel the need to call me at home on behalf of the reporter who takes over the piece. She'll be working closely with him on the fact checking, and they'll need my expertise on investigating Gavin's holdings stateside.

For the second time in minutes, Julius was dumbstruck. "Are you out of your mind? You are committing professional suicide," he hissed.

She looked at him steadily. "Do you know a better way? Correct me if I'm wrong, but is my father's firm not your one and only client, Julius? How long do you think you'll be kept on if Gavin disappears for good?"

Julius couldn't believe what he was hearing from the same young woman who had been in tears just minutes ago.

She leaned forward, looking directly into his eyes. "I know for a fact you were disbarred many years ago for 'financial impropriety.' It seems to me you have a great deal to lose if my father, and particularly millions of dollars of investors' funds, aren't found."

Shaking with rage, he barely trusted himself to speak. "You're serious. You actually think you can get away with this?"

"As serious as a heart attack. The only question is, are you? Are you willing to do whatever it takes to find Gavin and whoever murdered that private investigator?"

He looked at his watch, and this time made no secret of calling for their bill. "I need some time to think about this," he said, with a tight smile. He paused to scrawl his signature on the check. "I'm afraid I have another commitment I must attend to. I'll consider what you've said and get back to you."

"I wouldn't waste a lot of time if I were you," she said, meeting his eyes. "Oh, and Julius? Thank you for dinner."

Chapter Twenty-Eight

"I'm sorry Mr. Pinsette, but if Jordan isn't at home, I don't know where she would be. I know she had several doctors' appointments lined up. Have you tried texting her?" Dorothea asked.

"Uh, no," he replied. "But thank you."

It had been four days since he'd promised Jordan he would get back to her with his decision. Even as he placed the calls to her cell and office, he didn't know what that answer would be. It infuriated him that she knew about his disbarment. He was also frankly shocked at the stark change in her behavior when she smugly pointed out his lack of career options if Gavin was not located. Lost in thought, he was startled when his cell phone rang.

The caller ID said "private caller." He picked it up.

"I understand you've been looking for me. I was expecting to hear from you before this," she said.

"Jordan, I think we should meet. Trust me, this is not what you want to do. I can clear my calendar for this afternoon. What time can you make it to my office?"

"Impossible, I'm not in town at the moment."

"Well, when will you be back? I can wait, but please don't do anything rash until we've talked."

"I don't know when I'll be back. I'm in Italy. Tropea, actually," she replied.

His feet dropped from his desk with a thud. "You're what?"

"You heard me. I'm in Tropea doing some digging. I figured this was as good a place as any to start. Besides, I've always wanted to see where I was born." Her tone was animated, and her voice had a forced, almost manic edge to it.

Julius looked at his watch. It was eleven a.m. so it had to be eight p.m. where she was. "I thought we were going to talk about this again before you made any decisions."

"No, you were supposed to get back to me three days ago." She spoke more rapidly. "I had no intention of waiting for you to make up your mind. We don't have time to drag our feet. Besides, I've received some information that might help me figure out where things started falling apart with Gavin's La Thuile development. I'm going to try back-tracking from there."

He held the phone silently as he rubbed his head and let out a sigh.

"Julius, are you still there?"

"Yes, I'm here." He suddenly felt defeated. But at the same time, he was anxious to hear what she knew. "What do you want from me, Jordan?" he asked wearily.

"Does that mean you're going to help me?"

"I don't know what it means," he reluctantly admitted. "Why don't we start with what you need?"

He would figure the rest out later.

Chapter Twenty-Nine

Tropea, ITALY

It was late when Jordan finally shut down her laptop computer. Although she'd traveled for the past twenty-four hours, she knew she wouldn't sleep. When she'd felt this way in the past, she had often stayed up for forty-eight hours straight. And besides, there was so much to do.

The apartment, located in a former convent in the heart of Tropea's town center, felt cold and dank. The owner said he hadn't had any guests since the Christmas season and encouraged her to keep the windows open to air the place out. Easy for him to say, it felt almost as cold here as it did in Vancouver. Slipping on a cardigan, she picked up her fourth espresso and wandered up the stone steps that led from the kitchen to the building's common patio. She had her own terrace right off her flat, but although it afforded privacy, there was no view. With no other guests in the building, she thought she might as well take advantage of the large common one instead.

By daylight, the angled view from the rooftop terrazzo provided a stunning partial vista of the sea and the historic town, but tonight all she saw was a black void to the north. Off to the east were the glimmering lights of other residences nestled together along narrow cobblestone roads. Even at this late hour, she could hear laughter ringing out from the restaurants below and the occasional intimate murmurs of lovers passing by. Wistfully, she shivered and pulled her sweater closer. Reluctant to face the demons that would come to her in the dark, she knew she needed at least a couple hours of sleep. She turned and descended the stairs, leaving the crisp night air and tinkling laughter of the town center behind.

Chapter Thirty

For a moment, Jordan forgot where she was when she woke up warm and groggy from the sunlight that streamed into her bedroom. She was shocked to see the bedside clock registered 10 a.m. Throwing back the covers, she made her way to the flat's spacious kitchen and debated making herself an espresso. She thought better of it as she eyed the coffee grounds in the sink from the night before. Instead, she headed to the shower.

Her hair was still wet when she let herself out of her apartment and stepped into the bright sunlight in the street. The temperature was considerably warmer than the day of her arrival, and for a moment she stood idly on the sidewalk, face upturned, basking in the late morning sun. She looked around for the café the apartment manager told her about the night before. Sure enough, just across the cobblestone road and halfway down the block was Tropea Joe's, which boasted the world's best espresso, macchiato, and tartufo, Italy's unique version of two-flavored ice cream.

Unsure if she wanted breakfast or lunch, she ordered a double cappuccino and chocolate almond biscotti. She wished she'd brought along her laptop, but the danger of logging in to an unsecured network wasn't worth it. Checking her emails would have to wait until she returned to the flat. In the meantime, she listened to the busy chatter of the locals, who obviously were well acquainted with the proprietor, Joe.

By the time she'd drained her cup, the hustle in the café had escalated, and she feared she might be tying up a table for four that would become a precious commodity for lunch. Grabbing her purse, she was preparing to leave when she heard an urgent plea.

"Signorina, no, no! You must try our tartufo. This is your first time here, *si*?"

Puzzled, Jordan looked behind her. Presumably, the man urging that she try the world's best ice cream was speaking to her. "Oh thank you, but truly I'm not quite ready for anything else sweet. But the biscotti was delicious. Do you make it here?"

"But of course, signorina. We make everything fresh," he replied, a touch indignantly, but with a wide smile. "Please, you will insult me if you refuse my tartufo."

Before she could stop him, he'd dished out a generous portion and motioned for her to sit down.

"But you're so busy. I don't want to tie up a table you might need for lunch."

He looked around. "Busy? No, this is not busy. Sit, sit," he commanded. "Where are you from? America?" He pulled out a chair and sat across from her.

"No," she laughed. "I'm from Canada. Vancouver."

"Ah, is beautiful. I know someone who lives there."

"Really?" She waited for the usual declaration that he knew someone in Toronto and the ensuing question: did she know them? Europeans always seemed to underestimate the size of her country.

"Yes, some of my family moved there many years ago. They email me photographs all the time. They live near Stanley Park. You know it, yes?"

She smiled. "Yes, I know it very well. I drive through there every day to get to work."

"Over the Lions Gate Bridge, right?" He grinned delightedly, slapping his hand on the table.

"Yes, that's exactly right. You do know Vancouver."

The café, no matter what Joe said, was definitely getting busier. "Please, I think some of your customers need my table. The tartufo was delicious. How much do I owe you?"

He waved her hand away. "No, it is my treat. You must come again when you can stay longer. We serve dinner and have live music in the evening. You are staying nearby?"

"Yes, I'm at the Palazzo Convento, just across the street and down the block."

"How long you stay?"

Jordan hesitated. "I'm not sure," she said slowly. Her mind was working overtime as she anticipated his next question.

But instead, he said, "Ah, is a good time to be here. Not so many *touristi*."

"Hey, Joe," someone yelled from the bar.

Joe looked over his shoulder. "I must go, signorina, but you come back soon, eh?" He hurried off before she could thank him for the ice cream.

R ather than have to go out again for lunch, or dinner for that matter, Jordan stopped at a *specialita gastronomiche*, Italy's equivalent of a delicatessen. Back at her flat, she unwrapped her purchases and stored them in the refrigerator. Kicking off her shoes, she sat at the antique desk and powered up her laptop. Impatiently, she waited to be logged in to her virtual private network. Thanks to VPN technology, she was able to exchange emails with Dorothea, without her being aware Jordan was not, in fact, in Vancouver. The paper used the technology among its staff so data would be encrypted and secure. Until recently, it hadn't occurred to her that the same tool they used at the newspaper would come in handy in other ways.

Chapter Thirty-One

Jordan was unaware of the darkness that had befallen the apartment. She stretched her sore back and rubbed the chill from her arms. She hadn't eaten anything since the coffee and biscotti at Joe's and she suddenly realized she was famished. The thought of making something for herself, even from the goodies she'd bought from the local deli, was thoroughly unappealing. Although she intended to go back to Tropea Joe's, tonight she wanted something a little more substantial and with a quieter atmosphere. She vaguely remembered the apartment manager telling her about a good restaurant just around the corner, although she couldn't remember the name. No doubt, that was where she'd heard the music coming from the night before.

Her choice of clothes was easy, as she had brought very little. She slipped on a pair of slim fitting black jeans and a deep peacock blue jersey top that crossed flatteringly under her breasts. With no makeup other than some mascara and a fresh swipe of lip gloss, she quickly ran a brush through her hair. That's as good as it's going to get tonight, she thought as she let herself out of the apartment.

True to the convent manager's word, she found the restaurant easily, just in front of a beautiful twelfth-century Norman cathedral. She approached the restaurant's outer entrance, an arched, wrought iron opening enhanced by a blue-lit, double-cascade rock waterfall. There, she stood studying the menu board. She was delighted at the extensive range of menu items, as well as the relatively inexpensive prices. It was quite the contrast from Rome, where she had been shocked at the price of a café latte, which she drank standing up. It would have been even more expensive if she'd consumed her beverage at a table.

She peeked into the well-lit restaurant and uncharacteristically, felt shy about dining alone. At home, it never bothered her to eat by herself, but there she usually had her nose buried in a book or a stack of research files. For some reason, she felt strangely self-conscious and had second thoughts about going in. As she hesitated, a waiter noticed her and boisterously waved for her to come inside.

"Signorina," he beckoned. "Please, I have excellent table. I save it just for you." In spite of herself, she laughed. It seemed that to be a reasonably attractive female in Italy garnered special attention. Jordan wondered how the Italian women felt about the inordinate degree of admiration their men showed female tourists.

She allowed herself to be led into the spacious, multi-tiered restaurant, her eyes taking in the thick stone walls and Arabian-style draped ceilings. The tables were modestly decorated with Medici yellow and burnt-orange cloths, giving the entire room a warm glow. Welcoming as it was, she wondered if she'd made a mistake. The place was virtually deserted.

"Why is it so quiet?" Jordan asked the waiter.

"Is early, signorina," he said. "You are new here, *si*?"

"Yes, I came in the day before yesterday. The gentleman who looks after the Palazzo Convento, where I'm staying, suggested I come here."

"Ah yes, he is my nephew." He winked. She immediately felt embarrassed and hoped he hadn't realized she thought him to be a janitor.

"I am Roberto," he said, extending his hand. "My two brothers and I run this place. Please, where would you like to sit?"

Still feeling chilled, Jordan eyed a table toward the back of the mezzanine floor near the pizza oven. "Would up there be all right?" she asked.

"Anywhere you wish, signorina. Please allow me." He half bowed, politely stepping in front of her, and led her to the table. "Your waiter will be with you shortly. In the meantime, may I get you a glass of our specialty house wine?"

"Thank you that would be lovely, just so long as it's white." She suspected not ordering red wine in Italy might be considered treason, but she didn't have time for an episode with her stomach.

A s the time approached nine, Jordan was pleasantly surprised that indeed the restaurant had filled up, and she was actually enjoying the ambience and slow pace of her meal for one. Evidently, Don Rocco's was a place where the locals gathered *con famiglia*. She spotted at least three generations at a nearby table as well as a number of other large, animated groups of friends or family.

She finished the last of her wine while she waited for her check which like everything else, came in its own good time. Seeing her waiter approach, she pulled her wallet from her purse. But instead of handing her a bill, he placed a liqueur glass containing something yellow-colored on the table.

"Limóncello, signorina. From the gentleman at the bar," the waiter said.

Jordan looked across the restaurant and saw a good-looking, dark-haired man whom she estimated to be in his early to mid thirties smiling back at her. "Oh, no thank you, I've had enough, really."

As if sensing her discomfort he said, "If I may, signorina, the gentleman is a very good friend of our restaurant. We know him well. He is of very sound character. Please enjoy your *digestivo*."

Flustered, but not wishing to seem ungracious, Jordan accepted, much to the waiter's obvious relief. Slowly, she sipped the sweet liquid, feeling its warmth slide down her throat and radiate into her chest. She sneaked a look at the man at the bar, again. *Oh shit, he's coming over.*

She looked away as if she hadn't noticed him coming toward her and was fussing with something in her purse when he arrived at her table.

"Excuse me," he said in perfect English. "I should have introduced myself before sending over a drink. How very rude of me. Will you forgive me?" He extended his hand. "I am Giancarlo Vincente."

She could feel herself blushing. *God, it is suddenly very warm in here.* He continued standing as she reached up to shake his hand. As she debated whether to invite him to sit down—after all, he had bought her a drink—her waiter reappeared.

"Signor Vincente, may I get something for you? To join the young lady?"

"That would be lovely, Stefano," he replied. "But the lady

has not asked me to join her." His warm eyes crinkled with obvious amusement as he looked to her for permission.

Damn, how did I get myself into this? I just wanted to have a quiet dinner and go home unnoticed. "Please, you are welcome to sit down. But I was just getting ready to call it a night. I have a very long day tomorrow."

"Then I must not keep you," he said. "I hope I shall see you again." He bent to kiss her hand, and she smelled his subtle cologne. He smiled at her, showing impossibly white teeth, and turned to leave.

"Ah...thank you. For the drink. You have been very kind. I didn't mean to be rude," she stammered.

"The pleasure was mine, and you are not being rude at all," he said. "If I can be of assistance while you're in Tropea, here is my card. Please, don't hesitate to call."

Chapter Thirty-Two

The following morning, Jordan dumped the contents of her purse onto her unmade bed and fished frantically through the jumble for her apartment key. Already late for her first meeting in Tropea, she was relieved to find it tangled up with some cosmetics. She scooped everything back into her bag but for one lone business card. She turned it over. It read:

Vincente & Associati, Studio Legale
Giancarlo Vincente, Fondatore
Corso Vittorio Emanuele II, 184
00186 Roma, Italia
Tel. +39 06 96 03 81 00 Fax +39 06 96 52
*   60 71*
Skype: gcvincente email: studio@vincente.it

So Giancarlo was a lawyer and had his own firm in Rome. According to his card, his specialty was "Criminal Liability of Business Companies." It seemed an unlikely coincidence the first connection she'd made was a lawyer. The assistance of someone who obviously knew the ropes in

Italy would be invaluable, but how on earth would she approach him? Do you just call up a complete stranger and tell him your father, whom you haven't seen for ten years, has disappeared and is accused of embezzlement and murder back home? What a great way to make a first impression. Or technically, a second one.

J ordan knew where to find the Archivio di Stato di Cosenza—the office of births, marriages, and deaths—having consulted a map the night before. Thanking the barista for her coffee, she headed off in the direction of the main square.

The historic town of Tropea was stunningly beautiful. She learned it was older than Rome, which was some six hundred kilometers away. Particularly fascinating was the wide variety of architectural styles. The guidebook advised that over the years the town and its surrounding areas had succumbed to many earthquakes. In each period of history, the inhabitants rebuilt with whatever materials were available, hence the effect of mismatched buildings. With many renovations going on, some buildings were closed and roped off, apparently unsafe. She marveled at the designs of streets, most so narrow they could only accommodate one very small car at a time.

She longed to stray down one of the many steep steps and quaint lanes to discover where they led, but looking at her watch, she realized she was just going to make it in time to meet her interpreter. Jordan spotted an attractive, well-dressed young woman waiting at the top of the steps and ran up to meet her.

"You must be Jordan," she greeted her warmly. "I'm Angelina. Did you have any trouble finding this place?" Her well-spoken English had only a trace of an accent.

The two women shook hands. "No, your directions and my trusty guidebook were perfect," Jordan replied. "I just wish I'd had time to explore on my way here."

"I would be happy to show you around later. There is so much to see in Tropea. I hope you will be able to take some time from business to see our treasures while you're visiting." She looked at her watch. "I don't mean to rush you, but depending on how much information you need, we should go in. Soon, everything will shut down for *riposo*—our afternoon rest."

Jordan nodded. "Let's do it." Together, they hustled up the remaining steps and into the building.

They were shown into a reading area similar to a library and in rapid Italian were advised how to access the information they needed, some of which was computerized. Most was not. Jordan was grateful she had Angelina with her, as she hadn't understood a word of the clerk's instructions.

"You want to look for your birth record, correct?" Angelina asked.

"Yes, my parents obviously had it to get my original passport. In Canada I can renew it without my original birth certificate, but somewhere along the line it seems to have disappeared."

"Your birth date is February 19th, 1986 and that would be under the name "Leighton," yes?"

"No, I took my mother's maiden name a few years ago. It would be under 'Stone.'"

Angelina nodded and began pouring through information while Jordan thought back to when she'd changed her surname to that of her maternal Granny Leighton. She had changed from Stone solely to get back at her father after he'd left her and her mother for another woman. More than ten years after Gran's unexpected death, Jordan still missed her.

Gran's was the first funeral Jordan had attended. She recalled that in the church afterward, everyone came to give condolences to Cynthia on the loss of her mother. As usual, Jordan's father was on the other side of the world on a business trip. Her mother said he'd never have made it back in time, even if she could reach him. Recalling the tension between her parents in the months prior to Gran's death, she suspected her mother either couldn't track him down, or hadn't bothered to try.

The reception following the service was held at her grandmother's home. Overwhelmed by the number of guests in the house, Jordan had quietly slipped out to Gran's prize-winning garden. As she got part way down the path, she noticed a woman in a cream-colored dress standing alone, staring into the pond. Her face was partly visible and her beautiful, deep chestnut hair shone in the late afternoon sun.

She turned when she heard Jordan coming down the walk. Her warm smile was enhanced by striking emerald green eyes. She extended her hand. "It's very nice to meet you, I'm…" She looked over Jordan's shoulder, her smile vanishing.

Jordan followed the woman's anxious gaze and saw Julius Pinsette starting down the path toward them, his face shrouded in anger.

"Oh, please excuse me. I see I'm needed rather urgently," the woman said.

Jordan watched her hurry up the path leading to Gran's house. She remembered seeing Julius angrily clasp her forearm as she tried to pass him. When he caught sight of Jordan observing him, he quickly dropped the woman's arm, and she disappeared inside the house.

Later, when Jordan went looking for her, she was nowhere to be found.

Angelina's soft whisper interrupted her contemplation. "I'm sorry, but I have checked everywhere. There is nothing here that would indicate a birth certificate for you."

Jordan frowned.

"Are you sure you were born in Tropea proper? Could it have been one of the surrounding towns, perhaps?"

Jordan shook her head. "No, I'm positive it was Tropea. My mother always made it sound so exciting that I was born in this charming little place before she could make it back to Canada." She felt as if someone had knocked the wind from her.

"You said you'd changed your surname. Is it possible your mother would have registered your birth under her maiden name rather than 'Stone'?"

"I can't imagine why she would have. She never went by that name after she married."

"Let me check anyway, just to be sure," Angelina replied.

Assuming they'd find her birth certificate quickly, Jordan intended to ask Angelina where she could locate commercial permits and building records. If she could find something significant regarding her father's first project in La Thuile, she might be able to backtrack and find out where his business holdings began to unravel.

Angelina scanned further back under the Ls, but again came up empty. "I'm so sorry, I don't know where else to look. Is there anything else I can help you with while we're here? We still have about twenty minutes before closing time."

As she and Angelina reemerged into the sunlight, Jordan was grateful for the information they were able to glean on her father's building projects. However, she felt empty and confused as to the missing documentation on her birth.

Angelina smiled sympathetically. "May I take you for coffee nearby? I know a place very near here that doesn't close for *riposo*. It would be my honor," she added shyly.

The truth was, Jordan wanted to get back to her apartment and figure out what to do next, but she didn't want to hurt the young woman's feelings. "Thank you, Angelina, that would be lovely. But please, it's my treat, you've been so helpful today. I'm very grateful for everything you found on my father's businesses."

"Ah yes, but not so much about you. I am sorry, Jordan."

"Oh no, please. I know you did your best," she quickly assured her.

Once inside the café, Jordan succeeded in convincing Angelina to let her treat, and she stood in line while her new friend went to find a table. After ordering, she offered her money to the cashier only to be told it had already been paid for. The cashier tilted her head toward the person behind Jordan in line.

She turned and found herself looking into the smiling eyes of Giancarlo.

"It would appear we have a similar addiction," he said. "Asking for a triple shot of espresso in Italy could be putting your heart at risk."

She felt herself blush again. "Your heart can obviously stand it. What makes you think mine is weaker than yours?" she asked playfully.

"Touché, Jordan." He remembered her name. "Would it be rude this time for me to ask if I may join you?"

Not sure how to respond, she saw Angelina indicating she

had secured a table. Noticing Giancarlo beside her, she motioned that there were three chairs. I guess that decides it, Jordan thought.

As they approached the table, Angelina jumped up and gave Giancarlo a kiss on both cheeks. "*Ciao, sua cosi' bello vederti*! It's so good to see you," she said as they exchanged hugs.

"I see you two know each other," Jordan said. "Don't tell me. You're related, right?" She laughed as Giancarlo held out her chair and then Angelina's.

"No," replied Angelina, "but I went out with Giancarlo's best friend for awhile. Until he threw me over for another woman, that is."

"Oh now, bella, that's not true," Giancarlo replied. "You broke his heart when you turned down his proposal of marriage." He held his hands to his chest and sighed loudly.

"Yes, he was so heartbroken," Angelina turned to Jordan, "that within months, he had married another and now they have two bambinos, right, Giancarlo?" She laughed at his melodramatic gesture.

"Three actually," he corrected her, taking a sip of his coffee.

"Three? You see, Jordan. Italian men are very fickle. They profess their undying love to you one day, and the next they're breeding like little bunny rabbits with another woman."

She was enjoying this side of Angelina and was glad she had taken her up on her offer. Giancarlo also seemed particularly pleased. For the time being, she could forget her loneliness and the peculiar feeling of being a non-person in the local record archives.

After coffee and an hour of good-natured conversation, Giancarlo insisted on driving Jordan the short distance back to her apartment. As she and Angelina said their goodbyes at the café, she thought she caught a secretive smile between her two new friends.

Giancarlo's MINI Cooper careened around several corners before arriving with a squeal of tires outside her building. She turned to thank him but before she could, he'd catapulted from the car and opened her door. I could get used to his impeccable manners, she thought as she accepted his hand.

"I'm afraid I have to go to Rome tonight," he said. "But would you do me the honor of having dinner with me when I return?"

Searching frantically for an excuse, it dawned on her that she actually didn't want to find one. "That would be lovely, Giancarlo. Thank you."

"Excellent. May I have your phone number and I will call to arrange something?"

She fished in her purse for some paper only to come up with one of her business cards, on which she wrote the number of the cell phone she had purchased when arriving in Italy.

Giancarlo turned her card over. "You are a journalist. Why did you not tell me? Are you here working on a story?" He winked conspiratorially.

"I am a journalist," she laughed, ignoring his last question. "And you are a lawyer, as I discovered this morning when I read your card. I'm sure we'll have lots to talk about over dinner."

He looked at her earnestly, lingering on her eyes.

"Indeed," he replied. "Please, let me walk you to your door, and then I'm afraid I must be off. Thank you so much for a lovely afternoon, Jordan. I look forward to calling you in a couple of days."

She leaned against the door after letting herself into her flat. *What are you doing? You don't have time for romance or complications on this trip.* She instantly regretted her quick acceptance of a dinner date with this charismatic stranger.

Suddenly chilled, she changed quickly into some sweats, poured herself a glass of wine, and waited until her laptop logged in to the secure server. The information she'd requested was in her email inbox. Quickly, she scanned it for the salient details. *Dorothea, I love you!*

The last time she and Julius had spoken, his nervousness was palpable. Based on what she was reading, Jordan suspected the next installment would have an even greater effect.

Chapter Thirty-Three

West Vancouver, British Columbia

For the life of him, Julius could not figure out where Jordan was getting her information. It unnerved him that she knew things about Gavin and him that to the best of his knowledge no one else did. When she asked about Tommy Krochinski on their last telephone call, for a moment, Julius was caught off guard.

She obviously knew Kroch had been her father's former business partner, based on the scene he'd caused at the event honoring Gavin's contribution to the drug addiction center. But it was the additional details she had managed to glean that worried him. Perusing the last email from Jordan, Julius wavered between admiration of her tenacity and abject fear of what she had managed to uncover.

His world seemed to be tightening around him. The local and national newspapers continued to speculate about the connection between Manny Smith, the man found murdered at Stone's residence, and Stone himself. The Securities and Exchange Commission was hounding Julius daily for information on Gavin's whereabouts. That, together with John Barclay's public pleas to find the man responsible for fleecing dozens of his clients of their life savings, had Julius's stomach in knots. The fact he'd had no contact whatsoever from Gavin was the worst. The thought of falling face first into another professional chasm was not in his plans, and he felt more reason to worry about the latest details Jordan had uncovered. Would this debacle never go away?

In the short time she'd been in Italy, Jordan had managed to contact a number of individuals who had been instrumental in the success of Gavin's first European project in La Thuile. Many of the names she asked about in her emails rang faintly familiar, but it was so many years ago. Julius was beginning to realize his friend and client had many secrets he'd never shared with him. It was becoming abundantly clear why.

This last email made his pulse quicken. It contained the name of a man he would never—*could* never—forget.

How was it possible he was still alive?

Chapter Thirty-Four

Tropea, ITALY

J ordan had a difficult time admitting it, even to herself. The excitement of what she'd discovered about her father's business affairs within the last few days paled in comparison to the anticipation she felt as she dressed for dinner with Giancarlo. True to his word, he called her as soon as he returned from Rome.

From her meager wardrobe, she chose a cream-colored satin blouse and slim black pencil skirt. Paired with knee-length leather boots and a short wool jacket, she hoped she was dressed appropriately. It was a beautiful March day; one that beguiled with warm promises of spring and bedeviled with the cool, crisp evenings of winter. She couldn't remember the last time she'd dressed for a date, and was grateful that having packed light, her choices were limited.

. . .

Seated across from Giancarlo at the tiny restaurant table, she listened enthralled to his tales of Rome. His smile beamed from liquid brown eyes, framed by thick curly lashes. He had a full head of shiny, almost black hair. Although she was considerably shorter than his six-foot height, they'd matched each other's strides easily when he'd offered his arm as they walked to the nearby restaurant.

"Now, enough about me," he said. "Please, I have been waiting three days to find out about you. What has brought you to our sleepy little town of Tropea?"

Jordan didn't know if the warmth she felt creeping into her cheeks was from the fireplace or the wine she twirled thoughtfully around the bowl of her glass. "Compared with your life, I'm afraid there's not much to tell."

"Forgive me, I did not mean to pry. I just wondered if I might be of help to you while you're here." He fixed his gaze on her face and took a sip of his wine.

She wondered what she should tell him. *If* she should tell him. Although she had uncovered a lot about her father's business—and his life—she had run into a roadblock. She knew the name of the man who had been a major backer of Gavin's in his early days, but was at a loss how to contact him.

"Have you ever heard of a man named Vittorio Constantine?" she asked tentatively.

His gaze wavered ever so slightly. "Why do you ask?"

Now it was her turn to sit back and study him. Was it her imagination or did he seem wary?

"No real reason." *First rule of working a source, Jordan —don't seem too interested.* "Apparently he held a significant stake in a development project I'm looking into."

"Recently?" Giancarlo asked.

"Back in 1985. Did your family live here then?"

"So you *are* here working on a story, yes?" he countered, ignoring her question. His smile never wavered.

"Not per se. It's in relation to an old article my newspaper is thinking of resurrecting. I've been going back and doing some fact checking with the thought of turning it into a new series on tax evasion. It would appear that one of the individuals named in the original piece wasn't declaring all his income. As a lawyer, I'm sure you know that any investments held abroad are considered global income."

"Your card indicates you're a reporter on the City Desk. Do you also handle international affairs for your newspaper? That's unusual, isn't it?"

Their conversation was beginning to feel like a fencing match. "Giancarlo, I simply asked if you knew Mr. Constantine. Would that be a yes or a no?"

"Yes, I have heard of him. Tell me, have you had any success finding him?"

"No, as a matter of fact I haven't. I thought perhaps I could take you up on your offer of help. As a local, it shouldn't be that difficult for you to locate him."

"I can certainly try." He smiled disarmingly. "Forgive me, I should not have brought up business. You are too beautiful a dinner companion for us to be talking business. I want to know much more about you. How long will you be here, and will you have any time for sightseeing?"

The waiter arrived with their after-dinner liqueurs, and as much as she was charmed with Giancarlo's rapt attention to the parts of her life she selected to share, Jordan realized she wasn't going to get any further this evening.

. . .

The next morning she lay in bed a few more minutes, regretting the extra limoncello Giancarlo had talked her into. In spite of her concern about his reaction to hearing Constantine's name, she'd enjoyed a long overdue date, particularly with a man she found most intriguing. However, she'd have to ponder her feelings for him later. Her bedside clock told her she had a little over an hour to shower and get to her first appointment.

As promised, her rental car was waiting for her as she left her apartment. After a walk-around inspection and a few driving tips from the agent, she signed the leasing contract and made her way out of Tropea's historic area heading northeast on Viale Coniugi Crigna. With the luxury of GPS, she was able to savor the sunny, twenty-five-kilometer drive to Limbadi. Judging by the estimated time of arrival, she should only be ten minutes away from the Feudo Montalto Golf Club. Meeting with Mr. Grimaldi, her father's former solicitor, she hoped to make more progress toward finding Constantine than she had the previous night.

Looking at the map on the GPS, Jordan prepared to make a sharp right onto SP30. She tapped the brake lightly to slow the car as she went into the curve. She felt no resistance. No matter how hard she stepped down on the brake, nothing happened; the pedal went straight to the floor. Frantically, she pumped them again. She careened around the next bend, veering dangerously close to the edge of the road, throwing gravel against the right side of the car. Blood pulsed in her ears. She grabbed for the emergency brake and yanked it up as hard as she could. Nothing. Although the Nissan was an automatic, she remembered the leasing agent showing her how to gear down manually in the event she'd like more of a "sporty" ride.

She felt the car strain and buck as she dropped it into third and then into second. Although gearing down slowed her speed somewhat, she knew it wouldn't be enough to stop her before the next sharp turn indicated on the navigation screen. Her heart was in her mouth as she rounded the bend. Oversteering to avoid a car coming toward her, she skidded to the far edge of her lane, drifting ominously close to the natural rock wall. *Oh please, God, don't let me crash!* She heard the sickening sound of metal scraping on rock as she tried desperately to straighten out and get back in her lane. An oncoming car leaned on its horn as she fishtailed around the next corner. Again, she slid dangerously alongside the imposing granite cliff.

But this time she didn't bounce back onto the highway. It felt like a giant arm had reached out and grabbed the back end of the car. She heard the rear bumper peel off as if by a can opener. She thought she felt the car slow but wondered if it was just wishful thinking. Now on a straight stretch, she felt the vehicle list to the right. She jumped, letting out a scream as a driver behind her honked his horn and then skirted around her, narrowly missing another car before returning to its own lane.

Terrified her car was going to roll right into the cliff, Jordan realized she was driving in a rut between the road and the rock. And she was starting to lose speed. *Thank God.* More cars whizzed by as she felt several large boulders scrape along the undercarriage. Suddenly, the car came to a halt. Still clutching the steering wheel, she leaned her forehead against it and fought to slow her breath. Her trembling right foot was still on the brake pedal, which lay impotently against the floor.

Slowly, she eased herself from her rigid position and looked around. The odd jingle-jangle of an emergency vehicle sounded close. Looking into her rearview mirror, she took a deep breath for the first time in minutes, and gave silent thanks the police were behind her.

T he hustle of multiple ringing phones, and what seemed like the Italians' penchant for shouting was testing Jordan's patience to the limit. A clerk at the local police station had told her in broken English that they had to locate a translator before she could talk to an inspector. That had been over an hour ago. Her heightened sense of smell and roiling stomach confirmed she would soon be clutching her abdomen in agony.

Sitting on a hard wooden chair, a cup of cold, stale coffee in hand, Jordan was never so glad to see a familiar face in her life. When Giancarlo swung open the double doors to the police office, she could have sworn the cacophony dropped several notches in volume. Ignoring the solicitous greetings from police and staff alike, he bolted to her side. She wanted to get up but she couldn't.

He knelt beside her. "Jordan, what happened? Are you all right?"

She nodded, a lump rising in her throat. "How did you know I was here?" she asked, choking back tears.

"I was just finishing a meeting with a client upstairs when one of the clerks asked if I might be available to help an American with translation."

Despite her condition, she chuckled to herself at the Italians' collective idea that somehow Canada and the US were the same country.

"You look awful. Is there something else I can get you? Some bottled water perhaps?"

"Thank you, but no." She winced as pain pierced her

stomach. "If you could just find out how much longer I have to wait, that would be very helpful." She smiled weakly.

"Of course, let me talk to the inspector in charge. Will you be all right to stay here? I promise I won't be long."

On the drive back to Tropea, she closed her eyes and sank deeper into the soft leather seat of Giancarlo's MINI Cooper. She protested briefly about inconveniencing him further, but he had insisted on taking her home. Somehow, he had been able to fast-track her statement to the police with a promise she would make herself available again at their request. He even managed to cadge an anti-nausea pill from their first-aid kit to help make the half-hour drive to Tropea tolerable. She'd die of embarrassment if she threw up in his car. Her rental car had been towed to the station, the inspector agreeing there wasn't much more they could do until they'd gone over it. She sensed Giancarlo's presence motivated the inspector to become suddenly much more attentive to her situation.

She must have dozed off because the sound of her car door opening and his hand on her arm startled her. "We're here, Jordan. Do you have your key? I'll help you inside," he said, tucking his hand gently under her elbow.

"Oh no, I'll be fine. Thank you." As she struggled to her feet, she stumbled, falling against him.

"Please, let me help you. You are so pale, and I worry about you going up that steep flight of stairs to your apartment. Here, take my arm."

Too weak to protest, she fished in her purse for the large antique key and took his arm. Once inside her flat, he helped her out of her coat and over to the couch. "Can I make you some tea? Perhaps fix you something to eat?"

"That's so kind of you. I just need to take some medication and try to sleep. You've done too much already. I hope I haven't caused you to miss any other meetings today."

"Not at all. I'm just worried about you. Will you call me when you're feeling better? If you get my assistant just tell her your name and she will be sure to find me or put your call through."

"Of course, thank you, Giancarlo. You have no idea how much I appreciate your help." She tried unsuccessfully to stifle a yawn and her eyes watered.

"Get some rest and please call when you're up to it. I'm very worried about you with what happened today. I want you to lock the door behind me."

She was just getting into bed when she heard the muffled ring of her cell phone. It was Giancarlo.

"I'm sorry to disturb you, Jordan, but I thought I should tell you. When I pulled away from the curb in front of your apartment, I noticed a lot of oil on the road where I parked. I got out and looked, and I'm very sure what I saw was brake fluid. With your permission, I'd like to advise the Limbadi police and have them take a look at it. In the meantime, I've put a couple of caution cones over that spot so no one else can park there."

"Brake fluid? What are you saying?"

"I'm not sure. It's possible it could have been a leak, but usually the fluid would run out slowly and from what you said, your rental car wasn't parked there for more than a few minutes. Let's talk about it when you're feeling better. I just wanted you to know. More importantly," he added, "I want the police to know."

Jordan lay quietly in her darkened bedroom, feeling the

gradual abatement of her stomach pain. It suddenly dawned on her that in the ensuing chaos of what she now thought of as a near-death experience, she had neglected to contact Mr. Grimaldi to apologize for not showing up for their meeting at the golf course.

She would have to put that right in the morning, she thought, as she felt the medication kick in.

Chapter Thirty-Five

Without a phone number for Mr. Grimaldi the only thing Jordan could think to do was call the Feudo Montalto Golf Club, where they were to have met. Surely, someone there could tell her how to reach the solicitor.

"I'm very sorry, signorina," the concierge informed her. "I know of no one by that name,"

"But I was scheduled to meet with him yesterday," she pressed. "Perhaps he made reservations for lunch at noon. We were to meet in the restaurant."

"No, I do not have any reservation under that name," she replied, politely.

Unsuccessful, Jordan rang off. It was one more thing she'd put on her list to ask Giancarlo. With the ability to search the Internet for virtually anyone, what were the chances of not finding anything? Grimaldi's name had shown up frequently on permits and licenses her father's company had applied for back in the early eighties. He was obviously still around, so why could she not find anything about him?

. . .

She suspected Giancarlo had exerted considerable influence with the chief inspector of the Limbadi Police Department. Although she would have done so if necessary, the thought of driving back along that stretch of road anytime soon was unappealing. Grateful the police came to her, she was wholly unimpressed with the investigative skills of the officer sent to check the oily leak on the street outside her building. He quickly acknowledged it was brake fluid but couldn't tell her with any certainty when and how he intended to follow up. It seemed everything in Tropea progressed at a snail's pace. Or at least it did for foreigners. If it weren't for Giancarlo she thought, it might be time to wrap things up and move on.

Later that day, Jordan was surprised how disappointed she felt when Giancarlo abruptly canceled their dinner plans. She wouldn't even allow herself to think of it as another "date." She was initially reticent about accepting his invitation at all. Of equal concern was the brief text he had sent. *Can't meet tonight. Will call later. GC.* Previously, she'd observed he much preferred to pick up the phone and speak with her personally. He'd said on more than one occasion he hadn't acquired his peers' penchant for texting. "Too impersonal," he'd said, with a wrinkled frown and scornful shake of his head.

Absently, she flipped on the local television news, wandered into the kitchen, and poured herself a glass of wine. Might as well catch up on some social emails, she thought. Over the last few days, she'd ignored all but business communications. As she waited to connect to the network, she reached across the coffee table for her wineglass. Suddenly, she was looking at a close-up of her interpreter, Angelina, on the television screen. She grabbed the remote and turned up the sound. The commentary was in Italian so she couldn't understand all of it, but the photos told the story. Alternating between images of Angelina's smiling face were pictures of emergency workers and police coming out of a house. The television cameras lingered on groups of neighbors huddled nearby, many hugging each other, obviously distraught. A female reporter was trying to get a comment from one of the policemen, only to be dismissed with a brusque wave of his hand. Then, the newscast was thrown back to the anchor. *Oh my god!* Jordan recognized the written words scrolling across the bottom of the screen. "*Omicidio di Angelina Candiotti.*" The murder of Angelina Candiotti.

Her heart hammered as she dialed Giancarlo's number. *Pick up, dammit!* Mercifully, he did, on the fifth ring. "Pronto," he barked into the phone.

"Giancarlo, I just saw the news. Is it true? Is it Angelina?"

"Yes, Jordan. I cannot talk now. I must call you back."

She could barely hear him above the noise in the background. "What happened? Can you tell me…"

He had already hung up.

I t was several hours later when she heard the ring of the old-fashioned doorbell downstairs. She turned out the living room light before inching back the curtain to look out the window. Breathing a sigh of relief upon seeing Giancarlo's car parked at the curb, she ran downstairs to let him in.

Looking utterly defeated, he stood on the steps, his eyes red and bloodshot. He ran his fingers through his hair, leaving it flopped carelessly over his forehead. There was no sign of the warm mischievous smile she'd come to know.

"Giancarlo, I'm so sorry. Please, come in out of the cold." She pulled him through the door with more force than she'd meant. Without thinking, she put her arms around him in a hug, feeling the cold dampness of his overcoat against her cheek. He stood unyielding, arms at his side. Feeling awkward, she pulled away and looked into his eyes. They were filled with tears.

"Here, let me take your coat," she coaxed him. He stood still. "Just come upstairs with me. Please, Giancarlo." He nodded and followed her up to the apartment.

She hastily moved her laptop and papers off the couch. "Sit down. What can I get you? Can I make you something? Have you eaten?" Horrified, she realized she'd left the television on, and they were still covering Angelina's murder. She picked up the remote to switch it off.

"Leave it!" he demanded.

Startled, she looked at him and slowly put the remote on the coffee table.

"I'm sorry," he said. "I didn't mean to shout at you. I'm… I'm…I don't know." He sat on the edge of the couch, legs apart, hands dangling lifelessly between them. "Do you have something stronger than wine?" he asked.

"I'm not sure, let me check."

He turned up the sound on the television as she rifled through one of the kitchen cabinets. She remembered seeing bottles of something that resembled alcohol when she'd first arrived. "There appears to be some brandy here," she called out from the kitchen. "Would that do?" Not hearing an answer, she poured them both a glass—his more substantial —and took it into the living room. Thankfully, he had switched off the television. Unsure if she should ask for more details, she sat quietly and waited for him to speak.

Finally, he broke the silence. "Her mother checked her room to see if she had returned home from a party and found her in her bed, strangled. She is devastated, hysterical."

"I'm so sorry, Giancarlo. Why would anyone want to kill Angelina?"

"They never locked their door, you know. Life used to be like that in Tropea, but I've been telling them, it's not like it was when we were growing up as children." He took a gulp of his brandy and then another. "Nothing here is as it was."

"Do the police have any clues? Do they know why someone would have done this?" Jordan asked. She prayed Angelina had not been sexually assaulted but was loathe to ask.

"It's as if they were looking for something. Her mother said her room was a mess. Turned upside down. They must have gone through it after they killed her."

"May I have another?" he asked, holding out his empty glass.

"Of course." She fetched the brandy from the kitchen, poured him a refill, and put the bottle on the table in front of him.

It was two a.m. when he'd consumed the rest of the bottle. Knowing he shouldn't drive but reluctant to invite him to stay the night, Jordan contemplated what to do. As if sensing her dilemma, Giancarlo stood up to leave. "You've been so kind. I am very sorry if I've outstayed my welcome," he said. He wavered a little on his feet, and she wondered if she would ever see him look more beaten than he did at that moment.

"You were there to rescue me when I needed help. I only wish there was something more I could do. I know nothing will make up for losing Angelina in such a horrific way."

He nodded.

"Giancarlo, I don't think you should be alone tonight.

And you certainly shouldn't drive. If you don't mind sleeping on the couch..."

"You are very kind, but I must go. I want to look in on Auntie—Mrs. Candiotti. She's not my real aunt but she helped raise me. Angelina's sister and brother are with her, but she was so distraught, I know she will need me. There are so many things to attend to, and those at least I can do," he replied.

"But not tonight, you are exhausted. Please, Giancarlo, sleep here for at least a couple of hours. You will be no good to anyone if you don't get some rest." But she knew her words had no effect.

As they reached the downstairs door, he turned, and this time it was he who reached for her embrace. She felt his warm breath in her hair. "I am so grateful I could come here tonight, thank you, Jordan."

She stood back, encouraged to see a remnant of a tired smile. "Will you let me know when the arrangements are made for Angelina? I would like to be there."

"She would want you there. She was very fond of you," he replied.

For a moment, she thought he was going to kiss her. He looked in her eyes as if searching for something. Instead, he kissed her on both cheeks and squeezed her shoulders. "Get some sleep as well. You have been through a lot yourself in the past forty-eight hours. I will call you tomorrow. Good night."

She closed the door behind him and climbed the stairs. Too tired to clear up their dirty glasses, she turned off the lights, went to bed, and sank into a deep and dreamless sleep.

Chapter Thirty-Six

Little else dominated the news or the talk around town other than Angelina's murder. The locals at the markets and cafés clucked and shook their heads; news anchors frequently ended their broadcasts cautioning citizens to lock their doors.

The autopsy, which was mandatory in Italy in cases of sudden death, showed no toxic substances in Angelina's system and no signs of sexual assault. The body was released to the family, and the funeral was planned for the upcoming weekend. As was the custom in many small towns in Italy, everyone was welcome to attend, and posters were placed around Tropea and the surrounding villages, with details of the burial. Catering the reception following Italian funerals was unheard of. Food had been steadily arriving at the Candiotti residence immediately after the news of Angelina's death had broken. There would be more than enough to feed the immediate family and funeral guests, and still have left-overs to send home with everyone.

. . .

J ordan sat quietly in the cathedral, gazing up at the silver-framed painting of the dark-skinned Madonna of Romania, high upon the altar. The fifteenth-century Norman church was where the faithful of Tropea and the surrounding towns gathered. Unable to bring herself to approach the traditional Catholic open casket, where it was common practice, even for children, to kiss the cheek or forehead of the deceased, she stared at the polished white casket from her pew. Giancarlo, of course, was one of the pallbearers. He looked strikingly handsome in his dark suit, but his face was pale and crumpled. Before he joined the family in the front few rows of the church, she caught him looking at her and gave him an encouraging smile.

It was a beautiful, but heartbreaking service. The tributes to Angelina were endless and Jordan's chest tightened thinking of how quickly her new friend had been snatched from the world. *What would have been so valuable that someone killed for it?* The police had no leads and the family might have to live forever with the agony of not knowing why.

At the graveside, she sneaked a furtive glance at Giancarlo. After fulfilling his pallbearer duties, he was among the first guests, along with the family, to toss a handful of dirt on the casket and place a single white rose on top.

When the last of the mourners had departed, he joined her, taking her arm to lead her away. As they walked, Giancarlo explained that unlike in Italy's larger cities where coffins were stacked and placed in mausoleums, Angelina had been put to rest in the ground, where she would be surrounded by family members who had died before her. He seemed to take great comfort in telling Jordan how future visitors to the cemetery could wander through the tranquil, lush grounds and have picnics if they wished. There, her grave would be tended by generations of family for years to come. In death, he said, she would never be alone.

B ack at the Candiotti's home, Jordan was acutely aware of Giancarlo's presence at her elbow as she tried to make small talk with family members and guests. When she could politely bow out of the conversation, she turned to him. "I don't know how you managed to get through it, but you did a beautiful job of honoring her. Through you, I have a better sense of who Angelina was."

"It was hard," he agreed. "But thank you. You made quite an impression on Angelina as well. She was very excited the first time she met you, and I know she considered you a friend already." He smiled but his eyes remained sad. "Please, I don't want you to leave yet, but *Tia* looks overwhelmed. Would you excuse me? Please, eat. We have so much, we'll be sending everyone home with food," he lamented.

"Have the police found anything, Giancarlo? Anything at all? Why would anyone want to kill Angelina?"

"I wish I knew. We're frustrated, but I know the police are taking this very seriously. I have a meeting with the chief investigator tomorrow, but I am not hopeful. We all want answers, but most especially her mother. I think the little part of her that lived on after Angelina's father died, is gone. I cannot imagine *Tia* without her youngest daughter. In many ways she lived her life through Angelina."

"It must be awful for her," Jordan agreed. He turned to leave, and she watched as he discreetly rescued the woman he fondly referred to as *Tia*—Auntie—from the endless hugs of countless well-meaning guests.

. . .

They took the opportunity to duck out of the wake early. Much as she knew it tore at Giancarlo's heart to leave Mrs. Candiotti, Jordan suspected he needed a break from the cloying scene of the many mourners. He insisted on walking her the short way back to her flat.

It probably wasn't the best timing, but Jordan simply couldn't afford to wait any longer to ask what had been nagging at her for days. Since first meeting Giancarlo, she'd brought it up repeatedly, and each time he seemed to brush her off. She decided to take the plunge.

"Giancarlo, have you given any more thought to Vittorio Constantine, the man I asked you about that first night at the restaurant?"

He appeared to weigh his reply carefully. "What do you want with this man, Jordan?" His tone seemed irritated.

"Well," she began carefully, "Angelina and I found his name came up a lot in the public records office. Along with a Mr. Grimaldi, he seemed to be instrumental in my father's condo development in La Thuile. It appears he owned ten percent of the project. I realize that was prior to the Internet, but it seems odd I can't find anything on either one of them. And you say you don't know anything about him. Don't you think that's a little strange?"

Abruptly, he stopped walking and turned to face her. "You told me you were inquiring about Constantine in connection to an old newspaper article," he said, accusingly.

Shit! She feigned casualness. "I am. I just thought while I'm here I would check out a personal matter." Even to her, it sounded hollow.

He took both her shoulders and held her at arm's length. "Jordan, I don't know what game you're playing here, but I want you to stop looking for Constantine. Now."

She tilted her head questioningly. "That's ridiculous. I would have thought if you knew anything about either of them, you would have the decency to tell me. What are you hiding, Giancarlo?"

"What am *I* hiding? That's rich coming from you," he retorted.

"How could you say that? I've been completely honest with you. You're the one who seems to be playing games."

"You've been totally honest. Really?" A young couple holding hands parted and walked around them, smirking. Undoubtedly, they thought they were witnessing a lover's spat. "You had Angelina looking for a nonexistent birth certificate, you've changed your name—God knows why—and then you had her searching for records about your father's business. And you tell me you're here looking into the holdings of someone named in an article long ago. Just who is being less than truthful, Jordan?" His eyes narrowed and his jaw hardened.

She stood rooted to the spot, too shocked to reply. Angelina had told him her business. She had never asked her to keep her inquiries confidential; there didn't seem any need to. At the time, she had no idea Angelina even knew Giancarlo.

Angrily, she shrugged from his grasp. "You have no business telling me what I should and shouldn't do. I am not leaving here until I find out who these men are. No matter what it takes, Giancarlo, I *will* find out."

"No matter what it takes," he spat. "Even if you have to leave more bodies in your wake to do so?"

Stunned, she stood shaking, her throat so tight she could barely swallow. What was he saying? Did he somehow believe she was responsible for Angelina's death? The magnitude of what he'd implied appeared to hit him. Instantly, he looked remorseful.

"Jordan, I'm sorry. I didn't mean that. I…"

"Get away from me," she hissed from between clenched teeth. "Everything bad has happened since I met you. Tell me, was it just a coincidence we met that night at the restaurant, or did you plan it?"

"I owe you an explanation," he began, this time more contrite.

"You owe me nothing. Lose my number, Giancarlo, and don't ever call me again." She heard him call out to her as she ran the last half block to her apartment.

S he hadn't slept more than two hours when the sun came up, but she forced herself out of bed. Giancarlo had called and texted several times after she returned home, all of which she ignored. Overnight, she made the decision to hire a private investigator and leave Tropea. Whether she'd go straight back to Vancouver, she hadn't decided. Depending on what a PI could dig up, she might lay low somewhere nearby, but it was certainly going to be away from Giancarlo. As she made herself a strong Americano, she couldn't shake the familiar empty feeling of excising another potential lover from her life.

It took her twice as long as usual to get ready. When she finally left the apartment, she was so afraid of running into Giancarlo that she stuck her head tentatively out the door before stepping onto the street. *Damn, it's raining. I'd better go back and get my raincoat.* She silently cursed the steep staircase leading up to her apartment. Why hadn't she put her coat and umbrella in the common area at the bottom? It wasn't as if there were any other occupants to steal them.

Then, like a thunderbolt, it hit her.

When Giancarlo had brought her home from the police station in Limbadi the night her car spiraled out of control, he asked for her key to unlock the outside door for her. "I worry about you going up that steep flight of stairs to your apartment," he said.

He hadn't been inside her apartment building at that time. How would he have known about the stairs?

Chapter Thirty-Seven

Jordan scrolled down her computer screen, rejecting scores of private investigation firms specializing in, "Adultery or Infidelity Investigations (Marital), Unfaithful or Cheating Mate (Non-Marital), Cheating Husband Investigation, Cheating Spouse Investigation..." The list was repetitive and endless. It appeared there were enough cheated-on and surreptitious lovers and spouses in Italy to keep dozens of PI firms in business. She wondered which, if any, of the firms Veronica Lario, Prime Minister Berlusconi's long suffering wife of twenty years, might have engaged. Given his 'bunga bunga' parties, which allegedly involved having sex with underage girls, were a matter of public knowledge, the former first lady may have thought better of spending her hard-earned money. No doubt, she'd need every penny if her husband went to prison.

Finally, Jordan settled on an international firm, which claimed to be discreet and professional in all matters from business and finance to civil and private matters. Not only did it boast a large network of investigators throughout Italy, but they could also work seamlessly across the globe. Their website listed an entire page of industry-related accreditation, as well as membership in Italy's Better Business Bureau. Maybe while she was at it, she could find out more about Giancarlo Vincente. For the past twenty-four hours, she'd tried unsuccessfully to banish all thoughts of him from her mind.

A pparently, saying she was an investigative reporter, which wasn't strictly true— yet—afforded her much more personal attention in the procurement of a private investigator than the average citizen. Rather than fill out the confidential online form to make her initial contact with a PI, Jordan picked up the telephone and asked for the CEO himself. Upon providing her professional accreditation, and mentioning Canada, she was expeditiously transferred. One of the many upsides to the ensuing conversation was the firm had an investigator not far from Tropea who specialized in locating birth records. It was the CEO's opinion the same investigator could handle both of Jordan's needs: locating the two men associated with Gavin Stone's business, as well as uncovering the details of her birth.

Reluctant to meet Mr. Michele Abruzzese in Tropea, where she ran the risk of running into Giancarlo, Jordan arranged a rendezvous with the private investigator for the next morning at the Capo Vaticano Resort Thalasso & Spa. With the failed brake experience fresh in her mind, she decided to put her life in the hands of a private driver who would take her the short ten kilometers there and back. Not having to focus on driving gave her the opportunity to enjoy the breathtaking views of the Stromboli Volcano and Aeolian Islands. It was impossible not to be captivated by the vistas from the headland, the wild, unspoiled surroundings, and the crystal-clear sea of Capo Vaticano.

She found Mr. Abruzzese, who insisted she call him Michele (which he pronounced roughly as "mee–KAY–lay") to be personable and extremely professional. After discussing the details of what she required, she willingly paid his retainer and left the hotel with a list of what he would need from her in order to move forward. The clincher for her trusting both his ethics and professionalism was his expression when he spoke of his wife and baby daughter. He beamed enthusiastically as he showed her several photographs on his mobile phone. It was obvious that next to a passion for his work, they were the two loves of his life. For the first time in several days, she felt a sense of relief as Michele assured her he would have something for her within the next week, if not sooner.

Once back at her apartment, Jordan emailed Michele all the information he had requested. Then she got busy figuring out the best place to relocate where she wouldn't run into Giancarlo again. Though she had briefly considered changing her cell phone number, he'd had the decency to stop calling and texting her since their blow-up following Angelina's funeral.

Still, she couldn't get him out of her mind.

Chapter Thirty-Eight

She nearly bowled the short, stout woman over as she emptied her postal box and turned to leave. "Mrs. Candiotti, it's so good to see you. Jordan Leighton, Giancarlo's friend. We met at your daughter's funeral."

"*Si, si*, I remember." The woman's eyes brightened.

"I just came in to collect some mail," Jordan said. She hesitated to mention Angelina's death. "How are you managing?"

"Ah, some days not so well. But I am very blessed for my family."

As they spoke, Mrs. Candiotti seemed suddenly to remember something and rummaged through her purse.

Jordan's eyes darted around the busy foyer, half-hoping she'd see Giancarlo.

"I no see you in town anymore," the older woman said in her heavy accent.

"No, I...I have moved."

"Oh, is too bad. Very nice apartment. I clean for Giancarlo when he live there."

That's how he knew about the stairs! Why had he never said anything?

Recovering, Jordan said, "It's been lovely to see you, but I have a cab waiting, so I'd better go."

Angelina's mother urgently pulled something from her bag. "This is for you," she said, handing Jordan a photocopied newspaper clipping. "I find it in Angelina's diary. She think she hide it from me, but I always know where." She smiled and pointed at the article. "Your name is on it," she said.

Jordan scanned the article quickly. It was dated February 19th, 1986. Although it was difficult to see clearly, above the story was a photo of a twisted and mangled car being pulled up over a cliff by a huge crane. It was all in Italian but she could figure out enough to know it was a wreck involving a local woman, who apparently had been pregnant. Although she didn't recognize the name, it appeared that along with a "Sister Serafina," the accident victim had somehow been involved in helping children with autism. Handwritten at the bottom, presumably by Angelina, was: *For Jordan. Sr. Serafina —still alive.* Written underneath was an address.

"Mrs. Candiotti, have you shown this to the police?" Jordan asked.

"No, no one. I put in my purse to give Giancarlo but he in Rome." She put her hand to her chest and sighed. "He very good to me, looking after everything."

"Would it be all right if I take this?" Jordan asked.

"*Si, si.* My Angelina put it for you."

As Mrs. Candiotti didn't seem concerned about turning it over to the police, Jordan accepted it gratefully. She wished the little woman the best and left the post office. In the cab on the way back to the estate where she was staying, the newspaper clipping felt like it would sear a hole in her pocket.

Why would Angelina have wanted her to have it?

She tapped the driver on the shoulder and passed him the address. "Would you mind if we made a detour before taking me home?"

With trembling hands, Jordan pumped the solid metal doorknocker up and down. The sound of her impromptu arrival echoed throughout the imposing stone residence. Part of her hoped Angelina had given her the wrong address. Or, there was no one at home. Turning to leave, she heard someone coming to the door. When it opened, she found herself looking into a pair of exquisitely soulful, dark chocolate eyes. A woman Jordan guessed to be five years her senior pushed a thick tendril of dark hair from her olive-skinned face. Generous lips smiled warmly.

"Please come in, we've been expecting you," the woman said.

Surprised, Jordan extended her hand. "I'm Jordan Leighton. I'm here to see Sister Serafina."

"Yes, I know. I'm Thula." She thought she saw the woman glance cautiously over Jordan's shoulder as she ushered her inside and closed the door.

"I'd offer to take your jacket, but you might find it chilly upstairs. Sister likes to keep her room cool. Please follow me, I'll take you to her."

Jordan followed her along a cold, poorly lit hallway and up a short, curved stone staircase. Knocking lightly, Thula opened the bulky wooden door and stood aside for Jordan to enter. It took a few seconds for her eyes to adjust, the only illumination coming from the sunlight that danced through sheer lace curtains, projecting a kaleidoscope effect onto the opposite wall. Once she was able to focus, Jordan saw a tiny, wizened face lying, as if disembodied, on a pile of white pillows. The person in bed was barely large enough to disturb the bedclothes that covered her.

"Sister, Jordan has come to see you," Thula whispered.

"Please come closer, my dear," the elderly woman said, motioning her visitor toward the bed. "I'm afraid I am a feeble old woman and am not able to see well these days. *Quanti anni ho, Thula?*" she asked.

"You are ninety-seven, Sister," Thula answered, smiling at Jordan and motioning for her to take a chair by the nun's bedside.

"Sister, I'm so sorry to bother you," Jordan began tentatively, "but I was given a newspaper clipping of a woman who was in a car accident in 1986 and I…"

"I've been hoping you'd come soon," the sister interrupted, smiling ethereally.

"You knew I was coming?" Jordan asked, puzzled. This was the second time someone told her she was expected.

The sister looked at Thula. "Dear one, please bring me the box," she said.

Thula disappeared and minutes later, returned, and gently placed an intricately inlaid wooden box in Sister Serafina's hands. The nun's gnarled and twisted fingers trembled as she opened the lid and reached inside. As Thula held the lid open for her, she lifted a pink envelope from within and handed it to Jordan.

Miss Jordan Stone was written neatly on the front. Vaguely aware of the sister's voice in the background, Jordan's eyes were riveted to the envelope. She turned it over, saw it was sealed, and turned it back again.

"Open it, child," Sister Serafina said quietly. "It is time for you to know the truth."

Bewildered, Jordan gingerly tore open the envelope and began to read.

My dearest Jordan,

Without a doubt, this is the most difficult letter I will ever have to write. Each day, I pray I will be able to explain everything to you in person, but in case that is not possible I have given this to Sister Serafina, and a copy to your father's lawyer, Julius Pinsette. I don't know from which of these beloved people you will receive this, but I trust them both and have faith they will tell you the truth.

Jordan, being pregnant was the happiest time of my life. I savored every moment of feeling a new life growing inside me. I didn't know I was pregnant when I left Carmel to go back to Italy. I had tried to break off the affair with your father but I missed him terribly. As things turned out, Tropea was actually a wonderful place to prepare for such a joyous event.

In my eighth month, I was in a car accident while driving along the Amalfi highway on a particularly treacherous night. I was put on life-support and the doctors delivered the baby almost a month early, for fear both of us would die. As no one expected me to survive, your father had the enormous responsibility of making a decision about our child.

Cynthia was also in Italy at the time of my accident. Doctors were urging Gavin to take me off life-support. Unable to cope with the possibility of his child being raised without a mother, your father made the decision for Cynthia and him to take the baby back to Canada.

Yes, Jordan, you are my daughter. I have loved you every day since you were conceived, and I will continue to love you, no matter what happens. As long as I am alive, I will always wonder where you are and what you're doing. You, and your father, have made my life complete.

Contrary to everyone's expectations, I recovered from the accident but we realized there was no going back because we had let you go with Cynthia. Your father did the best he could in what seemed like a hopeless situation. It was not until after I had made a complete recovery that I fully realized I had, in effect, given you up permanently to the woman you have known as your mother for all these years. I thought I would literally die with you gone from my life, and when you became estranged from your father, I lost all hope. The heartbreak of you cutting the final thread that kept me bound to you nearly killed your father and me.

I pray that you can forgive me, Jordan. I pray that I can forgive myself. The only thing that has kept me going is your father's love and his unending devotion. Through him, I came to know you for the first 16 years of your life. Until then, I had only seen you in photographs. But, at your grandmother's funeral, I was so close I almost reached out and touched your angelic face. Julius has always been so very kind to me, considering the circumstances, but I remember how angry he became when he saw me there that day. Perhaps you remember. I ran from your Granny Leighton's house, as I simply couldn't bear to see you—such a beautiful young woman—and not be able to touch you and tell you who I was.

Jordan, as you read this letter, please don't hate me or your father. Cynthia did a good job of raising you and I can only imagine the shock you must feel at discovering she is not your biological mother. You must forgive her for not telling you the truth about your birth. Whatever may happen after you read this, just know that I love you more than my own life. I have prayed every day that before I die, I will get to hold you and tell you about all the things I have imagined for you, my daughter.

Please trust Sister Serafina or Julius—whoever has given you this letter. They are both good people who have put their own lives at risk to keep our secret.

With love never-ending, I will hold you in my heart forever.

Your mother,
Kathryn

Jordan could barely make out the signature through her tears. Slowly folding the letter, she looked at the old nun lying beside her. Eyes closed, the sister's lips moved silently as she fingered her rosary.

"Why?" Jordan asked quietly, her face hot with tears. Her throat tight, a ragged sob escaped. "Why did she give me away? How could she have done that?"

The nun reached for one of Jordan's hands. "My child, she sacrificed everything to keep you safe." She looked at Thula and asked, *"Come si dice?* How you say…*Eri la sua più grande gioia."*

Thula translated. "You were her greatest joy."

The room began to spin. Jordan felt as if someone had wiped her world clean, like a tsunami leveling everything in its wake. She grasped for some undefined emotion, but all she felt was emptiness.

The sister gazed at Jordan intently. "She loved you very much. You must promise you will find her."

"Why would I want to find her? She gave me away." Then came an afterthought. "She and my father aren't here in Tropea?"

"Oh, no, my dear, they have not lived here for some time. To stay here…would be great danger."

"I don't understand. Why would they be in danger? And what does that have to do with my birth twenty-seven years ago?"

"Your mother's…Kathryn's parents…were brutally murdered in Vancouver when she was just *una bambina*, a little girl," the sister explained.

"That's very sad, Sister, but…"

"The man responsible—he was evil. He had a summer home here in Tropea."

"But…"

"Please, my child, let me finish. I don't know when it might be my time. I must tell you before God takes me." She gave Jordan a weary but patient smile. "Vittorio Constantine —a vengeful man."

Constantine. His name kept coming up.

"He grew up with Kathryn's father, Enrico." She took a deep shuddering breath. "As boys, they spent all their summers together here. Like brothers, they shared everything. Until beautiful Francesca came along. Both fell hopelessly in love with her."

Thula offered the old woman some water to moisten her parched and cracked lips. She sucked weakly from the straw and then gently pushed it away. "They fight over Francesca's attention. Brings out worst in Vittorio. He forced Enrico to get involved in his family's criminal business."

"You mean the Mafia?" asked Jordan, incredulously.

Puzzled, Sister Serafina looked at Thula.

"It wasn't spoken about in those terms back then," Thula explained. Sister nodded in agreement.

"Things got bad that summer. Some say Vittorio forced

Enrico to kill someone. His parents sold their summer home in Tropea to get him away. *Cattiva influenza.* Bad influence."

Jordan wondered what this all had to do with Kathryn and her father.

Sister Serafina continued. "One day, no engagement, Enrico and Francesca came back from the city, married. Nine months later, Katarina was born. Your *madre.* After, the fight between the two men is terrible but Enrico kept working for Vittorio. One day, Katarina was about five, she and her parents just disappear. *Nonni*—grandparents, they stay. But they wouldn't tell where they went." She shifted uncomfortably, appearing to wince in pain.

"Sister, perhaps you should rest now. I'm sure Miss Leighton could come back another time," Thula urged.

Dismissing her concern, the sister continued. "Later, we find out they go to Canada. Changed their name from Belisarius to Bell. I think it was Enrico's way to start a new life away from *Vittorio e la sua famiglia.*" She closed her eyes and fingered the beads of her rosary again. Jordan waited for what seemed like minutes, wondering if perhaps the elderly nun had dozed off.

"They live in Vancouver for only one year before Enrico and Francesca were shot. Dear sweet Katarina saw it happen," the nun added, with a sigh. "People say her parents were killed because Enrico got away and some were afraid he would talk."

The nun's tale was fascinating but Jordan's patience was wearing thin. "Sister, I'm so sorry all these terrible things happened, but I simply don't understand what this has to do with me and why my father and…his wife…are in danger." *Or even why she should care.*

Jordan thought she saw a furtive glance between the sister and Thula. "Forgive me, my child. I must close my eyes.

Thula will tell you the rest. But before you go, may I say something to you?"

Getting up from her chair, Jordan bent closer in order to hear the nun's fading voice. "Yes, Sister, of course."

"Do not allow hatred or bitterness to run through your veins, my child. It will poison you and everyone you love, now and in the future. Kathryn loved you so much. She sacrificed her happiness to keep you safe. She trusted the woman you know as your mother, to raise you and give you all the love she wanted to give you herself."

Her translucent blue eyes searched Jordan's face. "*Cara*, you are as beautiful as your mother. You must find her." She reached out and tenderly ran a trembling, wizened hand down Jordan's cheek.

A fter tucking the sister in and giving her some medication, Thula ushered Jordan to a comfortable but equally cold sitting room. Grateful for the warm tea that helped steady her nerves, Jordan shivered in spite of the dwindling fire in the hearth. She listened in horror as Thula related how, as a child, she had hidden in a closet while Constantine did unspeakable things to her mother, forcing her father to watch. Then she saw him torture her father to death.

"Thula," Jordan asked, "how can you be so forgiving after seeing Vittorio Constantine murder your family in cold blood?"

The older woman smiled sweetly, as if placating an upset child. "You heard Sister, Jordan. There is no use poisoning myself and others with such anger and bitterness."

"But, I can't even imagine how you lived to tell about it. You were just a little girl—how could you not be scarred for life?"

"Well, I did live but I didn't tell about it."

"What do you mean? You said the police came and found you hours later cowering in the closet. You must have told them what happened."

"No, I couldn't. I didn't speak for two years after it happened." She paused to let her words sink in. "That's how I met your mother...I'm sorry...Kathryn. She brought me here to this house where I was able to work with psychologists and art therapists. That's what enabled me to speak again." She locked eyes with Jordan. "I owe her my life."

Jordan obstinately refused to acknowledge Thula's last remark.

"I made very slow progress at first. I remember wanting so badly to speak. I could form all the sounds in my head, but I just couldn't let go and say the words out loud. Kathryn taught me how to express myself through painting. Now, I have exhibits of my work. I am very blessed."

"But you still didn't speak. What happened?"

"When Kathryn came back, when she was pregnant with you, your father paid a full-time professional to come with her from Carmel to work with me. After working with Julia, I got so I could talk to myself when I was alone in my room at night. It was so strange to hear my own voice." She grinned shyly.

Jordan envied Thula's apparent sense of peace. How could anyone experience such horrific violence and not seethe with hatred and a desire for revenge?

As if reading her mind, Thula said, "I still hadn't spoken out loud to anyone. But one day I was at Kathryn's house when she had a visitor. I was out in her studio, painting, but I could hear her talking to a man inside the house. There was something about his voice that was so familiar." Thula stared past Jordan, as if in a trance.

Jordan held her breath, hoping she was wrong about what Thula was going to say next.

"I came into the kitchen just in time to see him reach out to give Kathryn a hug. He was facing me. I still don't remember doing it, but I must have grabbed a butcher knife off the counter and charged at him with it, screaming all my words over and over."

"Oh my god, Thula! It was *him?*" Jordan gasped.

"Yes," she nodded. "I recognized him. Of course, he had no idea who I was."

"What did he do?"

"Kathryn screamed at me to drop the knife and I did. She told him I was emotionally disturbed, and she apologized to him and begged him not to call the police. I was so hurt at the time—I felt betrayed by her. But she saved my life. He never knew I saw what he did to my parents. The police never released the information there had been a witness, much less a child, hiding in a closet."

"Why didn't you and Kathryn tell the police afterward?"

Thula fixed her eyes on Jordan. The silence was palpable. This time, it was Jordan who couldn't speak.

"You mean…" She couldn't say it. Thula remained silent. "You and Kathryn didn't tell because you knew it would put all of you in danger, including me." The magnitude of what she'd said felt like a hole had been bored right through her chest.

"You weren't born yet but yes, Constantine was so well connected that to report it would have been akin to signing our death warrants. He was a long-time friend of Kathryn's parents. He was like a godfather to her. He even invested in your father's business project in La Thuile."

All the references to his name on the permits made sense!

"Why would my father have had anything to do with

235

someone like that? How could Kathryn have let him get involved with someone like Constantine, after what he did to your family?"

Thula looked hurt.

"I'm sorry, Thula, but how could she?" Jordan asked, this time less harshly.

"At the time, Kathryn and Gavin didn't know the truth about Constantine. He was a trusted family friend when Kathryn introduced him to your father. It wasn't until she was pregnant with you that either of them knew who he really was and what he had done," she reminded Jordan. "By then it was too late. Constantine secured all the anti-Mafia permits your father required to get his development off the ground. In return, he owned ten percent of La Thuile. After that, everything Gavin touched turned to gold, so Constantine and his family invested more and more in your father's other projects. When the 2008 financial crisis hit and Gavin's project in Arizona went under, Constantine finally showed his true colors. By then, Kathryn knew he was the one who murdered my parents and she started an investigation into her mother and father's deaths. She was devastated, and of course she feared for her and your father's life."

"Thula, do you know how I might find Constantine?"

The woman's eyes widened. "Please, Jordan, you must promise me you won't try to find him. I beg you, use your energy to find Kathryn and your father. That is a far better use of your time. And much less dangerous."

"Do you know how I might find him?" Jordan repeated. She fixed her gaze on Thula.

"No I don't," she said, for the first time sounding curt. "There have been rumors for years that after he was shot, he went into hiding." She stood and started clearing the teacups.

"He was shot? When?"

Thula stopped what she was doing and sighed. "He was shot in an attempted execution. Even the Mafia tried to wash their hands of him. Some say he's dead—others don't know."

"What do *you* think?"

The other woman broke eye contact. "It's time for me to take Sister her tea." She picked up the tray and started down the hall. "Please follow me and I shall see you out."

"Thula, please—I have to find him. My father's life may depend on it, don't you understand?"

"I understand more than you know," she said, without turning around. As she opened the door, Thula warned, "Don't do anything you will regret, Jordan. I beg you."

Chapter Thirty-Nine

Jordan had slept very little after returning home from her meeting with Sister Serafina and Thula. Still reeling from the shock about her birth mother and with no one to confide in, she decided against canceling Michele's visit later in the morning. She prepared a tray with cold lemonade on the terraza of her new home base in San Domenica di Ricadi.

Just three kilometers from Tropea, the secluded residence Michele had discreetly leased for her was actually a small guesthouse located on an estate that guaranteed privacy and tranquility. Generations past had tended the land and a few acres were still devoted to a small organic farm. While maintaining her privacy, she could sit on the terrace and watch a few of the farm hands working in the valley between her house and the sea. Preferring to fend for herself, Jordan decided against having live-in domestic help. Instead, Michele hired a local woman to bring in groceries twice a week. She enjoyed preparing simple meals for herself, made from fish caught locally and much of the produce from the estate. Most days, she ate lunch outside but invariably the cooler temperatures of the evening forced her to enjoy dinner in the house, basking in the warmth of the cozy fireplace.

Though exhausted and feeling emotionally fragile, she was eager to hear what Michele had to report. And to tell him what she'd discovered. He had refused to discuss it on the phone, insisting he come to meet with her personally. Hearing the sound of a car coming up the driveway, she trudged around to the front of the house to greet him.

Forcing herself to appear normal, Jordan inquired about Michele's family, whereby he unabashedly showed her the latest pictures of his baby daughter as they sat across from each other, sipping their drinks.

"You said you have made some significant progress. Have you been able to locate Grimaldi and Constantine?" Jordan asked.

When he first sat down, the PI had taken a file from his briefcase. However, it remained closed on the table. As if reluctant to get into its contents, Michele folded his hands on top of the manila folder and looked at her earnestly. "Jordan," he began in a measured tone, "I had my suspicions about both these...er, gentlemen, but I didn't want to say anything until I was sure. But first, I know you have been anxious to find something about your birth. Perhaps we should start there." He loosened his tie but left the file untouched.

For some reason, she didn't jump in with what she had just discovered—that she no longer had a need to find her birth certificate.

"You were quite correct that your late friend, Miss Candiotti, was unable to find anything under either the name Stone or Leighton. So, using your birth date, I searched for any baby girls born in Tropea on that day."

"And?" She could feel her breathing becoming quick and shallow.

"There were no girls born that I could possibly link to either of your parents. They were all born to Italian families, most of whom were local. I was able to track down all the young women who had the same birth date and I spoke to or accounted for every one of them." He looked at her sympathetically. "I'm sorry, I know that isn't what you wanted to hear." It was the look Angelina had given her when she had told her the same thing.

Was it a morbid sense of curiosity that was stopping her from telling Michele the truth? "So you have nothing. You said you had some crucial information for me."

He nodded. "I do. Unfortunately, nothing that relates to your birth."

"Then what?"

"Jordan, the two men you are looking for—I don't think you want to pursue these individuals any further."

Giancarlo's words echoed in her head.

"If one more person tells me that, I'm going to slap them."

Michele cocked his head. "Someone else has told you this before?"

"What is it with you people? Is there some deep, dark secret here we foreigners aren't supposed to know?" Unlike with Giancarlo, she had told Michele the truth about her father, and why she was in Tropea. "These two men were instrumental in my father's first European development, which seems to be where his business started to go sideways. Now he's accused of murder and embezzlement back in Canada. Why is it such a big deal to find out anything about them?" She wanted to pull her hair out.

Michele looked down and slowly opened the manila folder on the table between them, swiveling it to face her. The air left her lungs and her stomach lurched.

On top of a half-inch pile of photographs was a full-color, glossy picture of a naked man who had been decapitated. His head, with an ice pick stuck in his ear, sat on the bloody pavement beside him. Michele lifted the photograph from the pile, exposing the next one. It showed a young man with a dark mop of hair, dangling precariously upside down from the front seat of an open car door. A pool of blood lay on the pavement beneath him. Michele thumbed to the next one.

"Stop it! Why are you showing me these? They are disgusting. I don't want to see any more, Michele. What do they have to do with my father?" Even after what Thula had told her, she couldn't conceive of Gavin being involved with such thugs.

Michele left the folder open and looked her squarely in the eyes. "This is what the two men who were your father's partners regularly did to people," he said quietly. "People who got in their way," he emphasized. "Jordan, I cannot expose my family to this." He tapped the photos in front of her. "I *will* not expose them to this."

"Constantine and Grimaldi did these things? My father would never have been involved with criminals like this. Michele, what are you saying?"

"They may or may not have carried out these hits themselves, but I can assure you they were behind them."

She pushed the photographs back in his direction. "Where did you get these?"

"They are part of a criminal case going back to 1987, before the Italian government got serious about trying to stamp out the Mafia, beginning in 1992. The one with the severed head was a former Mafia hit man before turning state's evidence. He had just said goodbye to his wife and children before going into protective custody. As you can see, he didn't live to testify, so the trial didn't go ahead."

She was having difficulty concentrating on Michele's voice.

"The second gentleman," he continued, "was found with eight bullets in the back of his head, his infant son screaming in the backseat. Apparently, he botched the hit of a rival boss during a contract killing."

She swallowed hard. "But you're talking about the underworld. How on earth would my father ever have gotten involved in that?" She had asked Thula the very same question.

"Jordan, these people only care about one thing and that's money. From what I can see, Constantine offered to secure the anti-mafia certificates for your father's project. That was his foot in the door. Once he realized he had hooked up with a successful—and legitimate—developer, he saw a perfect opportunity to invest in the La Thuile condos and your father's other projects. They provided a perfect way to disguise money transfers and launder cash. Grimaldi, supposedly Constantine's solicitor, was one of his henchmen. Your father would have had no idea he was being used."

So Thula was right.

"This is unbelievable. I was to meet with Grimaldi just over a week ago, but I nearly killed myself in that rental car. I haven't been able to reach him to explain why I didn't show up."

Michele froze, his drink halfway to his mouth.

"You were to meet with Grimaldi? How did that come about?"

"When Angelina and I were searching through the public records office, we noticed his name came up, along with Constantine's, in reference to permit applications. I asked her at the time about contacting him, but she said she couldn't help me. Then out of the blue I received a call from Grimaldi, offering to meet me. I just assumed Angelina had found him and given him my phone number." She put her hand to her mouth and gasped. "I never had a chance to ask Angelina about it. She died two days later."

"Be thankful you didn't make the meeting. I'd be shocked if he actually set it up himself, but your near accident may well have been what saved you. The last person he is said to have met with was found hanging in his apartment after the neighbors complained of the putrid smell."

They both sat in silence, staring at one another. Eventually, Jordan spoke. "You said you won't help me anymore. Michele, I understand your concern for your family—I do— but can you understand how I feel about mine? There seems to be no proof I was even born, my father has disappeared and..."

Numb, it suddenly hit her. She could barely form her question. "You don't think they've done something like this," she pointed to the file folder, "to him?" *This can't be happening.* She thought back to the night she found the dead body and had wondered initially if it was her father.

"I'd be lying if I said no. But honestly, I just don't know. Don't make the mistake of underestimating their reach, Jordan," Michele warned. "Outside of Italy, I am much more familiar with Mafia issues in the United States, but I do know your country has had a significant mob presence in the province of Quebec. Where you live, in British Columbia, I remember my parents talking about someone they went to school with in Tropea, who fled with his wife and child to Canada. They were gunned down while coming out of a restaurant. Even as a young boy, I remember the gossip that it was a Mafia family in Calabria, who ordered that hit. Today, things are quieter but the bosses still have power and are expert at wielding it wherever they need to."

Jordan pursed her lips and nodded. That certainly was consistent with what Sister Serafina and Thula had told her. If Michele wouldn't help her, and she could hardly blame him, who would she turn to? Based on the blasé attitude of the local police, even with Giancarlo's intervention, she knew she'd get little help from them.

"You mentioned someone else told you the same thing I did—not to pursue Constantine and Grimaldi. Do you mind telling me who that was?" Michele asked.

"For starters, an old nun and her caregiver. And..."

He raised his eyebrows expectantly.

She sighed, resigned to telling him the rest. "Someone by the name of Giancarlo."

"Giancarlo Vicente?"

She felt her pulse quicken. "Yes, do you know him?"

Chapter Forty

Two hours later, after switching from lemonade to espressos, Jordan tried to absorb what Michele was telling her.

"Giancarlo was new to the Public Prosecutors' Office. Unlike in your country, once a case has been assigned, the prosecutor is autonomous from the government. His predecessor," Michele rolled his eyes and gave a dismissive wave of his hand, "was totally corrupt, and finally got fired for accepting bribes. That alone, was quite a feat. Being fired, I mean. Not accepting bribes."

"But why would they have assigned such a high-profile case to someone so junior, as Giancarlo was at the time?" Jordan asked.

"Again, we do things quite differently in Italy. Prosecution cases are not assigned based on experience with a particular aspect of crime. It's all to do with territory. Constantine was living and operating his vast network here in Tropea, and that's where Giancarlo grew up and got his first job as a lawyer."

"Did you know him well?" she asked, trying to sound casual.

"At the beginning, only by reputation. He hired me to do some investigative work when he first tried to resurrect the old case against Constantine. Then, you know, we went for a beer on occasions. He never liked me to come into his office with my reports. He said it was too distracting, but I think it was because he didn't know whom he could trust. With good reason, I suspect."

Jordan thought back to her last conversation with Giancarlo. "What do you mean?"

"Well, right out of the gate, he clashed with one of the other prosecutors working on the same case, but in Rome."

"I thought you said each case was assigned solely by territory."

"It is, but when a crime is carried out in more than one location—and the tentacles of Constantine's empire were far reaching—you can end up with multiple prosecutors all acting independent of each other. And often at odds with one another. It drove Giancarlo nuts."

"I can see why. I can't imagine doing things that way in the Canadian court system." Jordan thought of the 2009 case against the young American woman who Italian authorities had hung out to dry for the alleged murder of her housemate. Based on that fiasco, nothing Michele said surprised her. "But that isn't why he quit the case and left the prosecutor's office, is it?" she asked.

"No." He appeared to be considering his answer.

"Michele, please just tell me the truth. You already showed me the photo of the witnesses you say Constantine ordered killed. Was that why Giancarlo left?" That would be enough to scare most people, she thought.

He sat back in his chair, put his fingers together in a tent, and touched them to his lips. When he looked up, the severity of his expression caught her off guard.

"No, those incidents happened long before Giancarlo's time. However, shortly after taking over the new case, he met a woman. She had a small child, and although they didn't live together all the time, she would often stay overnight."

Jordan had a sick feeling in the pit of her stomach.

"One such night, they were awakened by someone standing at the foot of their bed. A man warned if Giancarlo didn't drop the case against Constantine, he would rape and torture his girlfriend in front of him and her son."

"God, how awful."

Michele nodded. "The worst of it was her son was sleeping in the room next door. Until this man left—and he took his sweet time—she didn't know if he'd already killed her little boy. Thankfully, the child was untouched, but that was it for Giancarlo. He tendered his resignation the next day, and that's the last I heard about him until I saw he had opened his own law firm in Rome."

"What happened to his girlfriend and her son?"

"I'm not sure. I heard she never felt safe with him, even though by then he was only dealing with business clients in Rome. I think they just both moved on."

Jordan felt a twinge of guilt that she was relieved the woman and Giancarlo were no longer an item.

The time flew by, as Jordan and Michele continued to talk. However, after three calls from his wife within an hour, Michele made his somewhat sheepish apologies and left for home. The sun slipped slowly into the sea as Jordan cleared their dishes and brought them inside. It had been a beautiful afternoon, one in which she'd only worn a light sweater, but feeling the damp chill inside the house, she considered making a fire. There wasn't enough wood left in the alcove built into the stone hearth, but she could at least get it going while she figured out what to have for dinner.

Although the house was rustic in its charm, Jordan was grateful for the kitchen's modern updates. It seemed she was always defrosting something quickly, never thinking ahead of what she'd want to eat later in the day. The fire crackled as she popped a packet of fish in the microwave and grabbed her jacket off the hook by the kitchen door. Around the side of house, she was methodically loading split pieces of wood into the canvas tote, when she heard something from behind.

"Did you forget something, Michele?" she said without turning around. "Your wife is going to kill you..."

She felt a dull thud to the back of her neck and everything went black.

J ordan awoke with a crashing headache and the taste of a filthy rag tied tightly across her mouth. Lying on her back, her hands secured uncomfortably beneath her, her knuckles rubbed on the rough stone floor. Her shoulder throbbed as she tried to roll onto her side.

"Well, Sleeping Beauty is awake," a man said, in thickly accented English. "Go get Constantine," he ordered someone in the room.

Constantine? Where was she? She heard a door open and close. A hard-toed boot kicked her legs.

"Get up," he instructed, pulling her roughly to her feet. "You want to look good to meet your host." He grinned menacingly as he pushed her into a chair. This time she could see the door as it opened.

He looked to be about five foot eight or nine. His once

blond hair was now white and sparse, his face etched with lines, but there was no doubt it was Constantine. Having seen a picture of the younger version of the mobster in Michele's file, she recognized the eyes as unmistakably his. She remembered studying the photograph and thinking how completely devoid of any human emotion, they were. Heart hammering, she looked into the cold, calculating eyes mere inches from her face.

"It is so good of you to come. I understand you have been looking for me." He smiled at her and turned to the other man. "Take off the gag and leave us alone," he ordered.

"Mr. Constantine, perhaps I should..."

"Leave us!"

The man leaned over her, untied the knot behind her head and left.

Hands behind his back, Constantine circled the floor twice and stopped in front of her. "I have waited a long time to meet you, Jordan."

She kept her gaze fixed on the stone floor. He had surprisingly small feet.

"I knew your mother well. You have inherited her beauty." He leaned forward and gently put his forefinger under her chin, pulling her face upward. "I have no wish to hurt you, if that's what you're thinking. I only want to finish this nasty business between your father and me."

She licked her parched lips but remained silent.

"Would you like some water? I'm afraid I can't untie your hands, but with your cooperation, we can get this cleared up very quickly." He held a glass and let her take several gulps from it.

"There. Now that you're refreshed, you're going to make a phone call to our mutual friend, Giancarlo, and then you will be able to go home."

She tried to speak but nothing came out. She cleared her throat. "I have no idea how to reach Giancarlo," she said.

"Tsk-tsk, Jordan. We both know that's not true. I see several calls from him here on your phone." He brandished her cell in front of her face.

She berated herself for not erasing Giancarlo's previous calls. She shivered, thinking about the images Michele had shown her.

Chapter Forty-One

"I was hoping *you'd* know where she is," Michele said breathlessly into the phone as he continued his search around the ramshackle sheds on the estate. The woman he'd hired to take groceries to Jordan every few days had called him an hour ago, concerned that the kitchen door was wide open. She reported a strong smell of fish in the house.

"It's good to hear from you my friend," said Giancarlo, "but no, we haven't spoken since she left Tropea. I've been worried about her, but I didn't know if she was even still in the country."

Michele stopped to catch his breath. The time had come to reacquaint himself with the gym if he were to keep inhaling his wife's nightly homemade desserts. "I'm worried too. It's not like her to leave overnight without telling me." He had briefly filled Giancarlo in on his business relationship with Jordan.

"After our last conversation, I'm definitely not someone she would confide in," Giancarlo said.

Michele thought he heard a twinge of regret in his friend's

voice. He chuckled. "You can thank me later, but I think she might have a higher opinion of you now."

"Oh yeah, why's that?"

"Well, I hope you don't mind, but I told her about your brief stint as a public prosecutor." There was silence on the other end of the phone. "Giancarlo, are you there?"

"Yes, I'm still here. Why did you do that?"

"Hey, don't sound so pissed off. It's a matter of public record. It was the only thing I could do to make her give up on finding Constantine."

"You had that problem with her too. She's tenacious, I'll give her that," Giancarlo replied after a long silence.

"Listen, I have to go, but can you put some feelers out for me? Let me know if you hear anything?" Michele asked.

"Of course. Leave it with me. I'll see what I can dig up."

I n the outdoor café in the center of town, Giancarlo drained his espresso and scrolled through his mobile for one of his old contacts. Only a few minutes later, his phone rang again. Thinking it was Michele, he flipped it open without looking at the caller ID.

"Giancarlo? It's me, Jordan." She sounded strained and shrill.

"Jordan! Where are you?"

"I'm...I think I'm at a place outside town. I'm not sure..."

"Do you need me to come and get you?" He heard the scuffle of the phone changing hands.

"Why yes, Giancarlo, that would be exactly what she would like." The raspy voice was unmistakable. A familiar chill crept over him.

"What have you done with her, Constantine? I swear to God I will kill you myself if you lay a hand on her."

"My, my, you are in no position to threaten, Giancarlo. Now listen to me carefully, this is exactly what I want you to do..."

Shaking with rage, adrenaline pulsed through his body. Giancarlo threw some bills on the table and wove his way through the throng of patrons in the outdoor café. Just before exiting, he spotted a woman, her head turned in conversation with someone behind her. Casually, he pocketed the pink and rhinestone cell phone as he walked past her table. He ducked into the café's single-stall lavatory and made two calls in quick succession. After drying his hands, he threw the phone into the wastebasket and then placed a thick wad of paper towels on top. As he sprinted to his car, his mind searched for alternatives.

There weren't any.

He covered the distance in twenty minutes. The road was overgrown since he had last been there as a boy, but once he spotted a few old landmarks he felt calmer. His biggest fear was he might drive by the entrance to the old abandoned farm and vineyard. Glancing in his rear-view mirror, he left the Tyrrhenian Sea behind and turned right at a majestic grove of oak, chestnut, and acacia trees. Old and gnarled, they had stood as sentinels at the entrance to the rustic farm for centuries.

As he made his way up the meandering single-car drive-way, his hands drummed on the wheel. After Constantine had gotten Jordan to make the call, Giancarlo prayed the old man would keep her alive. He couldn't imagine what use Constantine would have for her once he'd used her to lure him to the property. A property that still gave him nightmares.

A late-model Mercedes sedan sat at the top of the

secluded drive. Off to the right was a ramshackle out-building. Giancarlo pulled in front and turned off the engine. The day had turned cold and a few drops of rain splattered the windshield. His phone rang. His body thrummed with tension as he pushed the talk button.

"What took you so long, Giancarlo? Don't tell me you forgot how to get here?" Constantine chided.

"Where are you, you son of a bitch?" Giancarlo yelled into the phone, twisting his head in both directions. "If you touch her I swear I will..."

"Cut the crap, Giancarlo. Get out of the car and walk twenty meters to your left. You will see a clearing, then a barn. Come inside. You are being watched every step of the way so don't even think about being a hero."

Giancarlo's shoes crunched on gravel as he approached the entrance to the barn. Cautiously, he stepped inside. He blinked rapidly, trying to adjust his eyes to the darkness, but all he could see was a black void. The flicker of what appeared to be a kerosene lamp suddenly appeared in the distance.

"Well, at last we meet again, Giancarlo. It's a pity it has to be under such circumstances. Please, come in. I'm sure Miss Leighton will be very pleased to see you."

Giancarlo stepped closer; the light illuminated Constantine's menacing face. Though the man appeared shorter than he remembered, the silhouette of his bullish frame was unmistakable. Constantine laid the lantern on something roughly shoulder height. As if in a spotlight, Jordan suddenly appeared, sitting rigidly upright on a wooden chair. Her hands were tied behind her and Giancarlo could see bindings around her ankles.

"So, this is what's going to happen," Constantine's voice echoed through the barn. "You're going to telephone Mr.

Stone for me." Standing behind her chair, he looked down at the top of her head. "If you behave well, Jordan, I will let you speak to your father one last time." Swiftly, a knife came into view. She flinched as Constantine held it across her neck. "That is if Giancarlo here does as he's told, quickly."

"I have no bloody idea where Gavin Stone is," Giancarlo shouted into the semi-darkness. "How the hell would I know? I've never even met the man."

"Ah, but you do know where he is," Constantine admonished. "I have been assured you helped the authorities locate him. And Kathryn. Ah yes, beautiful Kathryn."

For the first time, Jordan spoke. "Giancarlo, you've known all along where my father is? How..."

Constantine cut her off. "He knows a lot of things, don't you, Giancarlo? Tell her. Go ahead, I am a patient man." He lifted the knife and circled the air with a flourish.

"Jordan, I'm so sorry," Giancarlo said. "After you left Tropea I put some feelers out to an old contact in the prosecutor's office."

"Yes, he suddenly found some balls after slinking off like a pussy so many years ago," Constantine interjected.

Giancarlo continued. "They have been building a case against this scumbag for years." His heard jerked toward Constantine. "And they managed to locate your father. But I have no idea where he is. For Christ's sake, I don't even know if he's here in Italy." He held out his hands, imploring both of them to believe him.

"Enough," Constantine bellowed, erratically brandishing the knife. "All you have to do," he said slowly, as if speaking to a child, "is to make the call and you and your little girlfriend here can go free."

"Giancarlo, please, just tell him what you know."

"Don't trust him, Jordan," Giancarlo shouted. "He will kill both of us just as he killed my mother."

He heard a muted pop in the distance and hoped to god, it was the handiwork of one of the sharpshooters. By his calculation, they should have moved stealthily through the trees from the adjacent property and now be in place to strike. Constantine appeared to have heard it too. For a split second, the little man's steely gaze wavered.

Startled, Jordan heard a sound like that of an old-fashioned flash camera, and the barn was suddenly flooded with light. A cop in a bulletproof vest moved in to shield Giancarlo, followed by a line of uniformed officers who single-mindedly had their weapons trained on her and the old man.

"Your mother was a whore, Giancarlo. A wetback drug mule," Constantine railed. "But you—you could have had everything. You wanted for nothing but you turned on me. You could have inherited my empire." Jordan could feel his hot breath and spit on her ear. She tried not to move for fear the knife would cut into her throat.

"Put it down, Constantine," a second cop yelled. "You touch her and you're as good as dead."

"I'm going to die anyway." With surprising strength, he tilted Jordan onto the back legs of the chair, pulling her further away from the solid line of sharpshooters. "I always knew how to find you but I let you live, Giancarlo."

She felt more spittle on the side of her neck and the coarse stubble on his face brushed against her cheek. He reeked of stale tobacco and coffee.

"You have five seconds to put the knife down," instructed the lead cop, leveling his gun.

"Or what?" Constantine bent over the chair. His left arm was crooked around her neck, holding the knife. "I will slit her throat from ear to fucking ear, before you get off a shot," he shouted.

Jordan sat terrified, every muscle taut.

Then she saw it.

In her peripheral vision, she watched as the metal snout of a gun inched slowly from behind a stack of old gas cans to her right. *Oh God, he was going to take the shot.* She felt beads of perspiration trickle down her back, as she anticipated the knife slicing across her throat. She screamed when the bullet whizzed across her head, missing her. Constantine toppled sideways, knocking over the stepladder and with it, the kerosene lantern. With a loud whoosh, the tinder dry bales of hay around her exploded into balls of fire. She tried to wriggle free, but her chair threatened to tip over when she kicked against the ropes that bound her ankles. She struggled to breathe. Horrified, she watched the flames dance hypnotically across the floor toward her.

"Get out, now!" someone yelled. "The whole place is going up. We'll be incinerated within seconds."

"I'm not leaving her!" She recognized Giancarlo's voice.

The noise from the fire was deafening. She felt the heat searing her skin and fought not to hyperventilate and draw more smoke into her lungs. Through the haze, Giancarlo and a policeman ran through an opening in the flames. One grabbed her chair, the other reached for something off to the side. Someone threw a wet hood over her head as they dragged her through the acrid smoke. Greedily, she stole huge gulps of fresh air as she felt raindrops on her skin.

"Here, take her," she heard Giancarlo shout to someone. "I'm going back in."

"No!" She fought against her restraints. "Giancarlo, no!" She choked as the scream died in her throat.

Someone sliced the ropes that bound her to the chair and

removed the hood. They pulled her farther away from the barn now fully engulfed in flames. Two officers ran back into the structure after Giancarlo. With a deafening roar, the building caved in on itself, sending a giant fireball into the sky. *Giancarlo, why? Why did you go back in?*

As they all watched in horror, Giancarlo and the other two emerged from behind the fiery structure. They had Constantine with them. As they rushed past her to a waiting ambulance, she smelled the unmistakable stench of burnt human flesh.

Chapter Forty-Two

"Constantine is your *father*?" Jordan yanked the oxygen mask from her face as she struggled to get comfortable on the narrow cot in the emergency room. Grateful to have escaped with just some minor scrapes and burns, she couldn't get the acrid smell of human flesh out of her nostrils. As she watched a nurse tend to Giancarlo's wounds, she was torn between relief he was alive and anger that he'd gone back into the flames to rescue that useless piece of shit.

"You said you hated Constantine and now you're telling me you're his *son*?" She heard the near hysterical edge to her own voice. The ruckus caused a second nurse to appear and attempt to put Jordan's mask back on.

"Leave me alone!" she screamed at the nurse, who looked desperately to Giancarlo for direction. He said something quietly to her in Italian, and she slipped back through the curtains.

"I am not his son. I may be the product of his vicious assault on my mother, but he is not my father. I tried to warn you. Why didn't you listen?"

"*Me?* If you'd just told me the truth I might have," she

retorted. They stopped and stared at each other. A second nurse discreetly gathered her triage supplies and made a hasty retreat.

"Jordan, we are in this together," he said in a conciliatory tone. "I'm just glad you're safe."

In return for agreeing he and Jordan would stay in hospital overnight, Giancarlo coerced the hospital staff into allowing them to take over the patients' lounge at the end of the hall. With the privacy that afforded them, they talked late into the night.

Constantine, though badly burned, was still alive and under armed guard in the hospital's limited burn facility. At his advanced age, it remained to be seen if his body could withstand the multiple skin grafts that would be required to make him whole again. In any event, at daybreak he would be flown to the specialized burn center in Rome, where he would remain indeterminately under medical care and heavy security. Likely in excruciating pain, he would hopefully suffer for his sins, before his descent into purgatory.

Jordan shuddered as she recalled his raw and bubbled face when they'd whisked him past her at the farm. She still couldn't fathom why Giancarlo had gone back for him. It was nothing short of a miracle he had escaped the barn alive. As a boy who had spent his childhood playing on the property every summer, he knew there was a trap door in the cement floor, obscured by stacks of hay. The tunnel beneath, provided Constantine's cowardly right-hand man a perfect escape route after the rest of his boss's thugs had been shot by police. Giancarlo, and the two officers with Constantine in tow, had emerged safely after the barn lifted from its foundation in a final explosion. As distraught as she was, Jordan couldn't imagine anything more gratifying than seeing Giancarlo lead them out from behind the inferno.

Someone brought them each another cup of stale coffee. She waited while Giancarlo took a sip. "What happened to your mother?"

He rubbed his head and looked at her with limpid brown eyes. She had thought she'd never see those eyes again.

"Constantine met my mother when she was seventeen. She was working as a maid at a hotel in Mexico. He went there frequently when he was setting up his drug smuggling business in the early days. He promised her the world, and to get out of Mexico she went with him." He shook his head. "She thought she would be safe in Italy. Even her family gave their blessing."

"What happened?"

"Not long after she arrived in Tropea, he raped her and of course, she got pregnant. Ordinarily, he would have just tossed her out like garbage. But when she discovered she was expecting a boy, he kept her close." He tore a chunk from the rim of his Styrofoam cup.

"That boy was you," Jordan said softly.

"Yes. I'm sure everyone in town knew Constantine was the father, but he continued to keep my mother and me with him. Although he treated her terribly, she had no one to turn to so she stayed. When I was five, he got her pregnant again —this time it was a girl. He beat her so badly, she lost the baby." He ripped another chunk from the cup. "One night when Constantine was in Rome, she and her brother came and got me from my bed, and together we made it into Switzerland. But he found us. He had my uncle killed and brought my mother and me back to Tropea."

"How did he find you?" She saw the look on his face and

remembered the photographs Michele had shown her. "I'm sorry." She shook her head. "How stupid of me."

"Not stupid at all." He put down his cup and took her hand. "You remind me of her. My mother, I mean. She was very beautiful but she was...how do you say? Feisty?"

Jordan smiled, in spite of herself.

"Anyway, he beat her half to death, and then one day she just disappeared."

"You never saw her again? Did you know what happened to her?"

"He told me she had gone back to Mexico, but I knew she hadn't. She would never have abandoned me." A deep scowl darkened his face. "When we were in Switzerland she made me promise if anything ever happened to her that I wouldn't believe anything he told me. But she said to stay with him, that I would have a good life if I didn't cross him." He shrugged. "Or words to that effect. I was just five," he reminded Jordan.

"She was right. I hated him, but I took whatever he gave me. I wanted to become a lawyer so he sent me to law school. The best law school in the country. He was grooming me to take over the 'family business,' as he referred to it."

"But you went into the prosecutor's office," Jordan said, confused.

"Not at first I didn't. I started out in his organization. By running it like a respectable business, I helped him flourish. I saw things I should never have seen." He shuddered, as if reliving a nightmare. "When he was critically injured in an attempted execution, he thought he was going to die. Everyone did."

Jordan remembered Michele telling her about the incident.

"He had me go into his safe to retrieve his will and bring

it to his bedside for me to make changes to it." He shook his head.

"What happened?" She reached for his hand. "Giancarlo?"

He took a deep breath and eventually exhaled. "In amongst his papers, there was a home movie with my mother's name on it." He looked down at the floor, the words seemingly caught in his throat. On tenterhooks but not wanting to push, Jordan remained silent. When he looked up his eyes filled with tears. In a wavering voice he continued.

"He had put her in a room with a bunch of his drug mules. The camera followed her as they made her swallow one balloon after another of cocaine—or heroin—I don't know which."

Familiar with the process from one of her journalism assignments, Jordan felt the bile rise in her throat.

"And then they waited. They sent all the other mules out to smuggle the drugs but they kept her there. Until one of the balloons they'd deliberately packaged sub-standard burst in her stomach." His jaw hardened and tears coursed down his cheeks. "I watched my mother die of a drug overdose on a filthy mattress, while Constantine and his men watched."

Her heart broke for him as he recounted the nightmare. Neither of them spoke. They sat silently, in a state of utter exhaustion, listening to the sounds of the bustling hospital ward beyond the lounge door.

Chapter Forty-Three

Giancarlo had done his best to shield Jordan from the sickening details that would await her when she returned to Vancouver. But when an investigator from Interpol and another from the FBI came to the hospital to interview her, each new revelation assaulted her already raw emotions. The only positive note was her father had at last been located. Strike that. Authorities had known his location all along; it was just that Jordan had been the last to know. Had it not been for the murder of private investigator, Manny Smith, she might never have known Gavin's whereabouts.

"My father is in a witness protection program?" If this were someone else's life, it might have made for a titillating story. But it was her reality, and nothing about it was exciting. "What could he possibly know that would require him to go underground?" she asked, dumbfounded.

"May I?" Giancarlo asked the FBI agent, who nodded his consent.

"Jordan, for years, authorities in four countries have been trying to build a solid case against Constantine. They were always unsuccessful until recently, when they convinced your father to testify. Although Gavin possessed enough knowledge to put Constantine away, until *you* were grown up, Kathryn wouldn't allow him to divulge what he knew to the police."

"My father contacted me that night. That's why I was at his house. I hadn't talked to him for years, but he texted me that evening while I was at work and begged to meet me," Jordan said.

"I know," Giancarlo said. "Canadian authorities had everything ready to go. Kathryn was already in protection and your father was going in that night. The WPP guys had given him one last chance to pick up some documents from his house. He must have contacted you, afraid he'd never see you again."

That's why he'd pleaded with her. *Jordan, I know I'm asking a lot but pls meet me ASAP at 70 Seaspray Close in West Van. URGENT!* She swallowed the lump in her throat.

"Your father was on the way to his house when he texted you. He got there sometime before you arrived and discovered the body in his bed. He panicked, called his contact inside the program, and within minutes, they arrived and got him the hell out of there. It took a while before his handlers could share that information with the West Vancouver police."

She sat in her hospital bed, stunned. Giancarlo passed it back to the agents.

The first officer, whose name she couldn't recall, went first. "Miss Leighton, we're still putting all this together, but what we do know is your father's former partner, Tommy Krochinski, has been charged with Smith's murder.

Her mind careened back to the horrific scene at the Deer Ridge Country Club the night of the reception honoring her father. She could still see Krochinski grinning wildly at the crowd, shouting outrageous allegations against Gavin Stone. "How would Tommy Krochinski have gotten into my father's house and why would he murder Manny Smith?"

"Krochinski was under the impression your father was out of the country. Smith was killed elsewhere and his body was moved to where you found him at Mr. Stone's residence," the agent replied.

Jordan didn't tell him that was old news; the West Vancouver police had actually told her that quite early in their investigation. Something about bruising being present at the site of the needle mark in Smith's arm.

"It would appear Mr. Krochinski's drug habit had spiraled out of control, and last week, he was busted again for dealing. While in remand, he ran his mouth about how he'd taken out Smith, and framed Mr. Stone for it. He'd had a hate-on for your father since he was ousted from their company, allegedly for embezzling."

Finally, the Interpol investigator jumped in. "Seems Krochinski was overheard by the wrong guy, and in an attempt to get a shorter sentence for himself, he decided to snitch on him."

Jordan swallowed hard, trying desperately to absorb everything the agents were telling her. "So now that you have Tommy Krochinski for the murder, you have what you need. Why does my father have to go into witness protection?"

"We're pretty sure Constantine ordered the hit on the PI."

"*Constantine?*" Jordan's head started to throb. "What did he and Krochinski have to do with each other?"

"Near as we can figure, Tommy racked up some pretty steep gambling debts and as luck would have it, one of Constantine's friends in Vegas just 'happened' to run into him and took him under his wing. Before he knew who he was in bed with, Krochinski had obligated himself to doing some of the old man's dirty work. Smith had discovered that Constantine and Grimaldi were investing in your father's real estate developments in order to launder money. So, Constantine ordered Krochinski to take him out, and to frame your father for the murder. We suspect he had help—the fellow who befriended him in Vegas—and he's still at large."

Giancarlo leaned against the antiquated radiator in her hospital room. Although she was happy doctors had given him a clean bill of health, Jordan resented that they had released him, while keeping her for further observation. He cleared his throat self-consciously. "Jordan, there's something else we need to discuss with you."

"*Okay*," she said, dragging out the word. She looked at the three of them suspiciously.

The senior agent nodded for Giancarlo to proceed.

"Your mother has been booked as an accessory to Smith's murder."

She felt her heart turn to stone and her voice leapt a couple of octaves. "Why are you so uncomfortable, Giancarlo? Do you think anything *that woman*...Kathryn...did, would surprise me? She was probably just with my father for his money. I guess he got exactly what he deserved," she said smugly.

The agents traded glances with Giancarlo.

"*What?* Why are you all looking at me like that?"

"Jordan," Giancarlo spoke so quietly she had to strain to hear him. "I wasn't talking about Kathryn. The police in Vancouver have arrested your mother, Cynthia Stone."

Chapter Forty-Four

Jordan emerged from three days of excruciating pain, brought on by a severe stomach attack, which even morphine didn't take the edge off. Her Italian doctors insisted she stay in hospital another forty-eight hours to insure she was stabilized on her new medication before giving her the okay to fly. Armed with her test results the attending physician emphasized needed immediate follow up when she got back to Vancouver, she was finally released.

Giancarlo had driven her to the airport, all the while making strained small talk. She was so exhausted, it wasn't until she was somewhere over the Atlantic that it occurred to her she might not see him again. A week ago, that would have mattered. Now, all she could focus on was getting through the next few hours.

Following the thirteen-hour journey from Italy to Vancouver, a member of the West Vancouver Police Department was to meet her at YVR. Although she had managed to sleep a bit on the plane, the certain knowledge of what awaited her sapped the last bit of energy she could muster.

Jordan took as much time as possible disembarking the

plane and getting through customs. Only sheer will and determination would get her through her next meeting. She wondered if her life as she knew it would ever be normal again.

J ordan was beyond exhaustion as she sat slumped in the back of the unmarked police car. Thankful she didn't have to make conversation on the drive downtown, she struggled to make sense of what authorities had told her before she left the hospital.

Silently, she cursed that she'd have to deal with Inspector Dave Hunter again.

West Vancouver Police Department
March 2013

J ordan surveyed the dank ten-by-ten interrogation room in the holding center. Windowless, except for what she knew was a one-way mirror, wall-to-wall gunmetal grey swallowed the remnants of the early spring day she'd left outside. She shivered, a clammy blanket of bleakness clinging stubbornly to her skin.

"You knew all along he was leading a double life with this other woman and that I wasn't really yours?" Jordan asked Cynthia Stone. "Why didn't you *do* something?"

Staring across the chipped and dented Formica table, she searched her mother's face for something familiar. No, this wasn't her mother. Since seeing her just a month ago, the woman before her had become an empty shell. She reached across the table to touch her daughter's hand. Jordan snatched hers back. An officer standing guard just inside the doorway moved toward them. "No touching," he said.

"I did, my love. I *did* do something," Cynthia said, in answer to Jordan's question. "I got exactly what I wanted. I got the last laugh on Gavin and that bitch. He might have had her, but I got their daughter."

Jordan stole a furtive glance at the guard, aware they were being observed from behind the glass. "But they say you were involved in the private investigator's murder and you tried to frame Dad for it." Even as she said the words aloud, they defied comprehension.

"What was I to do?" Cynthia asked, seemingly oblivious to anyone overhearing. "He was blackmailing me, that PI— threatened to go to the press and tell everything he knew about your birth in Italy." She paused as if waiting for Jordan's approval. "He was blackmailing Tommy too. He had huge gambling debts as well as a drug habit, and neither of us could keep up with Smith's demands for money. It was the only way, Jordan. Can't you see that, my darling?"

"Conspiring to kill someone? Why didn't you go to Dad or the police? Why didn't you just tell me I was adopted? I'm twenty-seven years old, for god's sake."

"Your father," Cynthia shrilled with disdain, "washed his hands of me a long time ago. He said he'd come back and we'd raise you together, make a new start. And then that bitch survived the accident."

Jordan was startled at her venomous tone.

"I knew what he was doing, going back and forth to be with her, but I stayed with him for you, Jordan. I just wanted us to be a family." Just as quickly, her manner changed and she wrung her hands, her eyes pleading for her daughter to understand.

"None of this would have had to happen," Cynthia continued, without encouragement. "I tried to get rid of her earlier. But I'm glad I didn't. Otherwise, I would never have had you."

"You *didn't* have me," Jordan pointed out, bitterly. "You did one unconscionable thing after another. How can you call yourself a mother? You're unfit to be a mother. You are pure evil," Jordan said as she pushed back her chair. The guard moved aside to let her pass.

"Jordan, don't leave me. Please!" Cynthia Stone screamed after her. "I did it for you—for us."

Inspector Dave Hunter, whom Jordan hadn't seen since a few days after the murder, stood on the other side of the interrogation room door. Imperceptibly, he motioned for the officer to take the prisoner away. Her heart pounding, Jordan covered her ears to block out the screams as she watched the woman that once was her mother, disappear through double-locked doors. Several staff members looked up from their desks and then, discreetly went back to their work.

Hunter cleared his throat. "Can I get you a coffee or some water perhaps? I need a little more of your time, if you don't mind."

Though more polite than the last time they spoke, it wasn't a request. She dreaded going back into the interrogation room. Nevertheless, Jordan took Hunter's lead and walked past his outstretched arm as he held the door for her. "A coffee would be great, thank you," she said, trying to sound stronger than she felt.

He nodded to someone behind her and held up two fingers.

"Just so we're clear," he began, "Mrs. Stone will be held here until her first court appearance, and then she'll be transferred to the remand center. Normally, she wouldn't be allowed any visitors other than her lawyer. However, I pulled a few strings on your behalf, and we've made an exception."

"Thank you." Jordan took a sip of the strong, black coffee.

He nodded. She glimpsed the first trace of a smile.

"Your mother..." the inspector began, looking up from his yellow lined pad, "er, Mrs. Stone," he corrected himself, "has signed a full confession and will be formally charged with being an accessory to Mr. Smith's murder. That means..."

"I know what that means," she cut him off abruptly. "Did she actually...you know, physically...?"

"No, but she had full knowledge of what Krochinski planned to do and even encouraged him, both of which constitute being an accessory."

At least that gave Jordan some small measure of relief. Technically, her mother—or, correcting herself—the woman she'd thought of as her mother, wasn't a murderer.

"She has also confessed to two counts of attempted murder on Kathryn Bell," Hunter continued. "One in Carmel, California and the other in Italy."

Jordan slammed her cup down so abruptly that the liquid sloshed over the edges.

"That's going to be a little trickier. She committed those acts in two other countries, both of which we have extradition treaties with. Miss Bell...Kathryn," he clarified, "is refusing to press charges, but it's not up to her anymore. California and Italy can still prosecute Mrs. Stone for those crimes."

All at once, the events of the past forty-eight hours, strewn across two countries, smashed into Jordan with breathtaking force. The multiple cups of stale coffee she had consumed on an empty stomach roiled inside her like an angry cesspool, threatening to erupt at any second. She felt the familiar clamminess that preceded fainting. She opened her mouth to say something only to feel her jaw go slack.

"Oh shit," she vaguely heard Hunter yell to someone in the distance, "she's fainting—I need some help in here!"

W hen she came to, she was lying on the cold, polished cement floor. The chair she'd previously occupied lay toppled over, beside her.

"How are you feeling, Miss Leighton?" A concerned pair of eyes looked into hers as she felt someone take her blood pressure. "You fainted and bumped your head on the way down," one of the paramedics explained.

It was déjà vu. Like when she had awakened in an ambulance on the driveway of her father's house, where her whole nightmare began.

Someone had put a jacket over her, no doubt to protect her modesty, as she lay at an awkward angle on the floor. She turned her head and saw Hunter standing back from the fray, observing her. He actually looked concerned.

"Take all the time you need, Miss Leighton," he sighed. "We're not in any rush."

A fter the paramedics gave their thumbs up, Hunter showed Jordan to a more comfortable seat in a small staff lounge down the hall from the interrogation room. He sat patiently while she guzzled a bottle of orange juice but merely picked at a sandwich he had brought in. "You drink too much coffee," he pronounced.

"You smoke too much," Jordan replied, looking at his nicotine-stained fingers. She detected another slight smile.

"I'm glad you're feeling better." He flipped open his notebook. "So, as far as we can gather, back in 1985, Mrs. Stone suspected your father of infidelity. That's when she first hired a private investigator, Manny Smith. From what she told our officers, Smith informed her Mr. Stone had struck up a relationship with Kathryn Bell while he and your mother were vacationing in separate parts of Italy. She let it go but had Smith keep them under surveillance. It seems she was able to live with the knowledge her husband had been unfaithful. However, when Smith told her your father was about to leave her and marry his..." he cleared his throat, "mistress, it seems she went a little off the rails."

No kidding.

"Mr. Stone had moved out of the family home and was in the process of divorcing your mother."

Hunter's voice faded into the background as Jordan recalled the only time she knew of them talking about divorce. She was sixteen and they had just returned from their last summer as a family, on Saltspring Island after Gran had died.

"Miss Leighton?"

She snapped back to the present. "I'm sorry, go on."

"According to Mrs. Stone's confession, it was after your father's first visit to Carmel to see Ms. Bell, and following another of Smith's surveillance reports, that she entered Ms. Bell's unlocked home. She won't say if she planned to murder Ms. Bell at that time, but she says she spent considerable time in the house, eventually slashing a painting to pieces in a fit of rage." He stopped for a moment and rifled through the file. Jordan recognized her mother's handwriting on a sheet of yellow legal paper.

"After learning of her husband's plans to divorce her and marry Miss Bell..."

Jordan put her hand up to stop him. "Wait a minute, why

would she confess to all this? That just doesn't make sense to me."

Hunter nodded. "The reality is she didn't have much choice. First, Mrs. Stone appears to be severely emotionally disturbed. Second, once we told her Krochinski was trying to pin it all on her—the actual murder, I mean—she basically caved."

Jordan sighed, shaking her head in disbelief.

"As I was saying, she made a second trip to Carmel. Again, she can't, or won't say if she planned to murder Ms. Bell, but she does not dispute attacking her with a knife."

My mother attacked Kathryn with a knife? Hunter seemed so matter of fact about it.

"The injuries she inflicted put Ms. Bell in the hospital. It was after her attack that she decided to return to Italy, and your mother subsequently discovered she was pregnant."

"Pregnant with me, you mean." The words sounded foreign to her.

"Yes." He put his pen down and looked at her across the low coffee table. "I know this must be difficult for you. I just have a couple more things to go over and then I'll have someone drive you home."

Jordan nodded. "I understand that part, and now I know my mother...Cynthia... and my father came back to Canada. Kathryn was in a car accident and was on life support when I was born."

"Yes, well..." Hunter began awkwardly. "It seems...Cynthia," he said, taking her lead, "caused the accident that nearly killed her."

Could this get any worse? "But, by all accounts it was terrible weather on the Amalfi Coast Highway that night. Dark and rainy. They said Kathryn was going too fast and skidded off the road. It happens to tourists there all the time," Jordan said.

"That's true. But in this case, I'm afraid Ms. Bell had a little help."

"What do you mean?"

"The brake line in her car was cut."

Jordan felt the color drain from her face and tears stung her eyes. She willed herself not to faint again.

Hunter pushed a box of tissues in her direction. He closed the file and put down his pen, remaining silent for a moment. "In her statement she told us she knew you would disown her if you ever found out what she'd done. I'm sorry. In her own twisted way, I think she loves you."

"How can you say that after what she's done?" Jordan tried fruitlessly to stem the flow of tears as she got up to leave.

The detective gathered his things and stood to face her. "Well, I'd say she paid a pretty stiff price to hold on to you, wouldn't you?"

Jordan had no answer. Not one that would make sense, anyway.

"We're pretty much done here," he said. "Is there anything else before I get an officer to take you home?"

"How...how did she get involved with Tommy Krochinski? I mean, I know he and my dad were partners at one time, but..." She shook her head, baffled.

"Mr. Krochinski developed a nasty drug habit early on in their partnership. He also owed substantial gambling debts to some unsavory characters in Vegas. He began stealing money from the company, and Manny Smith got wind of it while tracking down funds your mother was convinced Mr. Stone was hiding offshore. It was pure dumb luck that Smith discovered Krochinski was stealing from your father's company. As Mrs. Stone admitted, Smith ended up black-mailing them both, so they each had their reasons for wanting him dead." He scratched his head. "Strange bedfellows, I know."

"Do you know who tried to run me off the road that night after the reception?" She wasn't sure she was ready to hear the truth, but it wasn't as if things could get any worse.

"It wasn't your mother, if that's what you're asking," Hunter replied. "We can't prove it, but we're pretty sure it was Krochinski. Mrs. Stone has an airtight alibi for that night."

Thank God, she thought, feeling the knot in her stomach.

He helped her on with her coat and signaled a female officer who waited nearby. "Constable Herera will take you home. Here's my card. If there's anything at all you need, just call."

She nodded her thanks and turned to leave.

"And Miss Leighton?"

"Yes?"

"We have some excellent counseling programs through our victim services department. Don't take this on all alone."

Was he suggesting she was as emotionally frail as her mother?

"I'm serious," he insisted. "I went through it when my wife and kid were killed. It will eat you from the inside out if you let it."

"I'm sorry," she stammered. "I had no idea."

Hunter shuffled his feet awkwardly. "Yeah well, I don't tell many people. I just thought perhaps this one time it might help."

"Thank you," Jordan said, extending her hand.

Chapter Forty-Five

After the confrontation with Cynthia at West Vancouver's holding facility, Jordan felt bruised and battered; the raw emotions threatened to swallow her whole. Operating on automatic pilot, she had fought wearily to get through the previous eighteen hours. Finally back in Vancouver, the last thing she wanted to do was hop on another plane and go to Sacramento, California. She held the faint hope that after this final leg of her journey, she could put this nightmare to rest and somehow begin rebuilding her life. But how?

Giancarlo had managed to convince American authorities and their international partners to allow a visit with her father and Kathryn before they were to be relocated through the Witness Protection Program. As they wouldn't allow Jordan to see the safe house in which they were staying, they had transported the couple, under extreme secrecy, to a large hotel in the capital. No matter how hard she tried, Jordan couldn't envision how she would act or what she would say when reunited with her father. Could she bring herself to meet Kathryn?

Having flown first-class, she was one of the first off the

plane, and she spotted her name on a sign held by a tall, athletic-looking woman in a navy pantsuit. "I'm Jordan Leighton," she said, approaching her.

The woman shook her hand firmly and casually ushered her to the edge of the arrival lounge. "If you'd be kind enough to follow me," she said, taking her elbow and steering her to an unmarked steel door. She quickly entered a key code and held open the door. Once inside, the woman showed Jordan a card identifying her as Special Agent Christine Heninger, with the FBI. "I just need to check your ID, Miss Leighton, and then we can be on our way."

Jordan handed the agent her passport as well as her Nexus card.

"Perfect," she smiled. "Now, there's a black SUV right outside. In case we're overheard, if you have any occasion to address me by name please just call me Chris, and for all intents and purposes I want you to act like we're old friends. Understood?"

Jordan nodded. Unexpectedly, the special agent took her by both shoulders. Her eyes were warm and encouraging. "I know you've been through a lot in the last couple of days, but in roughly forty minutes you'll be able to see your father, and it's entirely up to you if you want to meet Miss Bell, okay?"

Jordan's answer stuck in her throat and her eyes welled up. "I'm sorry, I guess I'm just tired and a bit overwhelmed."

"That's perfectly understandable." The agent handed back her ID. "Are you ready?"

They quickly exited the unmarked door and blended in with the last of the straggling international arrivals. Hooking her arm through Jordan's, Chris reached for her carry-on and inquired in a cheery voice, "How was your flight? Did you manage to sleep?"

"It was good. I think I dozed on and off."

"Here we are," Chris said, opening the back door of the SUV. "You and I will ride together." She closed the door behind Jordan and went around to the other side. Once in the car, she introduced the two men in the front seat. "Jordan, Paul there is our driver and beside him is Marco. Gentlemen, meet Miss Leighton."

They both turned in their seats. "Pleased to meet you, ma'am," Paul said first.

"Miss Leighton," Marco acknowledged her with a nod of his head.

As if sensing her question, Chris said, "Paul and Marco are both special agents. You're in good hands. Just sit back and enjoy the ride."

As promised, they reached their destination in approximately forty minutes. Along the way, Chris coached her on how they would enter the hotel and stressed the importance of moving swiftly and without question. Already wound up, Jordan looked out the rear window. Another black SUV swerved in behind them as they shot down the underground parking ramp. She looked at Chris nervously.

"Don't worry. They're with us," Chris said. "They've been with us all the way from the airport."

"Really? I just noticed them now," Jordan said.

The special agent gave a wry smile. "That's good."

Talking into a microphone at his wrist, Paul said to someone, "Unloading the cargo now. Will be in the elevator in thirty seconds."

Paul took the lead while Marco retrieved her luggage. Chris opened Jordan's car door and hustled her into a waiting elevator. Whoever was in the second SUV, parked at their rear bumper and remained inside the vehicle. Marco waved a special key card over a button that was simply marked "PH." After a silent elevator ride, the door opened. Two armed policemen stood immediately in front of them, blocking their exit. Once they recognized the agents, they quickly moved aside. Jordan observed two more armed officers, one at either end of the long hallway. The tension she had felt all the way from the airport increased to full-blown anxiety.

"This is our room." Chris unlocked the door. "See you guys later," she said to Paul and Marco as they headed farther down the hall. "Tell them we need a little time for Miss Leighton to freshen up, will you?"

"Sure thing," Paul called, without looking back.

Jordan stepped inside the lavishly appointed penthouse suite.

"Ladies' room is through there," Chris pointed. "Why don't you take a few minutes to yourself? Can I get you something cold to drink?" she asked, opening the well-stocked fridge behind the bar.

Jordan was tempted to ask for coffee instead, but thought of Hunter. "Is there any iced tea?"

"Absolutely. I'll have one ready for you by the time you come back."

When Jordan came out of the bathroom, Special Agent Heninger assessed her admiringly. "You look great. In fact, you look remarkable, all things considered."

"Thank you, you've been very kind."

"Just doing my job." The agent motioned to a chair across from her where she had set Jordan's iced tea on a sparkling glass coffee table. She took a sip from a bottle of Perrier and wiped her mouth with the back of her hand. "So here's the deal. Through that door," she pointed, "is your father."

Jordan felt her stomach turn over, and her hands became so sweaty she had to put her drink down.

"Through another door beyond that, is Miss Bell... Kathryn."

"I don't know if I can do this," Jordan interrupted. "Meet her, I mean."

"That's entirely up to you. No one is going to force you. We thought it would be best for you to meet with Mr. Stone first. Then you can decide together what you want to do, okay?"

Jordan nibbled her lower lip and nodded.

Chris leaned in, putting her Perrier on the table. "Jordan, here's what I want you to keep in mind. It's possible you will never see them again. So, you need to do what is right for you — something you can live with in the event that happens." Her look was deadly serious.

"But I thought with Constantine in custody they would be able to come out of the Witness Protection Program after they testify."

"That's a possibility, but until the dust settles and we know what we're dealing with regarding Constantine's associates, we are proceeding as previously planned."

Jordan wrapped her arms around her body, suddenly chilled. It hadn't occurred to her that this might be the first time in ten years she'd see her father, and possibly the last. And she would have to decide if she wanted to meet her mother. She held her hand to her mouth and rubbed her lips nervously.

"I'm going to go next door now and talk to Mr. Stone. Take your time and when you're ready, just tap on the adjoining door. Got it?"

She choked back a lump in her throat. Would this ever get any easier?

"You can do this, you know. I hear you're a pretty feisty gal," Chris said with a wink. She gave Jordan a reassuring smile and touched her shoulder as she got up. "I'll be right on the other side of the door. No pressure, right?" She grinned at her own joke.

J ordan stood on her side of the adjoining door, willing herself to knock. Heavily, she lifted her hand and tapped. She held her breath as she heard the lock turn on the other side. True to her word, Chris was right there. She stepped back for Jordan to enter.

There was only one other person in the room. He stood up the moment the door opened. Still tall and muscular, his full head of hair was slicked back the way he'd always worn it, but it had turned from black to pure white. Only his thick, bushy eyebrows were still black. His hair contrasted sharply with the deep tan of his lined, angular face. The compassionate brown eyes she remembered, though hooded with looser skin than ten years ago, met hers and he smiled tentatively. "Jordan," Gavin Stone said. His chin trembled and she saw the glisten of tears.

She hadn't moved from inside the threshold. How long had she been standing there? Chris gently guided her into the room. "I'm going to leave you two alone for awhile," she said, looking to Jordan for agreement. She nodded and Chris closed the door behind her.

"I want so desperately to give you a hug but I won't," he said. "Would you be willing to sit down and just talk?"

She nodded and moved stiffly to a loveseat across from him. There was a box of tissues and two glasses of water on the coffee table between them.

He tried to look casual as he brushed the moisture from

his eyes. "The truth is, Jordan, I don't quite know where to start."

The pain from holding herself so rigid was almost unbearable. Now she understood how Thula had felt; Jordan so desperately wanted to speak but couldn't seem to squeeze any words out. She reached for her water. "Perhaps you could start at the beginning," she said in a thin, reedy voice.

A n hour and wads of tissues later, Gavin had at last unburdened himself. His daughter had said very little while he spoke. She didn't need to; her face said it all—she was crushingly disappointed in him. "I never meant for these things to happen, Jordan. I hope you can believe me."

"Things didn't just *happen*," she reminded him bitterly. "You made them happen. You are one hundred percent responsible for this."

He opened his mouth to speak but stopped, then measured his words carefully. "You're right, I am responsible, but maybe once you have more living under your belt you'll understand things aren't just black and white." The moment the words left his lips, he knew he had hit a nerve.

"After I've had more living under my belt. Are you *kidding* me? Do you know what you put me, and my mother...Cynthia...through in the last ten years? In the last month? I can't believe you're saying that to me." He caught the ring of hysteria in her voice.

"I'm sorry, I didn't mean it like that," he said, floundering to put his remark in context. "You were just sixteen when your mother and I separated. It's not fair of me to expect you to have handled things differently."

She banged her glass on the table so abruptly he jumped.

"You and *that woman*," she said, looking toward the second adjoining door, "cooked this up long before I was sixteen and you know it. You betrayed both of us. And our entire family. If you couldn't stick by your marriage vows, why didn't you at least have the decency to divorce Cynthia before I came along?"

"I tried to," he said so quietly she barely heard him.

"You *tried* to?" Her voice had gone from shrill to condescendingly quiet.

"Your mother...Cynthia...started drinking and threatened to kill herself when I proposed divorce after we returned from Italy. I had hoped to get her through that initial rough period. I paid for her counseling—you know, to help her with the adjustment. And I tried to work out a more than generous settlement for us to go our separate ways." He paused and looked at his upturned palms as if to find the answers. "And then Kathryn became pregnant." His daughter stared at him with eyes of steel. "With you," he continued. "It was the happiest time of my life. I had always wanted children but Cynthia couldn't have them. We tried for years."

They sat in silence for what seemed like minutes. "You might not want to hear this, Jordan, but if I had it to do over again, I'd do the same thing, just to have you." He thought his heart would burst from his chest. He'd only felt like this twice before. Once, when he kissed Kathryn goodbye and had to leave her in the hospital on life support because he was too weak to make the decision to terminate her life. And again, when this beautiful young woman, from whom he was begging for forgiveness, was born.

When he looked up, Jordan's face had crumpled and she was quietly sobbing. Taking what felt like the biggest risk of his life, Gavin slowly got up, rounded the coffee table, and sat on the loveseat beside her. He gently lifted her hands from her lap and held them in his own. "I'm sorry for the pain I've caused you, Jordan, but I have never stopped loving you. I never stopped hoping for the moment when I could see you again and hold you in my arms. I couldn't go into hiding, possibly for the rest of my life, without seeing you just one more time."

Her body heaved with silent sobs and for a moment, he thought it was over. He couldn't blame her for being unwilling to forgive him, but at least he had been able to see and touch her.

"I know you want me to meet her, and I don't know how I can possibly do that," Jordan cried.

"She desperately wants to meet you, but it is entirely your decision. It took an enormous amount of strength for her to stay in the background while another woman...your mother...raised you."

"It was her fault. She knew you were married when she met you."

"It was both of our faults." He searched her eyes that reminded him so much of Kathryn's. "I don't know if you'll ever understand this—I hope you will. When I found Kathryn, it was as if she was my soul mate. The one and only person God had put aside for me. To have her and then to have you with her..." he trailed off, and shrugged helplessly. "It's more than one man deserves. If I were to die tomorrow, I would be complete."

Jordan looked down at her hands in his. "You really believe that. Even though what you did caused you not to have me in your life for ten years?"

"Yes, I do," he said, as if resigned to his fate. "But the next ten years hopefully won't be that way. Do you think you could ever find it in your heart to forgive me, Jordie?" He hadn't called her that since she was a child.

There was a discreet tap on the door and Chris peeked her head in. "We need to be leaving within the next half hour, Mr. Stone. Just wanted to give you the heads up." The door closed quietly.

Still holding her hands in his, Gavin sensed the change in Jordan. He had been dreading this moment, but he knew it must come. "We still have time for you to meet Kathryn. She's just on the other side of that door," he said, squeezing her hands a little tighter. "I will respect whatever decision you make."

Slowly, she pulled her hands away and dabbed her eyes with a tissue. He wondered if he might be witnessing a cataclysmic shift in his defiant daughter. He wanted this more than anything he could imagine. At the same time, he tried to maintain a poker face. Should he say one more thing? It could work, but it might also push her over the edge. She let him gently turn her face upward to meet his eyes.

"I hope against hope we will eventually be released from the Witness Protection Program but if we're not, will you be okay with the knowledge that the woman who gave birth to you was within ten feet and you chose not to meet her?"

He held his breath as he finished his question.

Gavin opened the door that separated them and tentatively placed his hand on the small of his daughter's back. Kathryn had been absently flipping through a magazine, and when she saw them enter the room, she tossed it aside. Jordan sensed she was about to rise and then appeared to think better of it. Instead, she sat erect on the white overstuffed sofa, her slim hands resting on each side of her lap. She wore a simple black sleeveless dress and around her shoulders, an aquamarine silk wrap, adorned with gold, raised chiffon butterflies. Her long, slim legs crossed demurely at the ankles above black patent leather pumps.

The sight of her took Jordan's breath away. Her warm smile illuminated an oval-shaped face, much like her own, but with a strong, square jaw and exquisitely high cheekbones. Her long, graceful neck was that of a ballerina's, and although Jordan could only guess at her age, she had just a hint of lines crinkling the outer edges of her striking green eyes. She took in Kathryn's full, expressively arched dark brows, above which was a slight widow's peak. Her hair, swept off her face and cut blunt just above her shoulders, shone deep chestnut. Jordan felt as if she were looking into a mirror. They could have been carbon copies of each other.

She felt her father tense as he led her further into the room. "Jordan, I'd like you to meet Kathryn." He squeezed her arm as if for his own reassurance.

"Jordan," Kathryn said warmly. "It's so good to meet you. Thank you for agreeing to this." She moved her hands to her lap and seemed to be trying hard to restrain herself.

"I don't think of you as my mother, you know," Jordan blurted. *God, I sound like a petulant twelve-year-old!*

Kathryn nodded and pressed her lips together, something Jordan was aware that she herself did whenever she was nervous. "I can understand that. Perhaps we can just chat a little in the few minutes before Gavin and I have to go." She frowned. "I'm sorry, that sounds so contrived. The truth is I don't know what to say to you either. Except, I think of you every day, and you have grown into a beautiful woman. I know you've made your father and your mother...Cynthia...very proud."

"My mother. Cynthia." Jordan didn't try to hide her disdain.

"She did a fine job raising you, Jordan. I know you must love her very much," Kathryn said generously, without a hint of jealousy. Gavin stood off to the side and remained silent.

"Well my mother is in prison right now." *And it's all your fault*, she wanted to say.

"Yes, I know that. It isn't your father or I, who wish to press charges. That has been completely taken out of our hands."

"But your actions caused all of this. You're still responsible."

"Jordan," Gavin interrupted, quietly. "We don't have time for this. Is there anything you want to ask Kathryn or me before our time together comes to an end?"

She leveled her gaze at the elegant woman who sat before her. "Why did you give me away?" she asked.

"Jordan..." Gavin interjected.

Kathryn reached behind her and patted his hand on the back of the couch. "It's all right, Gavin. I want to answer Jordan's question." She paused for a moment as if considering her words. "Constantine raped and killed Thula's mother and then tortured and killed her father when she was just a little girl," she said solemnly. "Then we found out he had murdered my parents in cold blood in Vancouver. By that time, he had become a partner in your father's real estate developments, and I was pregnant with you. The Italian authorities, as well as the FBI and Interpol, were trying to build a case against Constantine for racketeering, money-laundering, and murder." She broke eye contact and looked down at her hands. In a quieter voice, she continued. "I was eight months pregnant, coming home from a meeting with investigators when I had my car accident. At the time, we thought Constantine or his people were responsible."

Jordan felt sick knowing it was Cynthia who had sabotaged Kathryn's car. *They hadn't known they were handing their baby over to a murderer.*

"I understand Sister Serafina gave you my letter. So, as you know, I was not supposed to survive. The doctors delivered you early while I was on life support. Your father did the only thing he could have done to keep you safe from Constantine and to keep a piece of me with him." She looked up at Gavin and smiled. "He knew he would have my blessing for Cynthia and him to adopt you and take you back to Canada."

Gavin nodded. "We didn't list me as the father on the birth certificate, and we paid off the doctor who delivered you to issue a death certificate. We wanted Constantine to think you had died, just as Kathryn was expected to."

Jordan struggled to process the information they were throwing at her.

"From the time you were little, we told you your birthday was different than it actually was, just in case your birth could ever be traced." Gavin said. "Later, Julius forged a birth certificate that showed you being born in Italy to Cynthia and me."

So that's what Julius had to do with all this. That's why he was so angry when I went to Tropea. Now it all made sense.

There was another knock at the door. This time it was Marco, who stuck his head inside. "Five minutes, folks, and we need to be ready to roll."

Nausea and a sense of panic overcame Jordan. This was it. Anything she wanted to do or ask of her parents had to be done in the next few moments. "But Constantine is an old man and is in the hospital. Why do they still need you to go into the program?" she asked.

Kathryn answered. "Jordan, if his people tracked my parents all the way from Italy to Vancouver, you can be sure he still has associates who will go to great lengths to find us. But more than that, we want *you* to be safe. If we can help bring this case against him and his mob to a close, we can all get on with our lives." For the first time, she saw her mother's face harden. "With that monster captured, we've made a good start."

As all three glanced at the grandfather clock in the suite, Jordan tensed for the moment to come. Gavin came around from behind the couch and handed her an envelope.

"This is a package for Julius. It names you as my power of attorney and it leaves everything I have to you in the event of my death. The business, the house in West Vancouver, everything."

"But I can't..." Jordan stammered. "You'll need it all when you come back," she said half-heartedly, realizing that time may never come.

Gavin smiled and gently pulled her to her feet. "Then I know I'm placing everything in good hands for when that day comes. I can't think of anyone I trust more to handle my affairs in my absence."

"What about the SEC? You know, the embezzlement charges," Jordan asked.

"Julius has everything he needs to wrap up all the loose ends. I understand he's already had several meetings with the SEC and the police. It will still take some work, but they're confident they can prove it was Krochinski who mismanaged the funds. I'm hopeful they may even be able to recover some of the money for the investors."

While she and Gavin were talking, Kathryn had drawn

closer and the three of them were huddled together as Chris entered from one door, and Paul and Marco from another. "Jordan, one more thing," Gavin said. He took Kathryn's hand and gazed deeply into his daughter's eyes. "I want you to use whatever funds you need to defend Cynthia."

Jordan looked at him, stunned. She looked at Kathryn, who nodded in agreement. "But she's confessed to everything. And she doesn't deserve any help for the evil things she's done." She stared at Kathryn. "She tried to kill you, not once but twice."

Kathryn nodded. "I know I don't have the right to give you advice, but please don't live with bitterness and hatred toward her. It will only destroy you."

Sister Serafina and Thula had said the same thing, almost word for word.

"Cynthia has had a lot to contend with, and something inside her obviously snapped. Whether she ends up in prison in Canada or abroad, or possibly a mental facility where she can get help, she deserves to be treated like a human being. In spite of everything, she was a good mother to you, Jordan."

"Sorry, folks, but we gotta go," one of the agents said.

Gavin turned to his daughter. "Would it be possible to get a hug?" he asked. She nodded silently and moved into his arms, where their wet tears fell on each other's necks. After a warm embrace, he gently pulled away and kissed her cheek for the last time.

Kathryn stood still as if afraid to move a muscle. Jordan could see she was trying to make it easy for her. She held out her graceful, tapered hands. Jordan took them in hers and the two women moved toward each other. Foreheads together, Kathryn whispered to Jordan, "I will think of you every day, my darling. No matter what happens, please don't ever doubt that I love you. I have always loved you. That's why I stayed out of your life."

She touched her lips to her daughter's fingers and with tears streaming down her face, she turned and walked out the door.

Chapter Forty-Six

Vancouver, British Columbia
   Six weeks later

The sleeping pills her doctor had prescribed did their job, but Jordan hated the empty, groggy feeling when she awoke. Most of all, she hated not having a place to go to work each morning. After enduring the wrath of her editor, Ernie, as well as Dorothea's obvious disappointment in her—that hurt the most—the newspaper suspended her "indefinitely" while they investigated the events of the past few weeks.

Despite his anger, she knew Ernie was building a strong case for her reinstatement, but she was under no illusions it would be easy, or even possible. She struggled with the guilt of betraying poor Dorothea, who had trusted her implicitly. All the while she was sharing confidential information with her, she had no idea how Jordan was using it. Because of her, Dorothea was also cast under a black cloud of suspicion.

With her entire family gone, Jordan felt no particular purpose to her life. She had been sleeping too much, self-medicating with a bottle of wine a night, and generally contributing to her own downward mental spiral. In her heart of hearts, she knew her life was unraveling. Unexpectedly, it was Dorothea, who put her shock and anger aside to accompany Jordan to the specialist to get her test results. Only two weeks prior, she had let herself in with her spare key and found Jordan, having consumed almost two bottles of wine and an undetermined amount of pills, unconscious on the bathroom floor. With a firm but compassionate heart, Dorothea single-handedly nursed Jordan back to some semblance of health. She had checked on her daily, bringing her homemade meals at the end of her long workdays at the paper. The good news was Jordan's new medication had begun to take effect, holding further stomach attacks at bay. But the hard work of therapy for post-traumatic stress was still ahead of her. Her doctors had warned her she was operating on physical and mental overload.

J ordan had stayed in touch with Giancarlo by email. He and the various authorities involved, kept her abreast of any developments in Cynthia's case. Until her sentence was completed in Canada, it appeared highly unlikely she would be extradited to the US to face charges of attempted murder. In the meantime, she remained in a prison near Vancouver, where Jordan stubbornly refused to visit.

Then, out of the blue, Jordan received a phone call. It irritated her that the phone was ringing when all she wanted to do was sleep. It was four a.m. and as she tended to do of late, she let it go to voicemail. She rolled over and it rang again. Sitting up, she yanked the chain of the bedside table lamp and grabbed her phone. "What?"

"Jordan? I know it's late—well, early—but I thought you'd want to know." It was Giancarlo.

She felt a flutter in her stomach and sat up in bed. "Know what?" she asked as she reached for her robe.

"Constantine didn't make it through his first skin graft surgery. They said his advanced age, coupled with the bullet wound so close to his heart...well, his body couldn't withstand it. I got the call just a few minutes ago. I wanted to tell you right away."

She sat on the side of the bed, trying to get her bearings.

"Jordan," he said excitedly, "do you understand? This means your father and Kathryn might be able to come out of the Witness Protection Program."

Jordan was beginning to feel better as she stabilized on her meds, but she was grateful for the week between Giancarlo's call and his arrival in Vancouver. While suffering such debilitating physical and mental pain, her apartment had essentially descended into chaos. But with Dorothea's help, she had managed to get things spruced up in anticipation of Giancarlo's visit.

She trembled with electric energy as she paced back and forth between the international arrivals monitor and the waiting area. Having taken Hunter's remark to heart, not to mention her doctor's, she had quit the sleeping pills and her six daily Americanos; the latter, cold turkey. She was trying to eat regularly and was sipping on an herbal tea as she waited. *If Dorothea could see me now.* She checked on Giancarlo's flight one more time. It had landed.

She still couldn't quite grasp all that had happened in the short time since Giancarlo's phone call.

"I thought perhaps I could help with the transition," he'd

said on the phone that morning. "I know how alone I felt when I found out what happened to my mother at Constantine's hands. It must be devastating for you to face what Cynthia has done. Besides," he said, in a more upbeat tone, "I could use a vacation on the department's dollar."

Since rejoining the prosecutor's office, Giancarlo had been appointed as the special envoy charged with meeting the Canadian authorities regarding possible extradition proceedings against Cynthia Stone. He also had the final say on whether Kathryn and Gavin would come out of the Witness Protection Program. Even with Constantine dead, several of Italy's other prosecutors, as well as various international authorities, questioned whether Constantine's people posed a threat to her parents, who were valuable witnesses. Had one of Constantine's henchmen not taken out Grimaldi, there would have been no possibility of her parents' release. The faint chance Jordan might be reunited with her family, gave her renewed hope.

Her parents. Her family. She contemplated the strange words floating around in her head as she thought of her father and her mother, Kathryn.

"Ciao, bella!" she heard as she weaved her way through the throng of people waiting for their loved ones to arrive. Without thinking, she ran alongside the railing that separated well-wishers from incoming passengers. She stopped and waited for Giancarlo to walk the last few steps of the concourse. "I've missed you," he said as he caught her in his arms and twirled her around.

"I've missed you too," she said breathlessly, finally willing to admit and say it aloud.

He put her down and held her at arm's length, oblivious to

the passengers streaming past on each side. "You look fabulous, *cara.* You've gained a little weight, yes?"

She cuffed him playfully. "Are you saying I'm fat?"

"No. Just more *curvy,*" he replied with a wink. "How are you feeling?" In her emails, she'd told him about her illness.

"Okay, I guess. I'm trying to take it one day at a time," she admitted.

"Perfect!" he said, wrapping his arm around her waist. "Let's take it one day at a time together, *si?*"

T he fire crackled as they sat nursing their drinks at one of Jordan's favorite north shore restaurants. Though tired, Giancarlo looked more relaxed than she'd seen him. He had insisted on stopping for dinner on the way home from the airport.

"Can I ask you something?" Jordan said when the waiter brought Giancarlo's red wine and her sparkling apple juice.

"Anything, bella, I am all yours."

"Why didn't you tell me you used to live in my apartment in Tropea?"

"How did you know that?" He put down his glass but his warm smile remained.

"I ran into Mrs. Candiotti at the post office and she told me."

"Ah, *Tia.* She said to pass along her love. I think she is very fond of you."

"Giancarlo, you haven't answered my question. When did you live there?"

"I was only there briefly. Before I went to Rome to open my law firm."

After he and his girlfriend were threatened!

"What made you leave?" she asked, trying to sound casual.

He searched her eyes. "*Cara*, I know Michele told you what happened when I was special prosecutor the first time. What else do you want to know?"

She felt her eyes burn as she fought to hold back her tears. "Did you love her?" *Shit! Where did that come from?*

He appeared to be thinking carefully about his response. "I don't know. I was so intent on getting her away from Constantine's people that we never had the luxury of finding out. Even after we went to Rome, I think I pushed her away, for the sake of her little boy's safety." He moved her drink out of the way and took her hands in his. "Why do you ask?"

She didn't trust herself to speak and looked past him into the fire.

"*Cara*, are you afraid I will leave you too?" he asked gently.

"Everyone has," she said through her tears.

"Jordan, do you trust me?"

She thought back to everything they'd gone through together. How he had rescued her from Constantine at the barn. "Yes, Giancarlo, I trust you."

"*Cara,* I need you to trust me that I will do everything I can to put Constantine's mob away for good. So Kathryn and Gavin can come out of hiding. Will you help me?"

"But once you leave here, we'll be on separate continents. How will we manage?"

He flashed the devilish smile that she remembered the first night at the restaurant when he'd sent over a limoncello. He cupped her chin in his hand, and she saw the flames of the fire reflected in his eyes. The last of her doubts and misgivings melted away.

"Your parents had a long distance affair and now here you

are—the precious result. I'd say that worked out pretty well. Why don't *we* give it a try and see where it takes us, Jordan Leighton."

She toyed with her glass and made him wait for one long, delicious minute. "You're on," she said. "And by the way, that would be Jordan Katarina *Stone*."

Enjoyed Deadly Switch and want to find out what happens to Jordan Stone? Your next book is waiting!

SCARE AWAY THE DARK

A Stone Suspense Book 2

A mysterious text preluding murder. A globe-trotting suspect on the run. Can a young woman end the killing before her past buries her future?

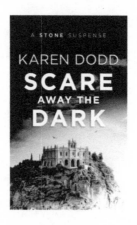

Vancouver, BC. Investigative reporter Jordan Stone loathes her estranged dad. But when he oddly messages her from out of the blue, she puts her bitterness aside for a slim chance to reconnect. Yet upon her arrival at his lavish mansion, all she finds is a stranger's cooling corpse.

With her missing father now accused of homicide and embezzling millions, Jordan's attempts to expose the truth only land her on the hit list. Desperate to discover who is really pulling the strings, she races to

Italy to revisit her miserable childhood... knowing she's drawing the attention of a cold-blooded killer.

Can she crack the case before she joins the skeletons in her family's closet?

"A riveting read; engrossing, entertaining, and clever. Extremely satisfying!" ~Amazon Review

GET MORE OF MY BOOKS FREE!

To say thank for this book, I'd like to invite you to exclusive *VIP Club,* and give you some of my books and short stories for FREE.

To join the club, head to karendodd.com/vip-club and a free book will be sent to you immediately! My promise to you is it will never cost you a penny—ever.

For more information, visit my website: karendodd.com

Acknowledgments

At times, with its long gestation period, this book felt like the birthing of a baby—or possibly, an elephant. I cried, I laughed. I gnashed my teeth. But ultimately, producing it was a labor of love.

The version that you hold in your hands today has become infinitely better because of some amazing people. First, my thanks go to Bernie Baigent (a.k.a "Agent Baigent) and Gerry Mazzei, both of whom provided me with invaluable expertise as the premise for *DEADLY SWITCH* began to percolate.

Secondly, I must thank my writing critique group: Karen Bower, Carl Hunter, Penny McDonald, and Cathy Scrimshaw. These kind and generous individuals have been there since the book's inception, for better or worse—often worse. I thank them for seeing depth in my story that I sometimes couldn't see myself.

The final group of staunch supporters consists of my dedicated beta readers. They are a special breed onto themselves. To—Liz Bell, Aubrey Duldalao, Dianna Jepson, Greg King, Barb and Jim English, Bonnie Hutchinson, Francine Legault,

Elaine Rivers, Joanie Chavalier, Maude Stephany, Diana Stevan, Rod Baker, Anna Axerio-Cilies, and Eric Lidemark— I thank each of them for guiding my manuscript with extraordinary insight and doing it with compassion.

I have had the tremendous good fortune of finding my editor, Laurie Boris, who helped me tighten my story without taking away my voice. As the yin to my yang, she was a joy to work with. And a huge thank you to award-winning cover designer, Stuart Bache, for the new and updated cover for this edition of Deadly Switch.

I am a firm believer that certain projects bring special people into our lives. For me, that person was Bethany Gould. In addition to being a gifted beta reader, she was the "mid-wife" who helped birth this book. Even though we've yet to meet in person, she inspired me on a daily basis, to keep going. She celebrated with me in joy, and she offered sage counsel when I experienced the grief of losing a precious soul sister to a senseless murder. I encourage you to find the blessing in each new relationship that comes your way. If you experience even half the sunshine that someone like Bethany can bring to your world, you will be rich indeed.

DEADLY SWITCH might never have been published if it weren't for a man who exemplifies the meaning of "pay it forward." Martin Crosbie was the one who sparked my interest in tackling the sometimes wild and wooly world of publishing. With unending patience, he taught me how to produce a book that would stand spine-to-spine with traditionally published books. More than that, he taught me how to do it with integrity. I will be forever grateful to him for inspiring me to push my dream out into the world.

Through Martin, I met many good people—one of whom was Robert Bidinotto. Having tread before both of us in the indie world, he never hesitated to answer my many questions and share his vast amount of knowledge. All because he had been where I was going, and like Martin, he wanted others to be successful. I believe both these gentlemen are on their way to becoming legends in what will one day, become the "traditional" way of publishing.

Finally, to my husband and soul mate, Glen. With unconditional love and support, he believed in me when I often didn't believe in myself. I know there is a reason why you were put in my path, my love—and I thank God every day for sending you to teach me what I most needed to learn. With profound gratitude, I dedicate *DEADLY SWITCH* to you.

—Karen Dodd
December 2013

About the Author

Karen Dodd is the author of the Stone Suspense novels. The second book in the series, Scare Away the Dark, won the 2018 Chanticleer CLUE award. *Everybody Knows,* is the first book in her new Nicoló Moretti Crime Thriller series. Karen lives in a small village on Canada's West Coast.

Visit her at www.karendodd.com

 facebook.com/karendodd.author

twitter.com/authorkarendodd

 instagram.com/karendodd.author